The Cursed Moon

THE CURSED MOON
BOOK I
BY LUIZA DOBRZYNSKA

ALL MATERIAL CONTAINED HEREIN IS
COPYRIGHT © LUIZA DOBRZYNSKA 2025
ALL RIGHTS RESERVED.
***
TRANSLATED AND PUBLISHED IN ENGLISH
WITH PERMISSION.
***
PAPERBACK ISBN: 979-8-9922051-2-1
EPUB ISBN: 979-8-2273956-7-2
***
WRITTEN BY LUIZA DOBRZYNSKA
PUBLISHED BY ROYAL HAWAIIAN PRESS
COVER ART BY TYRONE ROSHANTHA
TRANSLATED & PUBLISHING ASSISTANCE
BY DOROTA RESZKE
***
VERSION NUMBER 1.00

The Cursed Moon
Book I

by Luiza Dobrzyńska

Introduction

A spectacular chase down the streets of one of the main cities of the state was so unusual that people in shops crowded to the windows, while those on the sidewalks ran away and hid wherever they could. At a time when pedestrian traffic on the streets was limited for safety reasons to an absolute minimum, there weren't many of them, so everyone quickly found shelter. Public cars and relatively few corporate limousines swerved aside, sometimes narrowly avoiding a collision with a heavy police motorcycle or an elegant "private vehicle," as cars owned by high-ranking individuals were commonly referred to. Few could afford not just such a vehicle, but the registration fee, tax, and all mandatory insurance, and even fewer citizens had a chance to obtain the necessary permit to use such a mode of transport. The fact that one of these individuals was being chased by the police with sirens—modern motorcycles that the law enforcement officers were equipped with also had their own "screams"—caused quite understandable excitement. The officer quickly caught up with the "private vehicle," overtook it, and blocked its way. In a desperate attempt to evade, the driver skidded and crashed into one of the advertisement pillars, damaging both the post and his beautiful limousine. The officer jumped off the motorcycle, yanked the door of the "private vehicle" open with a strong tug, and pulled the fugitive out. Despite visible resistance, he handcuffed him and only then called for backup through his communicator. Witnesses to the event could still admire the well-dressed arrestee, struggling with the uniformed officer, until a prison van arrived at the scene. Dozens of theories were quickly hatched about what was happening, and everyone who saw it had something to talk about for the entire day. However, the next day, they futilely searched for any mention of the incident in news bulletins and gossip magazines.

"General, you can't do this to me!"

The young man stood straight, with his hands properly at his sides. Very tall and built like a wrestler, with sharp features of his lean face and short-cropped blond hair, he looked a bit like a model hero from a comic book. However, as he stood there, looking with a silent plea at the older man in uniform sitting behind the desk, he could evoke sympathy in any onlooker.

"Without hysteria, Lieutenant Wilder," the general tapped the desk with a stylus used for writing on informational foil. He seemed confident, but nevertheless consistently avoided the gaze of his subordinate.

"I know and you know that I acted correctly."

"Of course. No one is above the law."

"So why...?!"

"Wilder, please lower your voice. You are a fine officer, but you have one fundamental flaw. You don't understand certain subtleties of our profession and you don't realize that it sometimes requires being a diplomat, not a soldier. Publicly arresting the governor's son is something you should have spared yourself. If we were in some small town and you had caught the mayor's son, then perhaps... But we are in Texas! This is one of the most important pieces of land on our damn hemisphere and the people who govern it hold real power in their hands! They answer only to Number One. And you treated the son of one of them as if you were dealing with just another drunken miscreant."

"With all due respect, General... Mick Hoover caused an accident in which two young people died. He fled the scene and was brazenly confident that he would get away with it, just like his previous antics. The first better miscreant you graciously mentioned has less on their conscience and is more worthy of respect."

The state police general, Anthony Strikes, hissed impatiently and stood up from behind the desk. He quickly realized that reaching his subordinate only to his chin wouldn't allow him to look down at him, so he sat back down. His situation wasn't the best, even without having to deal with Wilder. He had barely reached one star on his general's epaulettes and his position was now in question.

"You don't understand anything. There is such a thing as politics. People in uniform must know this and not play lone riders from a children's movie, because it serves no purpose. Even if you belong to an elite unit. It was enough to hand young Hoover over to his father's custody. Don't you realize that people like him also don't want their family's issues to be too public?"

"Because what? Because once it gets into the press, it can't be swept under the rug, right?"

"When you have a family of your own, you may understand what it means to have your hands tied by an overeager officer when your son faces the death penalty!" Now the general accidentally raised his voice. "Surely you know that once the files are handed over to the courts, nothing can be done! Even the highest judge will only be able to sign the verdict and maybe add a recommendation to the appellate department, which in such a case does nothing."

"I know! And that's exactly why I personally delivered them to the courthouse, so they wouldn't accidentally-on-purpose get lost!"

Striker frowned, hearing the lieutenant's aggressive tone.

"Please do not shout in my office," he shook his head and adopted a sharp, official tone. "I have official papers regarding your case here. You are being reassigned."

"What?!" Clint Wilder's mind quickly flashed through possible locations for his reassignment, from a remote lost town on the plains to an Inuit village in Alaska. "Where? For what?!"

"For being too impulsive and not knowing when to back off!" The general's voice softened. "Please understand my situation. I'm being pressured from above. My career is also hanging by a thread, all because of your foolish, unnecessary stunt. Please lock the door, and then finally sit down and compose yourself. This is an official order. "Lieutenant Wilder listened without a word. He felt as if the whole world was crashing down on him, and completely unjustly. He had served in the police for six years. He was considered one of the best, and for good reason, he had quickly advanced, faster than any of his colleagues. Last year, he celebrated his acceptance into the Texas Rangers, which had been his dream since childhood. Although this "corps" had long since become just a kind of club for distinguished police officers, having lost its significance at least two hundred years ago, being accepted into it was still quite an honor, especially for someone as young as Wilder. He was really good. He had been trapped multiple times, tried to be bribed or intimidated – to no avail. He had managed to avoid all possible threats, only to finally stumble over his own honesty and commitment. This truly seemed like someone's cruel joke.

"You will be sent to the Moon," Strikes continued. "With a significant promotion to sweeten the deal. The documents arrived this morning. From now on, you are a captain and you are going to a new assignment. Immediately. To be exact, in thirty-two hours. I want to help you, so I will now pass on the information I have that might be useful to you to start."

"The Moon? You mean, the mining colony?" It was much worse than he had expected.

"Yes. The chief of police there was killed in the line of duty a few months ago; they need his successor. Currently, everything is being run by Lieutenant Juliette Ankes... you will replace her."

"Is she performing poorly?" Wilder asked this question mechanically, just to say something. He felt stunned. Lunnar? That forbidden hole? Is it that bad? To hell with the promotion if he has to end up there!

"Not really, I'm managing somehow so far, but she is simply both too young and too inexperienced for such a responsible position." The general touched a button on the computer keyboard, and a picture of a reddish, delicate-looking girl appeared on the television wall. "Here she is. A young lady from a really good, although social, background, trained as a librarian and a landscape technician at the same time. Initially B1, reclassified to A3. Previously worked at the Medical Academy in Palm Springs. Not suitable material for a police officer, do you think? Nothing could be further from the truth."

"I didn't say anything like that."

"But it's clear from you what you thought. No. This little one has a real detective talent. The previous chief was her supervising officer when she arrived in Lunnar as a key witness in some highly political case. I don't know what case; the files are classified."

"Well, it must have been serious." Not that he cared. He was too busy with his own suffering to think about others' troubles now.

"Probably so, but I don't know the details. Inspector Scott Cavanaugh took her under his wing, trained her, and after a while promoted her to his deputy. He probably also had an affair with her."

"So, a promotion through the bed?"

"I don't know... No, probably not. Cavanaugh wouldn't allow himself that. He had his faults, but he took the job very seriously. He wasn't just anyone; you can read about him in police annals. Juliette Kaphoolie has a knack for this work and is really sharp. And it's no wonder. A3 is a great rarity in uniformed service, especially on the Moon... You are B2, right? Exactly. That's still a lot. Although it varies. Please take a look."

The general changed the image. Now the screen displayed a photo of a dark-haired man with deeply sunken blue eyes and a face that seemed prematurely aged.

"The coroner and also the company doctor, Kelley Mc-Cave. A2. Exiled for violating genetic discipline. He married a B-class woman and pretended to be B1 for a while, even successfully. Competent and hardworking, and although he sometimes bends the rules and is undisciplined, overall he can be trusted."

He clicked the switch, bringing up the next slide. On the screen appeared a chubby blonde girl with a childlike face.

"Susana Herefort, A1, independent virtualist. Recently on a police payroll, "apparently a genius in their field. There is no information they couldn't reach, but they are a bit impulsive, like all virtualists. The niece of the current governor... I don't have any photos of them or any further details. A mysterious guy, also A1, you'd better watch out for him. Others are more typical.

Another photo change. A handsome man with a Southern appearance.

"Sergeant Feri Kuncz, C1. A former military member, left the army after some big scandal. He also had bad luck in the police, his partner died on what seemed to be an ordinary patrol, and he ended up behind a desk for a long time. However, he knows his job and can be relied on. He definitely won't be a nuisance to you."

Next change. A handsome, stocky middle-aged man with short facial hair.

"Neil Slavik, A3. A capable criminal lawyer, but no law firm on Earth wanted him. A cheerful guy and somewhat of a grabber. It's hard for him to keep his hands to himself around a pretty woman. Psychologists have concluded that it's a sort of tic for him, meaning he can't control it. He has the appropriate certificate; the matter is, overall, harmless, but I suppose you understand why no one wanted to work with him. He only found employment in Lunnar because there no one pays attention to such trivialities."

Another man, a Latino with an unreadable face, dressed in stormtrooper uniform.

"Alec Merino, C2, commander of the rapid response battalion. In Lunnar, stormtroopers also serve as transporters for prison ambulances; it's worth knowing. Merino is disciplined, effective, and there are no remarks on him. I don't know anything closer about him."

Now the screen showed a dark-skinned, stout woman with tightly pulled-back hair, round eyes, and distinctly African facial features.

"Lieutenant Rosanda Merrick, also C1. She heads the department for economic crimes," he grimaced sarcastically. "What's this department anyway, a few people and a local private detective, a loser... Merrick even earned the nickname Piranha while still on Earth. Once she finds a foothold, she won't let go. They say she has a grip like a bulldog. However, intelligence... well, at the upper level of a typical C, so not overwhelming. Like you, she caught the wrong person. He went to the gas chamber, and she was sent to Lunnar, supposedly as a sign of trust."

The next photo also showed a woman, in uniform, with hard features and broad shoulders. She looked more like a man, and although the bulges of the uniform hinted at breasts, the military bandana tied around her neck made it impossible to determine if there was perhaps an Adam's apple.

"Captain Lois Ann Sirtis, a professional soldier, commander of a military garrison, supposedly B2, though there's no proof of that. No markings due to an injury sustained in cartel wars. You need to be very careful around her. She'll be watching you. She was a close friend of Cavanaugh and quickly became fond of Lieutenant Ankes, perhaps even a little too fond. She likely has a preference for women over men. She won't like that some newcomer is replacing that little doll in the commander's position. She could make your life difficult, and she has the means to do so."

"Nice cast," Wilder muttered. Something about that Colonel Sirtis did not sit well with him, although he couldn't quite say what.

"That would basically be everyone you need to know about in advance; you will meet the others on-site. Oh, and there's also 'this.'"

A somewhat angular yet gentle and rather handsome face of a young man appeared on the screen. He had quite long, ash-blond hair that fell in strands across his cheeks and neck, narrow eyes, and dark, irregular eyebrows.

"Android. A prototype of a new line; supposedly, it thinks independently. At the main command of Lunnar, it serves as an assistant, which really means nothing. It belongs to Lieutenant Ankes and is something like her personal bodyguard."

"Android? So, what, a more advanced sexbot? My sister bought one to avoid going to dating centers, but she doesn't flaunt it."

The general shook his head.

"This is not a sexbot. Rather, it's an artificial human, from what I know. It thinks independently and can make independent decisions."

"An independent robot?!"

"I said it was a prototype."

"And isn't that... a bit dangerous? What if it rebels?"

Strikes reluctantly shrugged. He had never been interested in such issues before and had no intention of starting now.

"Apparently, it's not possible. Besides, I don't know; I'm not familiar with it," he closed the projector with a wave of his hand. "Wilder... Clint... I truly regret this. I don't like losing my best people, even on orders from above. You got reassigned despite my official objections. Maybe I can get you back when the storm quiets down a bit. For now, however, there's nothing that can be done."

I
CLINT WILDER
Personal Diary

If I say that Anna is everything to me, it will be as if I said nothing. We have known each other since school. She was never one of our cheerleaders or a Kardashian – I never liked that word. I knew it was derived from the name of three sisters who were incredibly popular back in the 21st century. Later, it started to be used to describe any girl from a very famous and very wealthy family, spoiled, silly, representing nothing, yet still being the object of widespread interest and adoration. To me, that word always sounded wrong, it grated like a broken mechanism, and that's why I don't use it. However, the phenomenon itself exists, for when and where has it not been? In our college, the main Kardashian was "the flawless Barbra Scott," the best of the cheerleaders supporting the school basketball team. Very pretty, a platinum blonde with light blue eyes and a figure straight out of a sports magazine, always dressed according to the current fashion, adorned with the latest gadgets like a Christmas tree, terrorizing her peers by pointing out their physical imperfections, seducing every boy in sight, but empty as a proverbial jar.

Anna was an entirely different type – dark-haired, fairly petite, with a tan complexion and slightly slanted, brown eyes. In my opinion, she was much more interesting, but significantly less glamorous than the girls from the cheerleading team, quiet, focused on studying. Since I had known her, she had one great ambition: to break free from the subordinate social class and become "someone" without the help of family connections, which Barbra could count on. She wholeheartedly believed that her future possibilities were poorly assessed in the delivery room, and I nodded whenever she talked about it. Did I really think she was much smarter than the average B3 that she was? I don't know. She wanted that, and I wanted her to succeed, though I would have to be blind to ignore the fact that as a student, she barely maintained her place in the official IQ tests around the school average. Even more astonishing was how quickly she shot to the top when it came to the grade rankings. However, she paid a high price for it. Every exam in which she received ninety-nine points out of one hundred instead of a perfect score became a reason for her hysteria and locking herself in her room for as long as a week until she improved her result to a hundred percent. That perfectionism seemed to me then something worthy of the highest admiration.

Over time, I noticed that the pursuit of absolute perfection was slowly destroying Anna. I joined the police, and other classmates quickly found their places in life, but for her, everything she could achieve as a B3 was not enough. The only concession she made for the lower classification was me. As she honestly admitted, she couldn't give me up, even though she should, since she aimed higher. It was for her that I studied like crazy and finally managed to get reclassified to B2, which did not so much please her as it motivated her to work *even harder. We had been inseparable almost since the start of our studies at the public college, and it is understandable that upon receiving a life sentence from General Striker, my first steps were directed straight to her. She couldn't meet me right away, but she promised to come to our favorite café an hour before my departure. Just that should have been a red flag for me, but I was too nervous to think clearly. I had to quickly pack clothes and all the necessary little things, sign the documents to release the apartment, arrange for the mail forwarding to the new place, and so on. I had a lot to do.*

Anna showed up on time. She looked gorgeous, and what she was wearing probably cost my entire monthly salary. They must have been paying her well at that corporation where she got a job, initially as a warehouse clerk, then as a secretary, and finally rising to the position of assistant to one of the directors. Barista looked at her in awe as she approached to place her order before heading to my table.

"I only have half an hour," she stated immediately, sitting across from me with a caffetino cup in hand. "So tell me, what's so important that you needed to see me right away?"

I told her everything as concisely as possible, while also observing the play of emotions on her face. For the first time, it occurred to me that I might not really know her at all. As I was going to this meeting, I was certain of how she would react, but now, even before she opened her mouth, I knew I was wrong.

"And what do you expect by telling me this?" she asked coldly.

I looked at her and felt my heart slowly freeze.

"We once planned a wedding. We could…" I stopped, already realizing that it made no sense.

"I worked hard for what I have," she said slowly. "I won't give it all up now to bury myself with you in a mining colony on the Moon."

"But that's only temporary!"

"Don't raise your voice," she admonished me. She took a sip of her drink, grimaced slightly, and put the cup down in disgust. "Only now do I see what awful stuff they're serving here. Not worth a single point."

I looked at her as if I were seeing her for the first time, and I could indeed regard it as such. This was not the Anna I knew. Or maybe it was, but I had simply failed to see her true face until now?

"I thought all along that there was something special between us," I tried weakly. "We've been together since high school. We faced all adversities together…"

"Don't try to blackmail me," she countered immediately, coldly and calculatingly. "The past can be as beautiful or as horrifying as one wishes, and it can be reminisced about on warm evenings on the terrace, but what truly matters is here and now. You can't expect me to throw away everything I've achieved just because you never know when to give up and keep getting yourself into trouble."

I fell silent for a long moment, unable to find the words.

"Anna, I don't recognize you," I finally whispered.

She shrugged. She took a mirror out from a pouch at her waist, checked her reflection, and touched up the outline of her lips with a pencil.

"That's your problem now," she said as she stood up from the chair. "I sincerely wish you good luck in your new job.

Write sometimes. And if you want, you can pay for my caffe-tino. I won't give a single point for this rubbish."

"I remember you used to like it, back when you couldn't really afford it," I wanted to remind her, but I held my tongue. I sat with my head leaning over the countertop and wondered whether to start banging my head against it or just burst into tears like a small child.

***

"Hello, Tomcat!" someone called from the back.

Wilder turned around. On the airport tarmac stood Elvis Greyfox, an experienced detective, his partner, mentor, and friend, known by colleagues as "Dakota." By the side of the older man was Salome Delaforrette, a rookie police officer who had been assigned to them as an intern a few months ago. They embraced warmly.

"We know how you were treated," Elvis said with compassion. "I want you to know that our entire precinct is going wild with anger. Striker is right not to show his face around here, because the guys would probably tear him apart.

"Tough luck," Wilder grumbled. Salome, nicknamed "Forest Nibble" by her colleagues on her first day of duty due to her short stature and as a play on her last name, was keeping her coal-black eyes glued to him, so he added bravely, "It happened. Tell everyone that I would do the same thing again in a heartbeat."

"Nobody doubts that, brother."

"It's nice of you to come to see me off."

Elvis smirked sarcastically.

"What see you off, Tomcat? We're flying with you."

Only now did the newly appointed captain notice that both of them had well-packed travel bags with them.

"What do you mean, you're flying? What are you talking about, Dakota?"

Elvis shrugged.

"Normally. I don't have any family or obligations, besides, as an intern, I've already been to Lunnar and I know what to expect there. And Sal said she'd love to have a big adventure. The Moon has fascinated her even before."

Clint suddenly felt something warm inside, and at the same time, the painful pressure around his heart that had been choking him for two days eased and melted away. He had been worried about this symptom. On the way between offices, he had even stopped by an automatic diagnostic station, but the results showed no signs of any pathology. This meant that the pain must be psychosomatic, and the sudden relief only confirmed that diagnosis.

"Listen, just because we're friends doesn't mean…" he started, but Elvis interrupted him immediately.

"Spare me. Yes, it does mean that. We're flying and that's it. We both got official assignments, so you have no say anymore."

The speaker above them announced in a warm, feminine voice.

"Passengers of flight 402 are asked to proceed to gate number five and prepare travel documents."

They exchanged glances. Elvis leaned down and threw his bag over his shoulder.

"Let's go," he said. "We don't want to miss the flight."

Clint followed him, still dazed. Actually, it was understandable that Elvis made such a decision. The aging and somewhat bitter cop had treated Wilder like a son from the start, like family he never had. But Salome? Young, pretty, and sociable, why did it occur to her to bury herself in Lunnar? There was some mystery in that. He decided to postpone solving it for later. Everything indicated that he would have plenty of time for such distractions. After all, what could possibly happen in such a hole?

On board, he settled into the seat indicated by the flight attendant and shut his eyes. He just wanted to rid his mind of the remnants of nervousness, but unexpectedly, he fell asleep. He was only awakened by a shake on his shoulder.

"We're here, Tomcat. But you were snoring."

He jumped up from his seat.

"I'm sorry, I haven't slept for over a day."

"Can't blame you. But now come on, someone is probably waiting for us."

"And what if not?" Salome piped up. She stood next to Elvis with her bag slung over her shoulder and shifted from foot to foot. It seemed that only now was she beginning to realize what she had decided.

"In that case, we'll order some transport. They surely have taxis here. Stop whining, Nibble." Elvis patted the younger colleague on the back and headed for the exit.

They were the last to leave the ferry. Outside, they were somewhat surprised by the sight of the airport, arranged just as modernly as the one they had departed from. They subconsciously expected greater primitiveness, after all, Lunnar still functioned in the collective consciousness as a mining colony and practically nothing more. The inhabitants of Earth seemed to know,"that the city is developed, but they still associated it with makeshift shacks for miners and slightly better buildings for administration. Snapshots from the Moon rarely appeared in the media. They were considered uninteresting, although – contrary to this attitude – spending a few days "on vacation" there was seen, due to the costs, as something to boast about, a kind of whim of wealthy snobs. Something like a very expensive camp in primitive conditions, where there are no conveniences of civilization. Soon this thinking was set to change, as Selenoport, a city of rest and recreation, was formally opened two weeks ago and was currently hosting the first group of thrill-seeking tourists.

After passing through customs, they were directed to the waiting area, where among all the signs held by the hands of residents' family and friends waiting for their arrival, they spotted the right one. It was being held by a tall, slender woman of mixed race with her hair styled in dreadlocks and the symbol C1 on her forehead. She was wearing a police uniform, adorned with a patch of a senior officer and a wide belt with many pockets, different from the one used on Earth.

"Captain Wilder?" she asked coolly and saluted upon receiving a positive response. "Senior Officer Kendra Maru. Welcome to Lunnar."

"Nice to meet you," Clint replied. "These are my officers, Lieutenant Elvis Greyfox and Officer Salome Delaforette."

"Please follow me to the service rover." Maru ignored the outstretched hand of the officer, turned on her heel, and moved ahead.

"Warm welcome," Greyfox muttered sarcastically. "Did you also get the impression that we are very welcome here?"

Salome smiled slightly.

"We'll have to win them over," she said quietly. "They can't love us on command. Let's understand them."

The senior officer looked at her with affection. Since this girl had been assigned to their squad, he had treated her like a daughter and that is why he was pleased that she had decided to move with them to the Moon. He lived under the impression, like almost all Earth residents, that nothing particularly dangerous or even interesting was happening there.

"You always try to explain everyone, Little One. They should train you to be a negotiator."

The service vehicle surprised them a lot. It looked heavy, almost awkward compared to Earth's chasers, which were sleek and elegant. It also seemed to lack the remote-control circuits from headquarters, like those on Earth. Behind the control panel, glowing with LED lights, sat a muscular, dark-skinned man with cheerful eyes and a shaved head, clearly the driver. He bore the C3 symbol on his forehead, distorted by an old scar.

"Welcome, welcome, boss!" he exclaimed. "Which one of you is it?"

He represented a polar opposite type than Maru, who took a seat next to him. He radiated friendliness towards the whole world and a joy for life.

"Me. Clint Wilder. Welcome, uh…?" the captain stumbled slightly.

"Officer Paul Idalgo, reporting for duty. Driver, barista, gofer, and generally fetch, carry, clean up."

Wilder introduced his companions mechanically.

"Nice to meet you, Sergeant, Miss," the officer started the engine. "Put your bags in the trunk and please load yourselves inside. Go on, go on, you'll fit. Trainee, huh? Our Kendra is also training to be a detective. Actually, she only has the final exam left. Maybe you two will become friends?"

"Shut your mouth, idiot," Maru growled through her teeth. She did not seem thrilled at such a prospect. Salome wisely refrained from making any comments.

The rover started and entered a tunnel illuminated by directional lights, joining a line of similar vehicles. For a long moment, nothing was visible except flashing lights, gray walls with information boards, and silhouettes of cars, then they emerged onto a wide highway leading to the city. The newcomers pressed against the windows. The highway was covered by a tunnel made of reinforced aluglass panels. Mogli therefore, with some effort, perceive the moonlit landscape shimmering behind the transparent metal plates – a dead space known from images and reports. Once they crossed the actual borders of the city, the view changed. Lunnar seemed primarily cramped to the newcomers. The buildings were certainly denser than in any contemporary earthly city, and also much squatter. There was no mention of skyscrapers typical of large metropolises and regularly arranged squares in such a place, so that did not come as a surprise. What left an unpleasant impression, however, was something else.

"How ugly and gloomy it is here," Salome finally whispered.

Since the synthesis of "smart paints," which do not require refreshing, earthly homes – whether in large metropolises or in the smallest towns – have been painted in cheerful, vibrant colors. Sometimes uniformly, and sometimes in patterns, depending on the consensus of the residents. People felt better among bright, contrasting colors than in the once-dominant cold grayness. Lunnar, however, was maintained in exactly that tone: concrete, steel, and glass.

"You'll get used to it, miss," Idalgo comforted her. "It's not that bad. Well, maybe at first. You just have to endure the first months, and then it will flow."

"How long have you been here, officer?" the girl asked after a moment.

"Just Paul, miss."

She offered him her hand.

"Salome."

"Nice. And how long have I been here? Soon a quarter of a century will pass."

"Seriously?"

"Yes."

"So how come…?"

"Still an officer?" he finished. "I haven't always been a policeman. I started at the helium-3 processing plant. It still exists, and it was established before it turned out that it's not such a super element as once thought and its use is rather limited."

"And didn't it tempt you to return to Earth?"

"Sometimes, at first. You see, Salome… I don't have anyone there. No family, no friends, just acquaintances, people I just say 'hi' and 'goodbye' to. But here I've made buddies, real buddies for drinking and fighting, right in the first year. For example, my roommate, Ira Smythe. He was a foreman then, now he sits on the factory council. We formed a bond in the early months of our acquaintance and to this day we are best friends, even though I left production and joined the police, and he has been promoted high. I may not be as close with others, but we generally stick together."

Maru's stony silence began to irritate Wilder. In contrast to Idalgo's cheerful, friendly chatter, it became not only strange but overtly hostile. On one hand, he understood this girl; on the other hand, the absurdity of her behavior was increasingly reaching him. He was not a usurper; he received a legal appointment. Not only did he not seek it, but it was actually a personal disaster for him. Did he really deserve such treatment, as if he had stolen something from someone? He felt like saying something unpleasant, but he held back. Instead, he asked in an official tone:

"Officer Maru, what types of crimes are most often reported here?"

The woman in the front seat slowly turned her head.

"Minor offenses are a daily occurrence," she said in a dry voice. "Bigger thefts happen every few days. At least once a week there are fights, often involving serious bodily harm. From time to time, there are raids by miners on one of the districts inhabited by factory workers or vice versa, which looks dangerous and is against the law, but usually, there are no victims, at most minor injuries. It's a kind of local social sport. More serious crimes are usually related to corporate rivalries, but there may be homicides in the heat of passion or under the influence of new types of drugs."

"Do you have a lot of them?" Elvis wondered. "Aren't they handling it excessively?"

Maru shrugged. The rover turned and descended into the next tunnel, stretching beneath the city center, obedient to the enormous neon arrow reading "Detour."

"Flight stations have nothing to do with this," she replied. "They operate with legal substances, tested and with assigned neutralizers. In Lunnar, there are laboratories developing new drugs and new narcotics, either created directly there or synthesized by the people working in them. They test them either on vagrants or on volunteers and distribute them illegally."

Wilder furrowed his brow.

"And you're not doing anything about it?" he asked.

The senior officer turned around even more and looked him straight in the eyes.

"How are we supposed to do that… captain? We lack personnel and legal capabilities. Lunnar is not Earth, you will see that. The Lunnar Company consists of seventeen mining corporations, five focused on processing, and ten manufacturing. Each of them has its own security, called industrial police, independent of us and their own internal regulations, approved by the court. These regulations differ significantly from each other, and we also have the criminal and civil code of Lunnar, which was not copied from Earth regulations. It was developed for the needs of a mining colony that was established in extremely hostile conditions, and it has never been changed. We must ensure compliance with A. The Law of Lunnar, B. The Laws of Earth and C. The internal codes of the corporations. Which sometimes is truly circus acrobatics." Maru visibly relaxed and thawed. "The main problem you will have to face is the lack of manpower. People with the appropriate qualifications prefer to join corporate police forces, where the work is safer and much better paid. Besides, you should know that miners do not get along with manufacturers, all the way from the lowest levels to the highest. Some dig holes under others and they are subject to a kind of omerta. When something happens, it is very difficult to find witnesses and get anything out of them."

"And how is the civil population's attitude toward the uniformed officers?"

"Like everywhere. They treat us like a necessary evil. Or even unnecessary."

The conversation, which was becoming increasingly friendly, was interrupted by a sound echoing through the tunnel. Idalgo slammed the brakes, and the other drivers did the same, almost at the same second. It was clear that they had been trained to respond immediately to alarm signals.

"What happened?" Salome shouted.

"I'll find out soon." Idalgo turned on the old-fashioned walkie-talkie. An irritated multi-voice burst from the speaker. It was the drivers' demanding explanations and cursing the unexpected delay.

After a moment, one voice rose above all the others.

"This is the monitoring operator speaking. Please remain calm and do not leave your vehicles. A serious crime has occurred on branch CE5, the road is closed. Please prepare for a stop until the appropriate services arrive."

Idalgo looked questioningly at Kendra Maru, then glanced at the passengers.

"CE5 starts just a few meters from here."

Clint Wilder made a decision in a fraction of a second.

"We're getting out. We'll take a look at this. Are masks needed?"

"No," Kendra unlocked the rover's door. "The tunnels are ventilated. It smells a bit, but you can breathe normally."

"Damn, I don't have my new badge yet. It should be waiting for me at the station."

"That's fine. I have mine, Paul does too, that's enough."

"Good. Grab your weapons." The captain checked his holster, which contained the latest model of the service pistol, the so-called dual gun: it fired both electric stun rounds and live ammunition.

They disembarked onto the roadway, ignoring the calls from the loudspeakers. Maru searched for the nearest camera and extended her hand with the badge towards it. The operator fell silent for a moment, then called out:

"Police on site! To everyone: do not interfere with the officers! I repeat: do not interfere…"

Bypassing the immobilized vehicles, they found a turn-off to branch CE5, which, if the signs were to be believed, led to one of the working-class districts. The damaged partition swayed on ripped fastenings.at a distance from the entrance in the corridor, one could see a truck tipped on its side and scattered packages with unknown contents. Clint drew his weapon from its holster and unlatched it, sliding the system switch to stun mode. The electric projectile, a type of battery that released a large impulse upon contact with the target, incapacitated anyone it hit in any part of the body. Wilder suspected that the mysterious assailant could not possibly be wearing armor against such projectiles, as civilians were not allowed to possess them, making stun weapons sufficient in this situation.

"Chief," Kendra addressed him for the first time in this way. "There were two explosions. One here, and the other in the main corridor, just further on."

"How do you know?" Wilder was surprised.

"I have absolute pitch. At first, I thought it was just an echo, but if that were the case, they wouldn't have blocked off the entire route."

"Right. Hey, is anyone here?! Police, please come out!"

No one answered. They didn't even hear a rustle that might indicate someone was trying to hide from their sight. There were no signs of blood on the ground or among the scattered packages that would suggest someone had fled.

Keeping his dual weapon ready, Wilder approached the overturned van and cautiously peered into the driver's seat.

"Someone's here!... though, actually, no. Oh crap..."

His companions, intrigued, also moved closer to the vehicle. Sitting rigidly in the driver's seat was a male figure – not a person, not even a robot, just a dummy. A male mannequin dressed in clothing and a cap pressed down on its forehead. A tangle of thin wires spiraled around the dashboard, connected to some device.

"What the hell?" Elvis huffed.

"Officer Maru, have you seen anything like this before?" Wilder turned to Kendra.

"Damn it, just call me by my first name," she snapped. "And no, I haven't seen it. I have no idea what's going on here."

"Don't you have any remote-controlled delivery vans?"

"No. Only drones from bars on the phone have their own programming. They deliver snacks all over the city."

"Why not vans? That would be logical."

Kendra sighed and wiped her sweaty forehead with her sleeve.

"Too dangerous. Autonomous control works for drones because they fly, and quite high too. They are also made of ultra-light materials. If one crashes, it might only splatter pedestrians with mayonnaise. A van with this kind of device would pose a serious threat to public traffic in case of even the slightest malfunction, and we can't have central control on the Moon," she paused for a moment. "Why is it so hot here? Usually, these corridors are cold like an industrial fridge."

Only now did the captain pay attention to the temperature around them. It was clearly rising. He suspiciously sniffed.

"I smell smoke! Something's burning nearby!"

Elvis looked around and went to the wall. He touched it with his hand and jumped back as if scalded.

"It's hot! What's going on there?!"

"Technical tunnels," Kendra looked around nervously. "I don't know what could be burning in there."

Wilder turned towards the visible camera under the ceiling.

"Hey, operator! We need technical support with fire extinguishers! Probable fire in the technical tunnels next to route CE5!"

The speaker crackled.

"I'm sending support. Evacuate the tunnel for your own safety."

"You all go," the captain directed his companions. "I'll check the driver's seat. Come on, that's an order!"

Elvis Greyfox clearly wanted to say something like "Not a chance," but glancing at Kendra and Idalgo, he changed his mind. He could not undermine his friend's authority in front of his new subordinates from the outset, so with a slight sigh, he firmly urged the rest to leave.

Clint peeked into the driver's seat again. He didn't have a sample collection kit with him, so he had to settle for a handy recorder. He took a series of photos, then gently tugged at the dummy's arm. Something told him it had to be important. It yielded easily. It was not very well secured, only by a strap with an automatic buckle, which soon gave way. A cable turned out to be just an additional security measure. It was not connected to anything.

He took the mannequin under his arm and retreated from the tunnel, where it was getting hotter and hotter. He was nearly bumped into by a woman in uniform, commanding a team of firefighters, supported by several technicians in civilian clothes.

"Get out of here," she ordered sternly. "We have started the evacuation of all vehicles from this route, go back to yours. We are taking over the area."

Kendra Maru pulled the captain by the elbow.

"Let's go. She's in charge here now. Later she will give us an official report, but for now, we mustn't interfere."

Weaving between vehicles, they reached the police SUV, beside which stood two clearly anxious firefighters.

"You're finally here," one of them said. "Get in and move. We've assigned an emergency route to the center, follow the green arrows. We will notify the command when it is safe to check everything for the investigation."

Wilder tossed the dummy into the trunk, which was dutifully opened by Idalgo, and got in, settling between Elvis and Salome.

"It's starting off nicely," he muttered under his breath and asked louder, "What could have caught fire? I mean, in those corridors?"

"Some technical stuff," Idalgo replied. He drove out behind the line of vehicles from the tunnel and directed the SUV onto the detour. "They store various things there. Only the service staff knows exactly what."

"We'll need to talk to them. Officer Maru, you are… you're a candidate for detective, as I've heard?" the captain addressed Kendra. "So, when the firefighters let us know it's safe to act, you will conduct the investigation. Let's treat it as a final test before the exam. You'll take Miss Delaforette with you, let her train."

The policewoman glanced at him over her shoulder.

"Roger that," she smiled wryly. "I'll take care of her."

The police vehicle emerged from the underground onto the city streets and shortly stopped in front of one of the buildings. It only differed from the others by a large sign with a shiny inscription "Headquarters" and the fact that there were two armed guards standing before the doors.

"We're here," Idalgo announced. "Let's get out."

II
CLINT WILDER
Personal Diary

Entering the headquarters, I felt a tightening in my throat. I was stepping onto foreign territory, which was to become my home for an unknown time, and a rush of gratitude washed over me for the friends who decided to support me with their presence at the cost of their own private lives. Without them, it would be much harder for me now.

A short, wide hall, bristling with all kinds of sensors, led to a huge room, from which two narrower corridors branched off further on. There were single desks with adjoining cabinets, not even cubicles. The local officers could probably only dream of their own offices. Crossing the threshold, I almost bumped into a very young, very pretty girl with the C3 symbol on her forehead. She wore a standard courier armband on her arm, navy blue, with a silver lightning bolt enclosed in a circle, and a small bag marked with the same symbol on a long strap, slung over her shoulder. She must have belonged to the police service. Nonetheless, she was dressed in civilian clothes—a floral sweatshirt, canvas shoes, and light shorts that boldly revealed absolutely fantastic legs. I gawked at them like a fool and only after a moment did, I pay attention to the rest. The girl had the looks of a Hawaiian or Tahitian—light brown skin, long black hair reaching past her waist and shimmering in the light like glass, a small nose, prominent cheekbones, and laughing black eyes shaped like almonds. I couldn't help but immediately picture her in a grass skirt and a garland of flowers around her neck, dancing hula on the beach.

"Oh wow, the new chief has arrived!" she shouted at my sight so loudly that it could probably be heard on the street, and she immediately disappeared somewhere.

The officers present at the headquarters left their work and turned towards me. Even the civilians being interrogated at several desks did the same. Under their gaze, I suddenly felt like an insect pinned to a pin and displayed in a case, or perhaps rather like a dangerous predator in a cage. They were watching me closely, like a zoo exhibit, where you never know what to expect, and rather unfriendly.

"Good morning, everyone," I said uncertainly. Then I pulled myself together. "My name is Clint Wilder and from now on I am the commander of the lunnar's police."

From the corridor to the left, a young guy in civilian clothes came out.

"That's disgusting," he stated emphatically. "A filthy disgrace."

I looked at him in surprise. He didn't look like a police officer. Judging by his build, he was definitely strong and athletic, but nothing about him hinted at a law enforcement officer. Especially his unshaven face and his hair, quite long, formed into curls over his forehead, and the earring with the gear symbol in his ear. So, an engineer?

"Who do I have the pleasure of speaking with?" I asked bluntly.

"None of your business," he shot back. He was clearly looking for a confrontation. He reminded me of a ruffled rooster.

"Come on, Chris," a policewoman with lieutenant insignia on her uniform emerged from behind him. She was carrying a large box, filled to the brim. "This isn't the captain's fault. He doesn't issue the nominations. Besides, it's really not your matter."

She had reddish hair, gray eyes, an A3 mark, and a somewhat freckled face, which could best be described as "the portrait of the girl next door." Definitely not a Kardashian or a Mary Sue, just a buddy. That was the first thought that came to mind when looking at her. I realized that this must be Juliette Ankes, whom I was to replace. I felt terribly foolish.

"I'll help," I offered before I could think about how that sounded in this situation.

"No need, captain," she replied casually. "These are all light items, plus Hallie is already helping me. The commander's office is down this hallway, first door on the right. I'll be back there shortly for my computer, for now, please make yourself comfortable."

The cutie in shorts just brought in a second box and set it on one of the desks.

"Can I do anything else for you?" she sweetly offered, winking at me.

"Take these documents to Judge Holstein," the lieutenant handed her a thick envelope taken from the box. "Have him sign the receipt. On the way, you'll deliver the supply order to the office supplies warehouse and the furniture storage," she handed the girl a bundle of informational sheets, "and then you'll go to the barracks and deliver this box to Colonel."

"Anything else?" the Hawaiian girl groaned. She clearly didn't want to leave the command during such an interesting moment.

Lieutenant Ankes gave her a light jab in the side.

"Tell Mabel that I'm inviting her to lunch on Saturday. Now, go on."

Hallie made the face of a petulant child, but she gathered the things handed to her into her bag and dashed out.

"Is she always like this?" I asked.

She smiled at me. Not out of obligation, sarcastically, or with cold politeness. She just smiled. She didn't seem worried about the demotion; rather, she accepted it calmly. I had to admit she had incredible class.

"Hallie is a bit childish. After all, she's only nineteen, so it's no wonder."

"Nineteen? Shouldn't she still be studying?" I wondered.

"She doesn't want to. What can you do? She's of age, it's her life, let her do what she wants. Please follow me, I'll show you the office."

I looked back at Elvis and Salome.

"Go on your own, Tomcat," my friend said. "That is, excuse me, Captain. And we'll find ourselves a corner with a desk for two. We'll definitely fit."

"Take that," Juliette pointed to a piece of furniture against the opposite wall. "It belonged to my friend, Silvana Evans. She fell in service... it happens. It's been empty ever since, so there's nothing to clean."

The sergeant extended his hand to her, which she shook firmly, manly. He liked that. He couldn't stand women who offered their hand as if it were a dead frog.

"Elvis Greyfox," he introduced himself. "Friends call me Dakota."

"Oh?"

"I'm from this state. At the capital command in Dallas, I was the only non-Texan."

"Juliette Ankes. Everyone calls me Leeta."

A connection immediately formed between them. It always happened like that. Elvis, incredibly communicative, easily won the affection of the entire environment and individual people.His openness and kindness, despite life's bitterness, endeared him to people, and few believed, not knowing him deeply, how sharp and uncompromising he could be.

Now Lieutenant Ankes looked at Salome, who hastily straightened up and saluted.

"Constable Salome Delaforette, Ma'am!"

"Just Leeta is enough. We're not too fussy here when it comes to ranks. We call each other by our first names; it makes things easier. You'll see for yourself. Alright, let's go to the office, captain... Of course, this familiarity doesn't apply to the commander," she added with a laugh.

"I'll go with you," the boy with bright curls growled defiantly.

"Out of the question. In any case, skedaddle. I really don't need your support; I can manage on my own."

"Not a chance. I'm not going anywhere." He settled into one of the chairs against the wall and made a face that said, "Just try to move me."

Ankes waved her hand.

"And what to do with such a stubborn one? Let him sit if he wants."

Elvis burst out laughing.

"We'll keep an eye on him, Tomcat. You can go peacefully."

The lieutenant headed down the hallway, and I followed her, wondering who this aggressive blonde was. After all, he certainly wasn't the android Striker had told me about. Finally, I couldn't hold back and asked directly.

"He's my younger brother," she replied. "A social brother. He's the chief engineer for the construction of Selenoport. The construction is finished and now awaits transfer. He's got it in his head that some terrible harm has befallen me."

"Really, I didn't ask for this nomination," I assured her hurriedly. "No one even asked me for my opinion. I got an order, and that's it."

She glanced back at me over her shoulder and smiled again.

"Well, I know," she said. "No sensible person would come here of their own accord."

"I'm sorry," I muttered. I felt miserable under her bright, friendly gaze.

"Unnecessary. I actually welcomed the news of your nomination with relief."

"Please, let's use first names. After all, you'll be my deputy, right?"

"I don't know. It's your decision, Clint. Get to know my files, and then think. Just don't think you owe me anything, because you don't." She opened the heavy, wood-styled door. "Here it is."

The office struck me as dark and overloaded with old-fashioned furniture, but after a moment I realized that it was very functional. The previous commander had everything at hand; he didn't need to look far and could work without being distracted by searching for an official replica of this or that piece of evidence or document. There were also quite a few traditional books on the shelves, with pages covered in thin plastic, mainly textbooks on forensics from various eras. Scott Cavanaugh must have been a true enthusiast of his work, and I wondered how I would ever manage to step into his shoes. I had already had such thoughts before. After my conversation with General Striker, at his suggestion, I had searched for materials on Cavanaugh, and honestly, it terrified me. Compared to a legend of that caliber, I felt so small and insignificant that I had no idea how I would earn the respect of his people, being who I am and nothing more.

"There's a staff apartment." Ankes pointed to the closed inner door. "We cleaned it up for your arrival, so you can move in right away. I just need to grab my data banks and I'm out of here." Seeing my surprise, she added, "We use a special type of computers. They don't have their own memory resources, just peripherals that the user disconnects each time after service. Security reasons."

"Don't you have any external penetration protection systems here?"

She shook her head.

"The really good ones require a lot of energy, which we have limited. Alright, I'm going to set up at the desk. Internal twelve, just so you know," she indicated the comlink to me. "The list of numbers is actually next to the lamp."

She left before I could say "Thank you" and ask her about that android of hers. I was still thinking about him, but so far, he was neither in sight nor had anyone mentioned him. Is Striker joking with me and nothing like that actually existed?

I was left alone in my new office, overwhelmed and completely unprepared for the role I was suddenly assigned to.

***

Elvis Grayfox would never let himself be dismissed by trivial things or intimidated by sour faces. His friendly demeanor and cheerful remarks finally broke through the armor of the blond engineer, who, albeit reluctantly and curtly, began to respond to the questions posed to him. The older officer skillfully steered the conversation, sticking to technical matters. Before the engineer knew it, he was drawn into a social discussion and completely forgot about his anger.

"The command equipment may seem unnecessarily primitive compared to what exists on Earth," he said. "But that's a misleading impression. Most modern equipment wouldn't work here because there's no necessary supporting infrastructure on the Moon. It simply couldn't be stabilized here. The first selenites…"

"Who are they?"

"Moon technicians. They developed systems that can be maintained in these conditions, based on older technology, outdated but much more durable than the latest circuits."

"For example, sir…?"

"Nikanov. My name is Chris Nikanov. For example, the internal communication system," the engineer indicated a miniature panel. "It doesn't work on voice commands.

It doesn't even have sensors, which for some reason perform poorly on the Moon. You'll find them in many panels throughout the city, and you'll see for yourself that insisting on them was a bad idea. Here, at the command, you just have to press buttons, and the voice and image travel over a cable."

"How? A cable? What is this, prehistory?"

"Yes indeed. Sometimes old solutions are the best. You'll find that to be true."

Elvis looked around.

"I immediately noticed that certain things here are, let's say, rustic. For example, the furniture, especially those chairs…"

Chris nodded.

"Systems that allow for hiding part of the equipment in the walls require too much energy," he explained. "On Earth, there's no issue with that, but here there is. The storage gets charged during the Lunnar day, and then, during the Lunnar night, Lunnar is essentially reliant only on it."

"And what if it gets damaged?"

Chris smiled.

"There is an emergency plan, but so far there's been no need to implement it…"

He was interrupted by a signal from the comlink.

"I'm receiving," Elvis said loudly.

"Not like that. You need to use the button," Chris showed him the appropriate button. "We don't have voice control," I remind you.

"Medieval times," muttered the older officer disapprovingly as he turned on the receiver. "I'm reporting in."

"Send me Salome, Dakota," came Wilder's baritone from the speaker. "Let her take her personal weapon."

Moments later, a command flowed from a similar device on Kendra Maru's desk.

"Officer Maru, please come to the commander's office. Also ask that engineer to join; I have a few questions for him."

Both policewomen appeared before the captain within seconds. He sat at his desk, leaning on his elbows and flipping through documents on one of the padds.

"I just received a message from the firefighters. The blast sites can now be investigated," he said. "One is in tunnel CE5, where we were, and the other is at the exit of tunnel CE2. It's not yet known if they are connected. Take a photographer with you."

"Understood," the women replied almost simultaneously.

"Good luck." The captain glanced at the engineer, who passed by the departing policewomen. "Mr. Nikanov, right? I looked at the Selenoport construction bulletin, you receive quite a bit of praise there. I have a request for you."

"Interesting. Where do you get the idea that I would want to fulfill it?" Chris scoffed. It was clear that he was still determined to treat the new commander as an enemy.

"Your sister confirmed that you are an expert in several fields, not just construction." Clint decided not to draw attention to that.

Chris raised his eyebrows and stiffened even more.

"I am a space electronics engineer, not a construction worker," he declared with dignity. "I oversaw the assembly of equipment and its proper settings, not the digging of foundations."

"I understand that well," the captain forced himself to hide a smile. Brother Leety reacted almost like a child, but there was a certain charm in that. He did not incite impatience. "I want to ask you for a favor, and I assure you that it will involve your actual talents."

The engineer seemed eager to immediately reject the proposal, but he was intrigued about what it might be and decided to wait.

"What is it about?"

Wilder stood up from behind the desk, straightening up. Chris was clearly surprised at how tall and sturdy the new commander was, as he measured him with his eyes with involuntary appreciation. He himself was thin-boned, very slim, and of average height, which he secretly lamented. His carefully hidden dream, which he did not even admit to his sister, was to have a physique like the captain's – something unattainable even with all the advancements in cosmetic medicine.

"Let's go to the storage room, Engineer Nikanov. I'll show you something."

In the small utility room filled with crates of spare equipment, on a wide bench, lay a mannequin, taken by Wilder from an overturned van.

"A retail mannequin, basic model," Chris assessed at first glance. "Very poor specimen, probably a reject. What's the deal?"

"Exactly. I'm convinced there's something in it…"

"Just ordinary mechanisms in these kinds of dolls."

"No, not just that. I would like you to perform what you might call an autopsy on this mannequin and check what's wrong with it."

The engineer looked at the captain in surprise.

"I don't quite understand."

"It replaced the driver in the delivery van that overturned due to an explosion in the side tunnel," the officer explained to him. "This is neither a common nor an acceptable practice. Someone put it behind the controls, and the vehicle somehow drove and probably didn't even break any laws. The accident that overturned the van probably had nothing to do with the controls… some explosion in the tunnel… Officer Maru is investigating it. But I'm intrigued by this mannequin."

"Now I'm intrigued too." Chris rubbed his hands together in satisfaction. "I just need some tools. Are there any here?"

"A full set." Wilder pointed to a plastic box in the corner. "I'm sure you'll find something suitable."

"I hope so."

The engineer opened the box and browsed through its contents, grimacing in discontent. It was clear he did not think highly of whoever assembled this set. Only the universal servo – a multi-tool for precision manipulation – drew his admiration. He finally picked a few small gadgets and methodically arranged them on the edge of the bench. Meanwhile, the captain brought a recorder from his office and attached it to the wall. Then he sat down on a stool in the corner and fixed his gaze on Chris.

First of all, the mannequin's shell needed to be cut open. Chris did this with a universal hobby knife, so sharp that he had to maneuver it very carefully to avoid damaging anything other than the hard rubber itself. As he pulled apart the shell, he whistled.

"Oh wow…"

"What do you see?" Wilder asked, intrigued.

"These aren't servomotors. I mean, they are here too, but besides them… Oh my…"

"What?" The sudden change in Nikanov's tone worried the officer. He stood up from the stool to see better.

"Just stay calm, captain. It's an explosive charge. It activated automatically. There are thirty seconds left… Do you have something thin and flat?"

Wilder looked around nervously, and his gaze fell on one of the thin envelopes used as labels for marking packages. Grabbing it, he threw out the cardboard description from inside and handed the empty plastic to Chris.

"That should be enough." The engineer slipped the envelope into the mannequin's interior and started some maneuver. Beads of sweat appeared on his forehead. The operation had to be delicate and required full concentration, as he held his breath during it. Wilder watched him, feeling as if time had stood still. Thirty seconds – can thirty seconds really stretch out that much? Finally, a slight crackle sounded, which in the silence of the storage room resonated like a gunshot. Both men flinched, involuntarily pulling their heads into their shoulders. However, the explosion did not occur.

"I blocked the contacts," Chris explained, gasping for air as if after a run. "A crude method, but it works with such detonators. Phew, but I got hot…"

He wiped his face with his sleeve.

"What now?" Wilder asked after a moment.

"I need to disassemble this. We could call in a sapper from one of the mines, but it's better not to wait, because the charge might have some additional detonator. Better not to take risks."

Nikanov bent over the cut mannequin again. Now he worked more calmly, not rushing. The captain watched his hands, admiring the precision and confidence of the engineer. He was disassembling a complicated mechanism with a long pair of tweezers and a universal servo into microscopic pieces without a single unnecessary movement, setting aside individual parts for later examination.

"Now it's no longer dangerous," he finally announced, straightening his bent back. "The charge itself is a synthxer, so if it went off, there wouldn't be a trace left of us, and this building would collapse like a house of cards. It's a very efficient explosive material."

"Easy to obtain?"

"No. It's not used in mines. It's too expensive and is not produced on an industrial scale." Chris looked at the commander attentively. "Now the technicians from your laboratory need to take care of this sausage, not me. Why didn't you call them right away instead of asking me?"

Wilder shrugged.

"I didn't want to embarrass myself," he explained with embarrassment. "I felt that this dummy was not just a dummy, but what if it was? I would have made a fool of myself right from the start."

Chris smiled broadly. The remnants of hostility vanished from his gaze, and it became clear and cheerful. He pushed his curls from his forehead and styled them back with his fingers.

"And you did well. If your technicians had started disassembling that mannequin, they would have probably triggered an explosion, because they probably don't know about such charges. But I do." Suddenly he grew serious. "It was close. What do you think about that?"

The captain was silent for a moment. The picture forming in his mind was not encouraging, but it seemed logically coherent.

"I need to wait for what Maru determines," he finally muttered. "However, it seems to me that it's a bigger operation. There were two explosions and a fire in the technical tunnel under the center. This charge you discovered was not activated, why?"

Nikanov picked up one of the parts of the disassembled mechanism with the tweezers. He studied it for a moment.

"The clamp failed," he concluded. "It got stuck. What did you say? The van overturned?"

"Yes, during the first explosion."

"The shock caused the blockage. Interesting, you know… I suspect the explosions were supposed to be correlated, but the timer in the mannequin was delayed by about two-tenths of a second, and then reset when the circuit was broken. The rubber used on the shells of such dolls minimally muffles the signals, and that was probably the reason for the delay. Later, I started messing with it and activated the backup system."

"In other words, someone was playing with it who knows what they are doing."

"Oh yes, without a doubt."

"So we have trouble." Wilder clenched his lips. After a moment, he looked at the engineer. "You can go. Thank you very much for your help."

The engineer returned his gaze with a shadow of previous defiance.

"Just don't think we've become friends. Because we haven't. You stole my sister's promotion, and I won't forget that."

Clint almost laughed despite his fresh concern. This young guy was growing on him, and unlike him, he was sure that they would become friends in the near future.

"Believe me, Nikanov, I did not seek this position. I also believe that your sister was treated unfairly, and if it were up to me, I would return to Earth in an instant. Unfortunately, neither I, nor you, nor she has any say in this matter."

III
LEETA
Personal Diary

When I came home for lunch, Sue was lying in the living room with a cloth on her head. Sid, curled up beside her, was purring intensely and didn't even perk up when I walked in.

"Another migraine?" I asked sympathetically. "Why don't you take a pill?"

"I'm not going to poison myself," she muttered. "A frozen towel does wonders too. I'm feeling a bit better now. Tell me, what's this guy sent from Earth like? Some loser, right?"

I sighed and sat down next to her.

"Actually, no," I said. "He seems younger than Chris and incredibly handsome. A real giant, he's definitely over two meters tall and built like a bodybuilder. He doesn't seem stupid either. An older policeman came along as well, looking a bit like the Indian from illustrations of old stories shown in the museum. You know, with a hooked nose, narrow eyes, prominent cheekbones, and his hair tied back. And there's a girl with them, maybe a bit older than Hallie, a fresh recruit. B3, interestingly. She's really tiny, such a little thing, French. A brunette, dark eyes, pale skin, typical 'little black

dress' style, she'd fit better in a café than in the police. She wears her hair in a bob, uses cherry lipstick, and has such eyes, they look like saucers. Half her face. They seem friendly."

She peeked at me from under the cloth.

"Do you like her?"

"Who, the Indian or the little one? Still, she's not that pretty, just those eyes are amazing."

"Don't be silly, new commander."

I couldn't help but laugh. Sue had always been surprisingly straightforward for a virtualist.

"Not my type, if that's what you mean. First of all, he's too young, just a brat. You can tell from a distance that it's his first time on the Moon and he knows nothing about it. I hope he manages somehow."

"If not, you'll help him. You're a good girl after all. Where's Monty?"

"I sent him to Sven Thorvald this morning. After that explosion in the mine, one of the servomotors in his arm is malfunctioning. He took quite a big hit from a rock. Sven adjusted the mechanism remotely once, but I think it needs direct intervention."

Sue sat up, taking off the cloth from her head. You could tell the headache was passing, though she still looked worn out. These symptoms must have been from using the helmet for the Integra program, but she never admitted to such practices, especially in front of doctors who would surely forbid her. She didn't want to take any risks. Integra allowed her to fish out the most well-guarded information from the net, which made her so effective.

"Just heat yourself something up," she said. *"I can't stand the smell of food for now. I'm going to my room, going to take a nap."*

It was always like this when my friend had a migraine. The pain eventually subsided and then she had to sleep, while I tiptoed around so as not to wake her and didn't cook anything but water for tea. Sensitivity to smells made her nauseous from the slightest scent on such days, and I wanted to spare her that. I also gave up on heating up the stew waiting for me in the closed sterilizer. I didn't even have to, actually—since food sterilizers were invented, there was no need to cool dishes to low temperatures to prevent spoilage. The stew might not have been warm, but I could eat it comfortably.

Comfortably? That would be too nice. I had barely swallowed a few spoonfuls when the intercom buzzed. Kendra Maru's face appeared on the screen.

"Boss, could you join us? We're at the 'Ocean' café by the entrance to the express tunnels. You know where that is?"

"Of course. Problem?"

"I'm afraid so."

I quickly ate a bit more stew, put the rest back in the sterilizer, refilled Sid's water bowl, and rushed out, calling a taxi on the way with my beeper. Recently, the lunnar's company "Seletaxi" had made a deal with the headquarters, providing us with vehicles out of turn at the agreed signal from the beeper. Sending my code, I knew that in a few minutes there would be a vehicle waiting outside the building where I was renting an apartment with Sue today, there will be a sleek vehicle with the "Seletax" logo that will take me wherever I want to go.

We were a bit sad to leave the police quarters, but we had to. We felt very safe there, but the assigned apartment was rather cramped and "awkward," as Sue put it. We needed something bigger, especially since the multi-part computer that my friend used for virtual surfing took up a lot of space. We managed to find a suitable apartment quite close to the station so I could walk to work.

I had already gotten used to these walks. On Earth, either nobody or very few people walk like that; it is even frowned upon because promenades and parks are meant for strolling, not streets. However, in Lunnar, police patrols do not check people loitering on sidewalks. Almost everything is different here, and I myself, if the café "Ocean" were closer, would not call for a taxi.

Kendra and the new police officer accompanying her were sitting at one of the tables with Zara Tagliani, the head of the fire department. All three looked deadly serious.

"What's going on?" I asked, joining them.

"Ms. Tagliani?" Kendra glanced at the firefighter.

Zara wiped her tired face.

"It wasn't an accident," she stated in a weary voice. "Someone planned this and not ad hoc, but with a longer perspective in mind. In the technical tunnels under the underground route, flammable materials were stored. They weren't brought in all at once because that would have drawn the attention of the technical supervision. They were brought in gradually and concealed under camouflage, mimicking walls or the ground. Whoever did this has good information about the tunnel maintenance system. They must have started acting after the last inspection and knew when the next one would be."

"And when is that supposed to be?" I asked.

"The day after tomorrow."

That indeed added up to one whole. And that meant the problem was truly very serious.

"What are the damages?" I asked.

"Less than one might expect," Tagliani replied. "Our mischief-maker is definitely clever and knows a lot about many things, but they're a poor chemist. It seems they wanted to destroy the city's underground transport, but they didn't take a rather basic matter into consideration. Fire needs oxygen, and in the technical tunnels, it's supplied by small compressors. Those devices shut down first, and the flames simply had no fuel. That's why the underground viaduct was not destroyed, and if it had collapsed, I'm sure you understand it would not only block transportation but also damage the above-ground infrastructure."

"Someone was indeed aiming for that," Kendra added. "It has a name, boss. Terrorism."

I knew that myself, though I preferred not to call it by name. But what could motivate the perpetrator? What did they want to achieve? Of course, I couldn't rule out that we were dealing with a maniac (such people don't need reasons), but it didn't seem like it to me. There are no coincidences on the Moon, and there are no random people.

"Have you gathered samples from all corners?" I asked.

"Yes, of course. Connie Benedict took photographic documentation and went to the station, while we stayed to talk with Ms. Tagliani. After all, she knows best about everything related to fires, explosions, etc. I thought I'd ask her a few questions."

In this regard, Kendra was undeniably right. The chief of the fire department in Lunnar had gone through the ranks, starting as an underage girl working as a cleaner in the firehouse and persistently climbing up despite all the obstacles. And there were plenty of them in this profession. After the mine accident where we met, we had seen each other several times, both professionally and privately. She told me a bit about herself, and I knew how hard it had been for her. In our times, there is no such thing as gender parity or separate standards like before the Ecological Catastrophe. I experienced this myself during physical fitness tests. To advance, Zara had to prove she was worth exactly the same.co her male colleagues in the profession and a little more. And she demonstrated. She was truly great and very effective, and her knowledge in her field was impressive.

"Zara, please," I started. "Remember if you have had any strange calls lately? Did anything unusual happen?"

She thought deeply.

"Maybe not completely," she finally replied. "However, three weeks ago, the new mayor asked me to have my people check the town hall and the closed neighborhood around it, where the government officials live. He didn't want to specify exactly what it was about, but we were supposed to look for explosives, flammables, and poisons."

"Did you find anything?"

"Nothing. And Mr. Kovacs just thanked us and threw us out onto the street. It intrigued me, so after work, I had a drink with one of the security guards at the town hall. I managed to get out of him that the mayor's office receives letters – not voice messages or emails – but plain, old-fashioned letters on square pieces of velum paper glued

at the edges. Someone leaves them on the doorstep of the town hall or in the doors. And Mr. Kovacs gets very nervous when he receives such a letter. He even assigned a reward to the guard who catches whoever is playing such nice games."

"Is there any idea what those letters contain?"

"The mayor doesn't confide in anyone. It's hard to talk to him at all. Don't think I haven't tried."

I didn't think so. Zara was stubborn and had enough curiosity in her to be a good detective if she only wanted to. However, Victor Kovacs, who replaced Prosecutor Cable as mayor of Lunnar, turned out to be a specific person, very difficult to deal with, closed off. It seemed, however, that I would have to find a way to break through to him.

"Thank you, Zara," I said. *"We'll stay in touch, because I might still need your help. Keep me informed about all suspicious calls, okay? And send me a description of your intervention as soon as possible."*

"Sure."

I looked at Kendra and Salome.

"Take the samples to the laboratory and compile a report," I instructed them. *"I'll talk to the mayor, but I need to have some evidence in hand first."*

Easy to say, I'll talk to the mayor... I immediately submitted the appropriate request on the official form, knowing that processing it would take the town hall's office at least a few days, and by that time, I would already have all the results from the lab. As soon as I finished writing, the technicians' report from the examination of the mannequin obtained by Captain Wilder arrived on my computer. I had already glanced at the brief message from Chris and knew that some-

thing very important had been detected, so I immediately started reading the document that had been sent to me. After studying it and checking a few more details, I decided that there was no point in waiting any longer and went to see the new chief.

***

Since the opening of Seleneport, the shuttle landing area had been under true siege. There was no shortage of those wanting to spend their holidays in a luxury resort, nor of those who simply wanted to receive treatment at the hospital built next to the recreational area, intended for the therapy of various diseases in controlled microgravity conditions. The latter were almost as numerous as those willing to pay enormous sums for a holiday package, so Chris Nikanov soon received a new task – overseeing the construction of a new lunnar's cosmodrome. Unfortunately, the capacity of the old landing area was only a minor issue. The primary concern turned out to be the immediate rise in crime. Although the Seleneport management employed its own security with industrial police powers, the main Lunnar command remained the superior unit and, as such, received all reports. They also had to intervene in more serious cases when arrests were made, which was not always appreciated by the "city of entertainment" management. Initial friction was soon replaced by forced cooperation between both agencies, as there was no other way to maintain order. The fairy-tale center generated huge profits for investors from the very first days, a and to maintain it at the current level and even increase it, one had to take care not only of luxury and entertainment but, above all, of the safety of the guests. It couldn't be done separately from Lunnar. The new governor reached an official agreement with the investors and the management of the resort appointed by them, which was supposed to end any misunderstandings. However, it did not end. The entrance of the police to the Selenoport was still being prevented for as long as possible, and Symeon Lange, the chief manager, made it clear that the lunnar command had no business there.

Something that could be called the criminal underground of Lunnar had been eyeing Selenoport from the very beginning. A clear act of terror, the first of its kind since the mining colony's inception, had to be somehow related to this. Captain Clint Wilder, a newcomer to this specific environment, was still not familiar with all the local arrangements, but being a good cop, he simply had to catch onto certain things.

"All the elements of the mechanism have been thoroughly examined by our technicians. Each of them can be somehow linked to the Juvenille Corporation, the youngest member of the Lunnar Company," Lieutenant Ankes said. "But that's not all. I thought about what Zara Tagliani told me…"

"And what did she say? And who is she?" Wilder interrupted her.

The lieutenant fell silent for a moment.

"Right, I haven't reported that yet," she admitted. "She's the commander of the lunnar's fire brigade. She told me that the new mayor is receiving some letters that really upset him. I emphasize, letters, not electronic messages."

"A bit old-fashioned, but some people like that."

"Of course. Especially since delivering such messages discreetly, bypassing a professional courier, reduces the chances of tracing the sender to almost zero."

"Don't exaggerate."

"And yet. These letters that Mr. Kovacs receives are written on vellum, not on electronic foil, which costs pennies."

The captain nodded.

"Yes, it costs pennies," he admitted, "but tracing who wrote anything on it, whether electronically or manually, is child's play. Vellum is basically anonymous. I understand now."

"Exactly. It's a very expensive material, one hundred percent natural, thick, smooth, glossy, and white as snow. The so-called 'rag paper' is much cheaper, although it's also costly, but lacks that elegance. It's used by smaller and poorer companies. Yet even they try to have at least a few sheets of vellum in stock. If one runs a good business aspiring to significance in the global economy, of course, more is needed. Among other things for prestige, but also because of that anonymity. You never know when it might come in handy."

Wilder smiled slightly, with some disapproval.

"Well, if someone assumes from the outset that they will want to outsmart the police one day…"

"No, why the police? Besides, that's beside the point. What I'm getting at is that the Juvenille Corporation ordered a whole dozen reams of this material at one time. Officially for printing diplomas and letters of gratitude on it. Fine, if they have such fancy ideas, let them print even on gold. After all, all the companies in the campaign order vellum for representative purposes, such as for business cards. Just not that much. The maximum order was one ream, and it was placed by the Horus Corporation, the largest and most significant in the entire Company. Others order in sheets. And suddenly Juvenille comes along and takes a dozen reams at once. That means six thousand sheets. Sure, it's not a crime, and it's none of our business how shareholders manage their profits. Something, however, doesn't add up."

The captain looked again at the laboratory report. He wasn't familiar with the technical details, but he didn't have to, as the document contained clear annotations.

"All these parts have a clear connection to mining, good," he said. "But how can we be sure that they were ordered by Juvenille,"'a or is this Horus or another company?"

Ankes pointed to the code designation present in the description of each element.

"Each element has energy signatures introduced. The analysis of the explosive charge showed that if it detonated, it would incinerate all parts of the detonator and there would be no chance of reading the signatures. But we have them now."

The commander scratched his ear.

"What about the vellum?"

"Ah right. Someone is writing letters to the mayor on it. We cannot rule out that this person is stealing property from any corporation, or even from a cosmetics manufacturer; you know, the labels of the most expensive ones are made of vellum… However, it would likely be someone at the very top who has to answer to no one, or it is unlikely because the excess expenditure would be too visible. Juvenille has a large supply and I can bet that it can document more use than others; ultimately, it could claim to sell small quantities to other entities and thus make extra profit. Merrick could look into this to see if there's any scam, but in my opinion, it would be a waste of time. We need to investigate a much thicker case than speculation on luxury goods used once in a blue moon for representation purposes."

There was much truth in what Leeta said. The author of the letters to the mayor certainly thought everything through well. The use of such an expensive material not only practically made it impossible to trace the sender, but also diluted any potential suspicions across all the companies that were part of the Lunnar's Company, and even on the cosmetics manufacturer mentioned by the policewoman or the upscale stores of Selenoport. Each of them used vellum for something, for example for quality certificates of high-end jewelry. The fact that the Juvenille corporation ordered a very large quantity of it could not be considered by the prosecution as any evidence in this particular case, even if the letters to the mayor indeed had any connection to the evident act of terrorism. However, the signature of the parts used to construct the bomb would certainly be such evidence.

"Okay. We officially start the investigation and simultaneous inquiry about Juvenille," Wilder decided. "Will you talk to the mayor?"

"As soon as they decide to see me. I've already sent a request."

"Excellent. By the way, I've thought it all through. You will be my deputy. I surely won't find a better one."

Leeta looked him straight in the eye.

"Are you sure you want this?"

"Absolutely," he assured.

He wanted to say something else, but just then there was a knock on the door.

"Come in!" he called.

A police officer in a uniform without rank insignia entered the office. He had a thin face and straight light hair falling to his nape.

"Monty!" Leeta exclaimed, embracing the newcomer warmly. "Finally, you're here. Is everything alright with your arm?"

"Yes," he replied, returning her embrace. "Mr. Thorvald wanted me to repeat that the repair was fully successful and there won't be any more problems."

Clint watched him with curiosity. So this was the android. He tried to imagine meeting him on the street or somewhere in a store – could he recognize that he was not dealing with a human? The skin did not seem artificial. Matte, of the color of a tanned human body, slightly too smooth for a male, but looking alive. It even had clearly defined blood vessels, not to mention details like nails. The eyes were bright, with careful features and an intelligent expression. Movements were fluid, natural. The voice was pleasant, with nothing mechanical about it. Maybe the expression was a bit too reserved... but it certainly wouldn't draw his attention. Normal, young, moderately handsome by his assessment, but athletic and definitely someone who took care of himself. An android? For sure?

Leeta looked at the captain and smiled at his expression.

"Allow me, this is my personal protection," she said. "Judging by the way you're looking, you've heard something about him."

Wilder stood up from the desk and instinctively extended his hand. This gesture seemed natural to him in the face of doubts about whom he was dealing with, because he had them.

Wilder had been seeing robots almost every day, like every inhabitant of Earth. Some were very similar to humans, but none so much that one could not identify them when standing in line with people. Even very sophisticated sexbots could not deceive a trained eye when placed among individuals for identification.

Monty solemnly shook the officer's hand.

"This is our new commander," Leeta said.

"Nice to meet you, Commander. I am Monty Romain, personal property of Lieutenant Juliette Ankes, assigned as a police assistant at the Lunnar headquarters."

"Is this really an android?" Wilder looked at the girl with skepticism. He could swear that under the cool, smooth skin of the hand, he felt normal bones. He held it and turned the palm up. "Yes, now I see. No fingerprints and the interior is not hardened like a human's. But… the skeleton?"

"Androids are created based on an accurately replicated human skeleton," she explained to him. "Otherwise, it wouldn't be possible to make it resemble a human at all. That's why they are so realistic. However, the greatest marvel of engineering is their brain. Monty is not a machine, Clint. He is a being. He presents himself as my property, but in reality, he is a friend."

Sergeant Greyfox peeked into the office.

"Tomcat, what do you want for dinner?" he asked. "Baby and I are getting gyros with soy sauce."

"I'll have the same plus two servings of lasagna. Do they have it here?"

"Oh yes, they have everything. And you, ma'am?" Greyfox turned to Leeta.

"Pitano resu with extra crackers."

"And you?" he looked at Monty.

Leeta chuckled.

"Androids don't eat, sergeant."

"Ooo... so...?" Elvis examined Monty with wide, astonished eyes. "Wow, good job. I'd be fooled. Unless... Are you pulling my leg?"

"I assure you, I am not."

"Alright then."

Greyfox left, shaking his head in doubt.

"I don't blame him," Wilder said. "It's really hard to believe that this is not a human. Does he bleed?"

"No way. If you really want, you can poke him with something. You'll see for yourself."

"No need, I was just curious about how far it has gone in imitating reality." Clint finally sat back down and looked into his mug. "Could you get me a caffetino? I plan to work at least until midnight."

"Monty, bring the captain a pot of caffetino and a plate of cookies," Leeta told the android. He nodded and left.

"Starting tomorrow, I begin working with your protégé. We will investigate the mayor's connections to Juvenile, and Juvenile's connection to the assassin." Leeta took her pad and the documents off the desk. She quickly wrote something on the pad's screen with a stylus. "Kendra and your friend will be looking for him. He's a dangerous guy, we need to locate him as soon as possible. Will you authorize such an assignment?"

Wilder nodded and signed on the device presented to him.

"Of course. Do you have any questions?"

Leeta was already leaving, but hearing the question, she paused. She turned to the new commander, narrowing her hazel eyes with a slightly mischievous smile.

"Why Tomcat?" she asked unexpectedly.

The captain blushed all the way to the roots of his closely cropped hair. He didn't like his nickname, although he did not protest loudly against it, reasoning that there was nothing he could do about how his colleagues called him. He had earned it in less than glorious, but justifiable circumstances of service that he would have preferred to forget if only he had been allowed. But he was not allowed. He pretended that it didn't bother him at all, not wanting to give reasons for new jabs, and before he knew it, the label stuck to him, and very few addressed him otherwise. He never imagined he would have to explain this to a stranger.

"I'll tell you one day," he muttered after a moment. "But not now."

IV
CLINT WILDER
Personal Diary

Lunnar never ceases to amaze me. It is cramped, dirty, primitive, and it seems no one cares to change its face. The fabulous profits of the mining corporations somehow do not translate into modernizing the city. Apartments do not have movable walls or the ability to change the color of internal coverings - they are permanently painted, which should not be surprising given the material they are made of. They are almost caves of concrete, not quarters for civilized people. Of course, those who live here have gotten used to it, not having much choice. Sometimes, maliciously, instead of "apartments," they say "residential units," and that is basically the only expression of criticism regarding the conditions in which they are forced to live.

The advantage of the Lunnar's command, poorly equipped, underfunded, and suffering from a perpetual shortage of staff, is the people. The vast majority are "exiles," perhaps not in the literal sense, as each of them ultimately has some choice. I also had one, strictly speaking, because I could have simply resigned from service and stayed on Earth. I could have found employment in one of the industrial police forces, in prison security, or just looked for another job. Well-paying. If it required further education, after all, I am not that stupid. Maybe then Anna would not have rejected me.

Yet I could not. The police has been my life since childhood, ever since at just twelve years old I started volunteering at the local station as a jack-of-all-trades, meaning fetch–hand over–clean up. While my peers attended sports activities and played on holoconsole games, I was receiving my first police lessons. When I was eighteen, I passed the fitness exam and was accepted as an intern. I had never been so proud in my life as I was then. And I quickly began to climb up, the fastest in the history of the city. I could not give this up, even for Anna, and that is why I found myself in this city sealed by a tight dome, on average 384,700 km from Earth (at perigee, of course, less, and at apogee, more). I could regret it and feel sorry for myself, but there was no time for that.

My arrival on Lunnar coincided with a terrorist attack, the first such incident in the history of the colony. I immediately had to roll up my sleeves and get to work, which in itself is quite a therapy. A huge support for me turned out to be, of course, Dakota and Salome, who despite her love for everything beautiful, elegant, and urban, tries hard to keep her composure in this dreary environment. It also turned out that I have Juliette Ankes on my side, whom, however, I slipped out of position, no matter how you look at it. She bears no grudge against me, or at least does not show it. She is a classy girl, there's really no other way to describe her. The boys from the assault battalion call her "princess" among themselves, and there is something to it. She stands out from the other female officers like a ruby from red glass, not insulting anyone, of course, and it is not just a matter of the

A symbol on her forehead. Even the way she speaks reveals her better background and careful upbringing. However, she shows no superiority over anyone, does not look down on anyone. She immediately called to order those who tried to treat me dismissively and made it clear to everyone that she would not tolerate a lack of respect for the new superior.

Ankes is - of course after me - the highest-ranking detective on Lunnar. Besides her, there is also Feri Kuncz working in that capacity at the station, a former military man, roughly forty years old, stocky, and perpetually unshaved brunette, his partner - an intern, Kathy Jouvenaux, a pretty blonde with gray eyes and a boyish figure (she has muscles like an athlete), and Kendra Maru, who has not yet received her license. She is partially African and partially Irish, and from what I noticed right away, she has a truly Irish temperament. She may not be a beauty, but there is something about her, and she seems to be popular among the male members of the local police. A handsome Somali, David Abumajid, who arrived on Lunnar just a week before me and has not yet settled in well, clearly has his eyes on her. He works for the economic department, so he is not one of my subordinates. However, Rosanda Merrick, the head of the department immediately announced that she would have no objections to him helping us if necessary. In addition to uniformed officers, she has a civilian at her disposal. This is private detective Kevin "Razor" Winslet, the only representative of this profession in Lunnar. Few people and rarely need his services here, but he has a few assignments and manages to make a living from them. Merrick herself looks exactly as she did in the slide shown to me by Striker; she is surly and unfriendly, but perhaps it shouldn't be surprising—she has a lot of work and very few people to carry it out. Besides detectives, we obviously have patrol officers who are responsible for patrols and simple interventions, as well as an intervention team under the command of Alec Merino. The sergeant in charge of the officers is Anthony Chekov. I have also already gotten acquainted with Neil Slavik, the department's full-time criminalist, while I still have not met our coroner. He is on vacation; in case of need, Dr. Larson, the chief of the local hospital, or one of his subordinates is supposed to take his place.

The investigation into the explosions on the underground route in downtown Lunnar is therefore my first in my new position. The procedures at the crime scenes were conducted by Kendra Maru and Salome, who were joined by Lieutenant Ankes. She also gathered information about the letters that someone has been sending anonymously to the mayor of Lunnar. A certain problem arose—Victor Kovacs agreed to speak, but his letter and the attached pass referred to him as the "chief of police of Lunnar." Did the mayor not know that Lieutenant Ankles, who signed the relevant form, no longer holds that position? Or maybe he knew and wanted to talk to me specifically? Not wanting to make a blunder, I decided to attend the meeting with my deputy, thus inaugurating my additional work at the department, in the capacity of a police detective, not just the main grump and taskmaster.

***

"The previous mayor was probably murdered, right?" Wilder asked, as Officer Ted Yamato was driving him and Leeta to the town hall. Monty was accompanying them, sitting next to Yamato in the front seat.

"Yes. He was also a prosecutor. In fact, combining those functions isn't entirely legal, but who cares."

"We don't have a new one yet?"

"No. Judge Holstein immediately submitted a request to appoint a new prosecutor, it's dragging a bit. I guess they don't have anyone to send for now." Leeta laughed despite herself. She had long learned to treat Lunnar's reality with humor, a skill her new superior still lacked.

"No one comes here voluntarily?" he asked.

"No one, as in no one. A lot of people are keen to come to Lunnar for work. But you know what kind? Like our Hallie. Uneducated and mostly very young. Or vice presidents of companies, which their contracts, amounting to a staggering sum, require. Sometimes it's the desperate ones for whom this is the last stop before suicide. Very, very rarely does someone not fit any of the above patterns."

Wilder nodded slightly. Leeta was looking at him seriously now, with sympathy.

"I've been told a bit about you," she resumed after a moment. "My friend and informant, who still lives on Earth, got a few people to spill the beans and learned why you are here. Of course, we weren't officially told this. Well, a new chief was appointed on Earth, and that's it. But I already know."

"And what do you think about it?"

"Well. You experienced what many others have. You acted honestly and were punished for it." She lowered her voice so the driver couldn't hear her. "Sandy warned me about something you should know too. Joseph Lee Hoover has put a bounty on your head. Two hundred thousand industrial points and ten thousand food points."

The captain's eyes widened.

"What?!"

"Lower your voice. Sandy stumbled upon this information totally by accident because, of course, such actions are prohibited and punishable."i officially such a place cannot exist. Such offers are circulated only in criminal environments, and you need someone there to hear about it. Don't ask how Sandy found out, because I don't know myself. However, I trust her. If she wrote me something like that, she must have been sure of her information." She paused for a moment. "I received the message from her half an hour before leaving home. That's why I took Monty, even though they might make it difficult for him to enter the town hall."

Wilder looked at the back of the android's head, sitting stiffly in the seat next to the driver. "As a bodyguard?"

"Yes. I'd advise you to take seriously what I'm saying."

"I take it seriously, but is he..." the captain hesitated, "programmed in any way? Trained in security? Does he know what to do in case of real danger?"

"You can bet all your points from both types of cards on that."

The police rover stopped in front of a round, stout building with two guard booths, guarding the barrier at the entrance. An armed man in a black uniform with a state service badge emerged from one of them. "Pass." He extended his gloved hand with a wide cuff.

Captain Wilder handed him the form received from the town hall through the partially opened window and showed his badge. The guard examined it closely.

"Hello, Commander," he said, saluting the helm with a tinted visor. "Who are you bringing with you?"

"My deputy and assistant."

"Just a moment."

The guard returned the pass to him, entered the booth and after a moment came out with three metal bracelets.

"Please put this on your left wrists," he instructed the guests. "Safety regulations require everyone except regular employees to wear a locator on the town hall premises. Even police officers."

"Of course," Clint replied briefly. He had encountered this kind of precaution before and did not consider it excessive. "Officer, please wait for us and don't go anywhere."

"Yes, sir!" answered the officer, Yamato.

The barrier went up, and the police vehicle entered the spot indicated by the guard.

The town hall of Lunnar was arranged inside similarly to any other government office, which made it look sterile and impersonal, almost like a hospital. All the doors appeared identical, except for those of the mayor's office. They had a museum-like quality. Unlike the plastic ones, these were made of real, intricately carved, darkened wood due to age – a true rarity not only on the Moon but even on Earth – and finished with brass. The decorative handle, polished to a shine, gleamed like pure gold. Even without the large plaque inscribed with "President of the City of Lunnar," anyone would have realized that they led to the most important room in the town hall. At the desk next to them worked a young woman, neatly coiffed and dressed in a perfectly tailored jumpsuit, busy entering some documents into the office computer's memory. She lifted her eyes to the guests and extended her hand wordlessly. Wilder handed her the pass. She glanced at it and pressed a button on the desk.

"Mr. President, Captain Wilder and two of his subordinates have arrived," she said into the microphone.

"Let them in," came the brief response from the speaker.

The beautiful, old-fashioned door turned out to be a kind of decoy. It didn't open in the usual way, but slid open upon entering a code on a cleverly hidden panel. This was unexpected, so Wilder raised his eyebrows in surprise and slight disappointment – like a false note in an artistically performed symphony.

The office behind the door matched the appearance of the door and was a faithful copy of the President of the United States' office from photographs found in textbooks. Stylish furniture, heavy curtains at the windows, an imitation Persian carpet on the floor, portraits on the walls. The first mayor of Lunnar who furnished it must have suffered from a kind of megalomania, or perhaps he was just trying to make this inhospitable place as comfortable as possible.

Victor Kovacs was waiting for his guests, standing in the middle. With hands clasped behind his back. He looked to be about forty years old. Of only average height, he appeared taller due to the unusual thinness that he attempted to mask with padding sewn into the shoulders of his jacket. He had black, closely cropped hair, small mustache, eyes as narrow as slits, and an eagle-like nose. There was something authoritative about him, and it felt like this man knew how to impose his will on others. Leeta looked at him, unconsciously furrowing her brow. He seemed familiar to her, although on the other hand, she could swear she was seeing him for the first time in her life. The mayor paid no attention to her persistent gaze.

"What can I do for you?" he asked curtly, not responding to the greeting. "Just please be brief. I don't have time for nonsense."

"We handle nonsense ourselves without bothering anyone," Wilder replied calmly. "Briefly means briefly. I would like the letters on letterhead that someone is sending to you anonymously."

The mayor sized him up.

"So you know about them."

"Otherwise, I wouldn't be here. Why didn't you come to the police with them right away?"

"I don't think I need to explain myself."

"Actually, you should. I know that there are threats in these letters because upon receiving one, you ordered the fire department to check the conference center. Now someone has blown up part of the underground overpass. So far, no one has died. For now. I believe, however, that it's only a matter of time. You ordered the center to be checked because someone warned you. You probably received a warning before the attack in the underground too."

Kovacs sighed and walked behind the old-fashioned desk. He sat down in a high armchair, tilting his head back and closing his eyes.

"These letters really only annoyed me at first," he began after a moment. "Each one contained some threat: arson, the release of toxic gas, or something similar. The guards, at my command, thoroughly checked every location where the announced attack was supposed to take place. They found nothing. Not even the fire department... I called them in because I started to get seriously worried. And still nothing."

"Then why didn't you notify the police?"

"About what? That someone is playing tricks on me?"

The captain stepped closer.

"As you can see for yourself, these were not tricks," he said emphatically. "Rather a carefully planned operation. Please give me those letters, we need to investigate them. Whoever is behind this is very dangerous. I believe you understand just how much now."

Kovacs wiped his face with both hands.

"Can I offer you a drink?" he suggested. "Because I need one."

"We're on duty, I and my people," Wilder mumbled reluctantly, adding more politely, "But you should feel free."

The mayor opened a cabinet next to the desk, took out a square bottle, and poured himself half a glass of amber liquid. He drank it in one gulp and refilled.

"I usually don't drink in the middle of the day," he justified himself. "This matter has frayed my nerves. I can't understand why someone is stalking me and for what purpose."

"Does the author of the anonymous letters make any demands?" Leeta asked. The mayor shot her a tortured glance.

"If they were making demands, I would at least have a starting point." He pulled out a drawer from the desk and took out a stack of papers bound together. "Check for yourselves, if you don't believe me."

Wilder put on a latex glove and carefully placed the letters into a standard evidence bag.

"The laboratory must examine this. Afterwards, you will receive your property back, unless it is classified as evidence in the case," he said in an official tone. "You really have no idea who is slipping you these letters?"

Kovacs shook his head and took another drink.

"If I knew, I wouldn't be hiding it. I don't understand any of this, I swear. I'm not claiming to be an angel, but I can't figure out who would want to take such revenge on me and why."

"I don't think this is really about you at all," Leeta felt a pang of sympathy for this man. For some reason, he seemed extraordinarily lonely in a position he neither desired nor fully accepted. "You have only been on the Moon for a short time, so you likely haven't had the chance to offend anyone yet."

You might suspect that someone has it in for your position, but who? After all, they tried to hold a competition after Prosecutor Cable's death, considering Lunnar's specificity, any candidacy would have been accepted for review, but there simply weren't any volunteers. A lot of problems, a dubious honor, and meager pay. In some random subsidiary, the third deputy CEO earns about three times what you do here, and doesn't have to answer to the government in case of any catastrophe. So neither social position nor money is at play here; what else could someone have against you? Unless you have some personal issues, back from Earth.

"I don't recall, miss. Excuse me, Lieutenant," the mayor smiled faintly. "Surely you won't have a drink?"

Leeta returned the smile.

"Thank you, Mr. President, not on duty and not in the presence of a superior."

Victor Kovacs gestured with his chin towards Monty.

"And what about him? Can't he speak?"

The policewoman looked at her android, who stood still and kept watch over the entire office, barely moving his head. His polymer eyes were equipped with a very wide field of view, which often came in handy.

"This is our assistant. He is supposed to listen and learn, not chatter. For now, he has nothing wise to say."

Monty performed a slight bow towards the mayor, who replied with a nod.

"Since you have nothing more to tell us, thank you for your time," Wilder decided to interrupt this exchange of pleasantries. "We will, of course, stay in touch, Mr. President. Please notify us immediately when you receive another letter like this. This is really no joke."

"I know that. Just understand me: I don't want to look foolish. The local journalists are just waiting for that."

After exiting the town hall, the captain remained silent until they released the locators and boarded the police hovercraft. It wasn't until they were on the way back that he looked at his companion.

"I think he liked you."

"Really?" Leeta shrugged nonchalantly.

"What do you think of him?"

"Nothing specific. He reminds me of someone, but I just can't recall who."

"Didn't you notice anything particular?"

The girl looked at the captain with curiosity and thought for a moment.

"No, not really. And you?"

"He's an alcoholic."

"Because he had a drink? Don't exaggerate. Many politicians have a drink, thinking it adds seriousness in the eyes of their interlocutor."

The captain shook his head.

"It's not about that. Did you notice what he drank?"

"I'm not very knowledgeable, but it was probably brandy. Nothing unusual."

"No brandy. Original Scotch whisky, Ledaig Triple Wood. Full 53.8 percent. And he drank it like water, without even a cough. I assure you, the new mayor of Lunnar is a drunkard and hardly hides it."

There was silence in the car for a moment.

"What does that tell us?" Leeta finally broke the silence. And answered herself. "Probably nobody drinks without a reason. Kovacs must have started much earlier, not just when he got to Lunnar. Perhaps whoever is harassing him now knows the cause of this situation."

"Yes, but notice, it doesn't look like typical blackmail," the captain glanced at the letters in the plastic bag. "Which complicates our case because it could be about revenge, and we don't know who or for what. You know what? Let's hand these papers over to the techs and properly check our mayor. I have a feeling we'll uncover something interesting."

"Possible," Leeta nodded. "We'll need to use the main computer at the precinct. It has really good spying software. I'm not as skilled as Sue, but I can find most of what's hidden in the virtual space. She taught me a lot."

"A valuable acquaintance."

"Oh, you can say that. A wonderful girl."

"Is she your... partner?"

Leeta first made a surprised face and then broke into a hearty laugh.

"And how can you not love you men?" she said, amused. "You are so uncomplicated, straightforward in your conclusions. No, my dear, to is just a friend and roommate. If that's what you're asking, we both prefer guys."

"I'm sorry..." Wilder mumbled, blushing all the way to his short-cropped hairline. He didn't know where that question had come from or why. He wasn't used to interfering in other people's lives more than necessary.

Lieutenant Ankes patted him on the shoulder in a manner more like an older sister than a subordinate or colleague. He suddenly realized that she saw him that way – as a younger brother.

"Let's deal with more important issues for now, chief. You can delve into all our personal lives when there's nothing serious happening. Contrary to appearances, there are plenty of those moments here."

V
LEETA
PERSONAL DIARY

I'm not as good as Sue. It's unlikely anyone is. She's brilliant by birth and through hard work; there's no one quite like her. However, she's taught me enough to navigate the virtual world fairly well for someone without a directional distortion. So, I found information on Victor Kovacs relatively quickly. The new boss wasn't helping me, just watching with visible fascination at what I was doing. He probably had never seen such advanced network searching methods. Scotty called people like him "cowboys," in the sense that they rely on the simplest solutions, preferably brute force, without indulging in subtleties. "They won't reinvent the wheel," he used to say. "But no one will slip past them once they catch a scent." The problem is that the chief commander of Lunnar shouldn't be such a cowboy, but someone who understands all aspects of our work. Someone like Scott. But he's no longer here. One can only hope that perhaps in time Clint Wilder will grow into his position, which he never asked for.

After a few hours, we already had a substantial collection of documents, press releases, and ordinary gossip. The new mayor of Lunnar turned out to be an extraordinarily color-

ful person, to put it mildly. As a politician, he seemed very promising. A graduate of the Department of Economics and Political Science at the Australian National University at the age of just nineteen, he quickly established himself as an energetic and inventive person, almost obsessively ambitious. He was active, winning local elections and rising rapidly. By the age of twenty-four, he became the mayor of Melbourne, and shortly after – a member of the local parliament. A few years later, he caught attention on Central Island and began to be entrusted with increasingly significant tasks. With each promotion, his ambition grew. From allusive mentions, we soon gathered that his opponents, if they hadn't withdrawn from the competition themselves, were literally crushed, but there was nothing concrete in that. We kept digging through reports about Kovacs's successes, looking for a reason why this man, surely extremely intelligent and determined to achieve life success, enjoying support on Central Island, had ultimately been sent to the Moon. Why? The fact that he was ruthless in eliminating competition could not be the direct cause of his downfall, as there is neither mercy nor chivalry in the world of politics. Something else must have happened.

Eventually, we divided the work. While the captain focused on Kovacs's career, I concentrated on reports about his personal life. There was quite a bit of it, mainly further romances and marriages, ending in divorce no later than six months. But there were also lawsuits over various issues, usually rather trivial, yet ensuring that Kovacs never backed down. In addition, he was an avid sportsman. He practiced windsurfing, kendo, and aerobatics, even winning awards at national competitions. However, all of this collapsed at some point. Two years ago, gossip magazines and daily newspapers stopped publishing notes about him. Moreover, the name Ko-

vacs virtually ceased to appear in any columns. We noticed this almost simultaneously.

"Whatever happened, it had to take place in May 205 AEC," Wilder decided, and I nodded. "In April, we had one, two…five mentions in the 'Today in Politics' column and two in the 'Parliamentary Herald'."

"And at least as many articles in the tabloids," I added. "A new romance, this time with the adult magazine model, Satin White, a car accident, an altercation with journalists at a conference, an interview with his former neighbor, and an analysis of family ties. Those are the longer ones; I didn't even count the shorter notes. And in May, silence like a poppy seed. And since then, not a word."

"Exactly. As if he was erased from the world."

For a moment, we were both silent.

"We won't come up with anything for now," Wilder finally sighed. "Let's wait for what the technicians say, and then we'll dig deeper. For now, let's go grab a bite to eat, what do you think? Lunch time has long passed."

I looked at my watch. It was almost four in the afternoon.

"We could go to 'Favorite'," I suggested. "It's a little diner around the corner. They have quite a good menu and it's cheap. We usually order takeout from there, but I feel like stretching my legs."

We left, being watched by Salome, who was black as coal, writing a report at her desk. The quiet little Frenchwoman hardly made her presence known at the precinct, but I had noticed earlier that she looked at me suspiciously whenever she saw me with Wilder. I thought that at our earliest opportunity, just the two of us, I would need to explain to her that as far as I was concerned, there was nothing to worry about.

The object of her affections did not exist for me as a man even for a moment.

At this hour, 'Favorite' was almost full. We barely found a couple of seats for ourselves and ordered lunch. Eating greedily – I was really very hungry – I remembered something.

"What day of the week is it today?" I asked.

"Wednesday," the captain replied somewhat indistinctly, with his mouth full of soy cubes in barbecue sauce.

"Oh, my goodness! I forgot," I grabbed the menu and quickly placed a takeout order. "Sorry, I have to visit someone. And bring them lunch. It's my turn today."

Wilder frowned in surprise.

"Our team is taking care of Inspector Collins," I explained. "He's an old man, a former policeman, completely alone in the world. He refuses to go to the retirement community, so he moved to the Moon while Scott was still alive. That is, Inspector Cavanaugh. They knew each other well. He lived near the precinct, at 4B12 Center Street... that's how we refer to it, they don't have proper names, only the name of the district and the number. The houses are designated by letters of the alphabet. Scott visited him every day and helped him as much as he could... We didn't know about this, you see, he was very secretive. But after his death, Neil Slavik, our lawyer, found out everything. We discussed the matter and decided that we would be the Collins family. So, he wouldn't be lonely."

"I'll go with you," he offered eagerly. "Now that I'm one of you, I'll join in."

The waiter brought our neatly packaged lunch. We paid and left, heading to 4B Street. People glanced back at us a lit-

tle – no wonder, after all, it's rare to see a giant like the new commander in person. He commanded both curiosity and respect. However, he didn't pay attention to the looks thrown his way, lost in his thoughts.

"I still can't get used to the fact that you can just walk around the streets like this," he finally said. "Like a few hundred years ago. And it's not like someone just jumps out for a moment to a store two houses down, but in general… even without a particular need, people walk, stop, turn back, chat while standing against the wall… On Earth, they would be immediately ID'd and reprimanded."

I understood his astonishment well. I remember how I initially perceived normal pedestrian traffic in Lunnar.

"You get used to it quickly," I reassured him. "That's the house. Second floor."

Collins opened the door for us, I had barely touched the doorbell. It was clear he had been waiting, and I felt guilty.

"Sorry, John, we have a difficult case and it took us a while," I said in a justifying tone. "This is the new commander, Clint Wilder".

I kissed the old man on the cheek and handed him a box with lunch. He accepted it, not taking his eyes off Wilder. The captain was also looking at him, probably surprised by his appearance. People that wrinkled from old age are rarely seen today, anti-aging pills masking the signs of aging almost until death. Unfortunately, John, like Scotty, is allergic to those medications – a condition that is not extremely rare, but many who are affected somehow cope with it. He apparently does not, though I have never asked why.

"Impressive size, son" he said, extending his hand. "It's a wonder you haven't become a wrestler in school yet. You'd be famous by now."

"Circus performances never interested me" the captain shook the offered hand with such caution, as if afraid that an unwary move would crush it. Understandable, next to him Collins, though certainly not weak, could seem as fragile as Chinese porcelain. "Nice to meet you. John Collins, right? I'm recalling you now, 'When was that… Almost half a century ago. Old times. Come in, kids, I'll brew us some tea."

"You'd better eat something. I'm sure you're hungry" I suggested.

"First I'll get you something to drink. Quiet, kid. I know the duties of a host better than you know the instructions for operating an automatic curling iron."

He poured three cups of aromatic brew, handed us two, and took a seat at the table with the third, finally opening the container I had brought. He dug into the food with a healthy appetite.

"Tell me what's new" he encouraged me between bites. "What about those explosions, do you have any leads yet?"

The captain shot me a worried glance. He was still mentally on Earth and didn't understand the specifics of Lunnar.

"Here everyone knows everything" I explained to him. "Word of mouth works excellently, and the local TV station, Golden Ether, has very efficient reporters. They can sniff out anything in a few seconds. Keeping a secret is nearly impossible here."

"That's bad. Bad for our work."

"You're right, but what can we do?" Collins smiled from over the lunch box. "So how's it going for you?"

"We're waiting for the lab results" I answered. "It seems that someone is trying to intimidate the new mayor. The only thing is, we don't know yet what they want or who they might be."

"Someone who, first of all, has knowledge, secondly, access to explosives, and thirdly, a lot of money" Collins washed down the stew with tea. "Without money, no one would dare attempt something like this. And besides that, what's new?"

It was a kind of ritual. Each of us who visited "the resident," as we called him among ourselves, told him not only about daily life at the precinct but also about everything that had happened anywhere. The old man practically never left his apartment, spending his days reading and watching television. He said he was waiting for death in the most pleasant way available to him.

When we stepped out onto the street, Wilder looked at me and asked

"How old is he, actually?"

He surprised me. I didn't know myself. I thought about it.

"Well, I don't know, quite a bit. Was there a birth date in the Annals?"

"I don't remember. I don't think so. Since the introduction of the sensitive data law, such things are not provided in the public domain, so they avoid it even in the Annals. I asked because I happened to remember the date of the entry about Collins. I had to because I took an exam in the history of the state police. That was almost sixty years ago, and he was described as experienced and awarded by the then Number One sniper of the elite intervention group. He was the one *who prevented a massacre during the incident at Fort Worth airport by killing the attacker before he could detonate the bomb. Those who later reconstructed the events had difficulty believing that anyone could shoot accurately from such a distance."*

I furrowed my brow. I had heard about that incident, but rather vaguely. I didn't know the details.

"So, he's quite a hero?"

He smiled sadly.

"A hero is a big word. He just did his duty. Just like we all do. Society usually does not see this at all, and that's how it should be. People need to feel safe, which is why the media cannot mention such issues in detail," they looked at me. "Is this not observed here?"

"It's hard to enforce the law in such a place," I sighed. "You'll see for yourself. So, what? Shall we get back to work?"

***

The man who was brought to the station by one of the patrols appeared to be under the influence of strong narcotics. He was constantly shaking, staggering, and drooling, his face was red, unshaved, hair drenched in sweat and tousled, and his eyes were darting around like a drunkard in withdrawal. Despite this, his clothing indicated someone well-off and respected in society. He wore expensive shoes, a well-tailored suit, and a watch that certainly cost three standard salaries of an average clerk. He must have been someone important.

"Another golden rain?" Lieutenant Ankes asked.

"Probably not," the patrol officer shook his head. The other one nodded in agreement. "Golden rain doesn't cause these symptoms. This is some new filth. He went berserk on the street, smashed a store window, and created a traffic hazard. He almost ran under a van from the chalcopyrite processing plant."

Salome left her work and approached the detainee. She studied him closely, then took an electronic thermometer out of a small pouch attached to her belt. She pointed the sensor at the man.

"39 degrees," she read. "These are not drugs at all, this is some disease. Possibly contagious."

The lieutenant took the device from her hand and repeated the measurement.

"You are right." Her face hardened. "Call the commander and the doctor. Lock the doors. No one is allowed to leave the building or enter until further notice."

Elvis Greyfox pressed the button on the comlink.

"Tomcat, you need to come here quickly," he said into the microphone. "We have a problem."

"You're good, Salome. You caught on right away," Ankes addressed the intern. She smiled faintly. She tried to cover the fear that had taken hold of her, but she couldn't. Not without reason.

Contagious diseases had mostly been eradicated from public space. Occasional cases of sore throat or "ordinary cold" were immediately isolated, just like typical childhood diseases, which were now very rare. The vast majority of pathogens had been eliminated from the Earth's ecosystem due to the synthesis of substances called "external vaccines." Sprayed in the stratosphere, they slowly descended, causing microorganisms responsible for contagious diseases to start combating each other from within, at the RNA level. This didn't work for all, but for most. A few very stubborn, rapidly mutating viruses causing the "ordinary cold" survived, although in a severely weakened form. They no longer posed a significant threat, though the "atmospheric vaccination" procedure was still repeated every year due to those capable of rapid mutation. The fact that malicious microbes had practically ceased to exist paradoxically caused them to evoke panic in society. Scientific programs and publications about past epidemics reinforced this fear in people, and the symptoms of infection in one person could cause panic in the entire area. No wonder the people present in the station turned pale and stiffened, struggling against the urge to escape anywhere.

"I... I... I am a nurse by training, Lieutenant," Salome finally stammered. "I just really wanted to be a police detective; it has been my dream since childhood and..."

"Please, call me by my first name, like everyone else. You are a valuable asset to the police and you will surely be a great detective. If the captain signs off, I would like to be your supervising officer." Leeta handed her the thermometer back. "I think we will work well together."

"As long as we survive."

"A bit of optimism."

Captain Wilder and Doctor McCave, who had just returned from vacation and appeared at the station only a few minutes ago, entered the room. He hadn't even had time to change into his duty uniform, which he always wore at work.

"What have you come up with this time?" he shouted with displeasure. "I'm gone for a few weeks and it's a mess right away?"

Ankes showed him the detainee. The doctor took a fresh pair of gloves and a mask from his pocket. He put both on and then approached the man sitting in the chair.

"Everyone, step back." He raised the arrestee's chin with his hand. "What is your name?"

"Your... name?" the man mumbled.

"First name, last name?"

"...last name?"

The doctor shone a flashlight in his eyes and examined his abdomen with his fingers.

"Does it hurt here? And here? No?" he looked at the captain. "A new commander, huh? Well, you're starting with a bang. This is probably not an appendicitis attack, peritonitis, or kidney stones. The liver is a bit tender, it might be irritated, but that couldn't cause such a strong reaction. I also rule out a stroke or hemorrhage. We must assume the worst. Please arrange a quarantine."

"Of course, doctor...?"

"Kelley McCave. You know the procedures in case of an epidemic suspicion, right?"

Clint Wilder shook his head helplessly. He wanted very much to look like a commander holding everything together, but the situation overwhelmed him.

"Just a week ago, I was an ordinary homicide detective," he explained. "Assigned to the district command in Dallas. My nomination is a sudden issue and... essentially a punitive assignment. No one prepared me for this. I didn't have time to familiarize myself with lunnar's procedures."

"In this matter, they are just like earth ones, though you may not know them if you haven't been in a management position before." McCave sighed in despair. "Leeta, help him. After all, you're the deputy commander, right?"

"The captain hasn't signed the official…"

"No time for sulking, girl! We have a crisis situation. I'm taking this individual to the sick bay, and I will soon give you all the immunoglobulin and gamma globulin. And no panic. For now, we don't even know what it is. It might not be anything particularly dangerous."

It cannot be said that his speech visibly reassured people, but silently they returned to work, and Leeta firmly pulled Wilder with her to the commandant's office.

"The quarantine procedures are in the binder," she said. "Inspector Cavanaugh made sure that all important documents were printed and laminated in case of electronic device malfunction. He was a bit old-fashioned, but it came in handy." She took the appropriate sheet from the binder. "Here's everything you need. If you allow me, I'll contact Hallie now. We will need support, and outside, it's just her, the patrol officers, and Detective Kuncz on a covert mission. It's a bit unfortunate…"

The captain looked at the document handed to him. It was formulated clearly, precisely, and succinctly. Absolutely follow the doctors' orders, remain calm, strictly adhere to regulations, block any information that could reach civilians.

"What can a courier do in this situation?" he asked, just to say something.

"Even notify the military. We must act before the journalists, Sirtis will know how to silence them."

"Can't we just call? Or use a walkie-talkie?"

She shook her head.

"Definitely not. On Lunnar, everyone listens to everyone. Only home intercoms are relatively safe… they were installed on outdated fiber optics, it's a paradox, but it's much easier to shield them than modern communication. And a personal phone is almost useless here, there's only one network operating on the Moon, and the signal drops out all the time."

"So bad?"

"No, not really, the company invests a lot in equipment, but the conditions here are poor. Theoretically, it should be great because we have a vacuum outside the dome, but only theoretically. Something causes the signal to bend and reflect multiple times when transitioning from a vacuum to the biosphere. It's very hard to deal with, although experts keep trying. Chris can explain it better, he knows just about everything."

"So what will we do?" the captain felt increasingly helpless. He had prepared for various things, but not for a possible epidemic. Lieutenant Ankes seemed calmer.

"I'll send a call to Hallie via my personal pager. She will contact us from the nearest video communication point."

"Aren't you worried?" Wilder couldn't hold back. She looked at him and he immediately understood he was wrong.

"And what do you think? I'm going crazy with fear; I just can't show it. Can you imagine what would happen, what if there was a panic at the main command on the Moon and the news of our illness got out? Lunnar is a specific place. Claustrophobic, because there's nowhere to escape. Psychosis spreads here for the slightest reason like a fire, uncontrollable. There would be such chaos that we wouldn't manage."

She took a small device from her belt pocket and pressed the button on it several times. A modulated beep sounded.

"This is terribly archaic. When was this last used?" the captain asked, looking at the beeper.

"At the end of the twentieth century of the old era... or maybe at the beginning of the twenty-first. Sometimes you have to draw from the past... even though there isn't always much to draw from. We lost a lot of good technology during the Ecological Catastrophe and the wars that broke out then. Just before that disaster, almost all documentation was stored in virtual form, and when the internet, as it was then called, went down and servers were destroyed, everything was lost. Our devices have a good function, they are also location trackers. I don't know the technical details, but they can be pinpointed even when the connection is breaking and there's no way to have a conversation. This has already saved many lives."

Wilder listened and looked at her with admiration, almost forgetting the situation he was currently facing.

"You're really very educated. What are you doing in the police?"

Leeta smiled.

"Appearances can be deceiving. I was a librarian at the Medical Academy. Not much work, a lot of time. I read everything that came into my hands, mainly things I really had no right to read. When I became a police officer, I found that everything a person has read can come in handy in this job."

The captain sank into a chair and stared at the shiny new badge lying on the desk.

"You would be a much better commander than I am, Leeta. I'm B2, you're A3. It makes no sense for me to give you orders instead of you giving them to me. It's… unnatural."

Lieutenant Ankes laughed heartily. In reality, she wasn't in the mood to laugh, just like everyone at the station at that moment, but the new commander's disappointment over reasons of a more social than formal nature amused her.

"Nothing is natural on the Moon. You'll get used to it."

A message alert blinked on the videophone screen. Wilder hurriedly pressed the receive button. An excited face appeared on the screen—Hallie's. Her black eyes sparkled with curiosity.

"What happened, boss?" she exclaimed. "I'm calling from the café on Sixth Avenue. You can speak freely."

"They have soundproof booths by the videophones," Leeta whispered and nudged Wilder aside. "Listen, Hallie, very carefully. Go back to the precinct. Tell Colonel Sirtis to take charge of maintaining order in the city temporarily according to procedure number seventy-one, and then go home. You have the day off. The main command is, for now, closed; we need to deal with a certain problem. All patrols that are currently on the streets will come under Colonel Sirtis's command until further notice. Do you remember?"

"Of course, boss. But what happened?"

"Nothing special, we'll manage. And remember, mum's the word."

"Boss!" she pouted. "Have I ever leaked anything outside?"

"Not so far, and let's keep it that way. Now run! It can't wait!"

"Yes, ma'am!"

And the videophone went dark.

"Will she really remember?" Wilder asked skeptically.

"Oh, of course," Leeta reassured him. "That little one has an eidetic memory; she doesn't forget anything, which is why she's an excellent runner. And she will be a good police officer... as soon as she grows up. So, what now, commander? Let's get to work. We have a really tough task ahead, everything else has to wait."

An hour later, the commander received a brief message from Colonel Sirtis. The military had temporarily taken over responsibility for public order, meaning the police no longer had to worry about anything other than what was happening at the command.

VI
CLINT WILDER
Personal Diary

The hardest part was dealing with civilians, called in for questioning or reporting something that day. The doctor had to administer sedatives along with the immunity vaccine to keep them from panicking. The police officers were holding up better. They buried themselves in work to avoid thinking about what they had no control over, catching up on paperwork. This most unpopular task seemed never-ending, as evident, even here.

Chris Nikanov, who came to visit his sister and also couldn't leave the station, occupied himself with fixing what was malfunctioning at the station as soon as he managed to find a toolbox. He whistled through his teeth and seemed the least bothered by what was happening.

"Is your brother always like this?" I asked, looking at the surveillance screen.

"Most of the time, yes," Leeta replied, lifting her head from the emergency situation report she was filling out. "He's not easily frightened. Oh, he's fiddling with the freight elevator. Good, maybe it will finally get moving and stop breaking down every few minutes."

"Don't we have a handyman?"

"There was one until recently, but he had a nervous breakdown and returned to Earth. We don't see a replacement yet." She looked at me thoughtfully. "You don't seem like the sensitive type, but just remember to mention it to Kelley if needed. It's nothing to be ashamed of. Many of us go through a phase of 'moon depression.' Generally, it can be managed relatively quickly."

I scoffed. What a thought! I'm not a damsel in a romance novel to succumb to some nervous breakdowns. Usually, I handled bad moods, even very serious ones, on my own and had no intention of changing that. Even here, in this rundown hole where I was sent so everyone would forget about my existence. I had no intention of crying on the sleeve of a doctor I had just met and who did not inspire my trust at all.

I turned on the external monitoring and watched the streets for a while. However, I didn't spot any signs of panic, so nothing had leaked out for now. People were glancing a bit at the military patrols, but without any particular interest—just a slight surprise. They probably thought it was some kind of maneuvers, and that was for the best. The question was, did everyone? It wasn't long before an incoming call flashed on the video phone.

"Barbara Bain from the Golden Ether channel," introduced a pretty brunette on the screen. "Can you provide me with some information?"

"What kind?" I asked with resignation. Unfortunately, the law obliges me as a public official to cooperate to some extent with the media. I couldn't simply tell her to get lost, which I was very much inclined to do.

"Has the police established anything regarding the explosions in the city center?"

"All details are classified and I cannot provide explanations on this matter."

"Can we expect further acts of terror?"

I took a deep breath.

"There is no talk of acts of terror," I declared, trying to sound credible. "It's rather a vandalistic act by an individual with a disturbed psyche. We already have a lead and apprehending this vandal is a matter of hours, days at most."

I was lying, and the journalist knew I was lying, but according to press law, she could not make the slightest hint of it until she had hard evidence that contradicted what I was saying. At that moment, we were both playing our roles as best as we could.

"There are patrols made up of soldiers on the streets," Ms. Bain further inquired. "Is this related to the explosions?"

"No," I firmly denied. "These are just periodic joint maneuvers of the uniformed services. There is no reason to instill any fear among the civilian population."

"Is that why the main police station has just been closed, and those civilians who came there for various matters can't return home?"

"Yes," I realized this sounded implausible, but tough. "Once the maneuvers are concluded, everyone will be released. Isn't this an unjustified restriction of their freedom, violating civil rights?"

Ankes slightly slid a piece of foil with a short note "Robbles $4" under the desk. For a moment, I felt like I was back in elementary school, where kids pass notes to each other in *class in similar ways. Pretending to be busy with her work, she watched me out of the corner of her eye and seemed to realize that I was in some trouble. She was right. I recalled that this law indeed regulates the possibility of suspending civil liberties for a short period in exceptional situations and precisely describes the circumstances.*

"Robbles Law, paragraph four," I said. "During exercises, civil liberties can be suspended for a short time. This is in accordance with the New Constitution. Is that all? Excuse me, but I have a lot of work."

"For now, that's everything," Bain mumbled, dissatisfied. "Thank you.

And the screen went dark."

"That nasty woman, damn her..." I blurted out. Leeta ignored my ungracious words.

"That's her job," she said, not looking up from the report. "She always sticks her nose in everything because she gets paid for it. You'll get used to her nosiness. Besides her, there are two more such smart alecks who also work for Ether, Karlsson and Pinky. You'll definitely meet them soon."

I groaned.

"I can't stand journalists."

I had no reason to love them. If it weren't for a certain nosy reporter, Hoover wouldn't have found out that it was I who arrested his degenerate son, and therefore, I probably wouldn't be serving time in Lunnar now. My details were disclosed—unfortunately, as a police officer, I don't fully qualify for civil protection. I once thought it was a trivial matter, that it meant nothing because an honest person has nothing to hide. However, it turned out that things in life aren't always that simple.

There was a knock on the office door, and at the same time, the nervous tenor of the doctor came through the speaker, asking if he could come in.

"Open," I said into the microphone.

The doctor entered and closed the door behind him.

"I have the test results," he declared, placing the printouts on my desk. "On one hand, they are reassuring; on the other, not so much."

He casually settled into the chair, took a piece of cigar from the inner pocket of his jacket, and lit it without asking for my opinion. With visible, almost perverse pleasure, he blew a thick cloud of foul-smelling smoke toward the ceiling and sighed deeply. I looked at the sheet of information foil, but what was on it didn't mean anything to me.

"What does this mean?" I asked, trying not to sound too helpless.

He turned his eyes to me.

"Malaria," he replied briefly. "It's good in terms of the infection vector. It's a disease transmitted not by droplet, airborne, or foodborne routes, but by insects, which are no longer even on Earth, let alone on the Moon. They were eradicated over two hundred years ago, which ended the career of Plasmodium parasites."

"So?"

"The malaria parasite. There were at least five species, and all needed mosquitoes and midges as hosts to maintain their developmental cycle. These little beasts caused the deaths of up to a million people per year, yes, because it's a fatal disease. They had to be dealt with to control the situation."

"So where...?"

"Yes, that's a good question," he interrupted me. "In several laboratories, frozen samples of infected blood survived, as well as batches of larval parasites, stored in liquid nitrogen. It's a rather complicated matter because the destruction of these samples was mandated worldwide, but you know scientists. Something might have survived. I'll say more, something definitely survived because live parasites are now in the blood of that unfortunate person, confined in the sick room."

Ankes pushed the keyboard she had been working on away from herself.

"Will he die?" she asked.

McCave scoffed.

"No. I've already sent a request for the appropriate medications to Earth; the guy will survive. I've also called an ambulance; they'll take him to the hospital and put him in isolation. Just to prevent him from frightening other patients, because the situation is safe. And we can lift the quarantine because, as I said, it's impossible to get infected without the mediation of mosquitoes."

"So how did he get infected?"

"Probably he was deliberately given infected plasma in an injection. In fact, it's almost certain, because I don't see any other way. Anyway, this is quite a crime story and not only that. We are dealing with a potential public health threat."

I shook my head.

"If they don't resurrect mosquitoes, then probably not," I suggested.

"Theoretically, you are right. However, please consider: someone has live larvae and it's unknown who they will inject next. It can be done very easily, with a so-called dart," he pulled a tiny object out of his pocket. "They are mainly used in veterinary medicine, but not only. Sometimes it's necessary to pacify some dangerous madman, and it's probably better to do it with a dart containing a sedative than something more brutal. I think our patient was given the parasite using such a little device. I found a mark from a needle on his neck."

For a moment, the three of us fell silent. The situation looked bad. Infectious diseases used to be treated as a regular part of life; now they evoke terror in people. Someone decided to take advantage of this. It was almost impossible for a mysterious assassin to want to strike only at the unfortunate person they infected. They probably wanted to demonstrate their determination and abilities. Perhaps it was also to incite panic in the city, an impression that the residents were facing an epidemic. Somehow, this connected strangely in my mind with the letters to the mayor and the explosions under the center. From Leety's expression, I could see she was drawing similar conclusions and didn't like them at all.

"Are you sure we are not facing an epidemic?" I asked the doctor.

"Absolutely," he assured me. "Civilians can be released; let them go back to their homes. Just don't let them gossip."

"About what? About maneuvers?" I turned on the PA system and blew into the microphone. "Attention! This is the commander speaking. I am declaring the end of the exercises. Thank you for your engagement and discipline. Everyone is returning to normal work; civilians may exit the building."

McCave snorted with laughter and took another puff from his cigar stump.

"Clever. Exercises... Actually, why not? Leeta," he turned to Ankes, "do you want to look at these samples under a microscope? They are quite interesting."

"I'd love to. I'm done already."

The lieutenant closed the report, and they both left me with my thoughts. And they were not cheerful.

The fact that someone was playing with explosives was itself a very disturbing matter. However, infectious diseases, oh, that's something of much larger caliber. No one had done that for ages, and the publicly available information stated that fear-inducing pathogens simply no longer existed. They had been destroyed by an external vaccine and in laboratories by lasers. Could it be untrue? If so, the problem was serious and not just concerning Lunnar. I hope I'm wrong.

I took a sip of caffettino, already quite cold. I could have turned on the heater, but I waved it off. Sometimes it's better to cool down than to heat up. I nearly choked when someone opened the office door without ringing or announcing themselves. A woman in a military uniform with colonel insignia entered as if she owned the place. Lois Ann Sirtis, I guessed immediately. It couldn't have been anyone else. Instinctively, I got up from behind the desk.

"Good afternoon, ma'am," I said, trying to adopt the most official tone possible.

She didn't respond immediately. She pulled up a chair and sat comfortably in it, crossing her legs. I tried to assess her as I was taught, with one look. I had to admit, she looked impressive: very tall and sturdy for a woman, fairly attractive despite her buzz cut, perhaps just a bit too muscular. She must have been very strong. She could be appealing, although she was certainly over fifty. She probably wasn't tak-

ing anti-aging pills, judging by the crow's feet at her temples – these products work best where the skin is thinnest, and therefore most around the eyes. I wonder why. Women, even those very allergic, would rather stuff themselves with anti-histamines and endure side effects than give up the effect of "freezing" their youth.

"So, you are the new boss of this flea circus," she stated rather than asked. "Congratulations, though I don't envy you."

Her voice was deep, slightly hoarse, not feminine, but nonetheless attention-grabbing. Remembering Striker's warning, I tried to find unfriendly notes in it, but there didn't seem to be any. Also, the colonel's gaze, while cold, didn't seem to reveal any hostile feelings. Trying to maintain a dignified posture, I sat down in my chair, resting my elbows on the desk.

"I got this nomination against my will," I said, wanting to make things clear right away. "If you believe Lieutenant Ankes suffered an injustice, I think so too, but I had no influence over it."

She waved her hand dismissively.

"It's well known how this works. I thought from the start that Leeta wouldn't keep her position for long. I like her, but she's too soft to run the Lunnar's police. Or any other. In the long run, she wouldn't be able to keep it all together. You," she examined me with a scrutinizing look, "might work. I inquired about you as soon as you were sent here."

"And?"

"The opinions are unanimous. You're a tough guy, though also a bit of a hothead."

I raised my eyebrows because I didn't know that word. She understood the expression on my face, adding with a tone of condescension:

"It means you act under the influence of emotions, without thinking. It's sometimes a valuable trait, though it can also lead to trouble."

"I know," I muttered reluctantly. "Would you like something to drink?"

"I don't see any lady here. Call me by my name. Why not?"

I must admit that the local trend for familiarity somewhat depresses me – everyone, from the orderlies to the directors, calls each other by their first names and no one finds it strange.

"And what do you wish for... Lois Ann?" I asked. She winked at me friendly.

"A caffettino would be fine, but something better than that sludge from the machine, with double caffeine and no sweetener. We'll chat over a cup like elegant people."

***

The malaria-infected man, after a brief investigation, turned out to be a member of the board of the Juvenille corporation. Although he had no documents on him, Salome Delaforette, who took on his case, quickly handled it.

"I thought to myself, how much could his clothing cost," she told Leeta, bringing her a printout from the computer, "and based on that, I calculated the likely amount of his salary. He definitely couldn't have been either a miner or just some low-level clerk. Then, I sent his photo to the directors of all the companies and the management of the Lunnar Company. And I got his information. Harry Gelbart, deputy vice president of Juvenille, an economics graduate from Harvard, has been working in Lunnar for two years. His direct superior was very concerned; I said Gelbart had fainted on the street and is now undergoing tests."

"Very good," Leeta praised her. "Get ready."

"Where to?" Salome wondered. She sat down in the chair next to the deputy commander's desk.

"Not where, but where to. We are going to check on the important man's headquarters. We will try to find out who he has stepped on. Of course, you know where he lives?"

"Of course. Here's the address." The intern pointed to the bottom of the printout.

Lieutenant Ankes frowned.

"Are you sure?"

"I have confirmation from the management office, and what?"

Leeta muttered something in discontent and thought for a moment.

"We won't go there alone," she said after a while. "Workers' Angles is an old mining district, one of those places where it's better not to show up in uniform without an appropriate escort. Why did Gelbart rent an apartment there instead of staying at an official corporate hotel? Juvenille is relatively new to the market, but offers very good accommodation conditions for the management staff, even better than Horus. Where's your buddy the Indian?"

"Dakota?" Salome looked around. "Dakota!"

Elvis Greyfox peeked out from the archive room.

"What's the matter, Baby? Lieutenant..."

"Oh dear, call me Leeta, like the others. Don't go anywhere, you're coming with us to the search as soon as Judge Holstein signs the warrant." Saying this, the lieutenant hurriedly filled out the strict inventory form. "Uniform and weapon are mandatory."

"Okay, I'll just finish here and I'll come to you."

"Finish calmly, I'll call you. Hallie! Where is that girl again? Hallie! Find her for me, and quickly."

The pretty Hawaiian only appeared after a while, finishing the substitute cookie she was holding, added for free at "Favorite" to the standard meal sets.

"I was at lunch," she announced in an offended tone. "I have to eat too, boss."

"And am I saying you can't? Take the scooter and rush to the judge's office. Let him sign it, and come back fast."

"Yes, ma'am!"

Hallie swallowed the rest of the cookie in one bite, wiped her hands on her sweatshirt, grabbed the form handed to her, and ran out, bouncing like a little girl.

"A scooter?" Salome looked questioningly at Leeta. "You use such toys here?"

"Only for couriers, every company has its own. They're usually kids, so it's hard to entrust any of them a company sled, and the scooter uses very little energy, is fast and agile. Perfect for a courier."

"Weird place. I really feel like I've been transported back in time. Like in the Wild West."

Leeta laughed and patted her on the back.

"You'll get used to it. I felt the same way at first. It really is a bit… Western here, especially on raid days."

"Raid days?"

"When miners fight with factory workers and vice versa. Or those from one corporation raid the neighborhood of those from another."

"Seriously?" Salome's eyes widened, clearly shocked. "Such things happen here?"

"Well, what do you want, on their days off the boys get bored. Anyway, it's not our concern, but the stormtroopers from the intervention company," Leeta reassured her. "They take care of maintaining order, they only call us when something really serious happens. But raids rarely end badly. Just a lot of shouting, a bit of destruction, lots of bruises, a few broken noses, and at most a broken arm or leg."

The young policewoman flinched slightly.

"Like savages."

"Maybe a bit," Leeta admitted and returned to her computer. She checked the duty schedule. "Today Yamato is on duty, he'll take us. We'll also bring Monty with us."

"Oh!" slipped out of the intern. The lieutenant looked at her, intrigued.

"What's wrong?"

"Do we have to?"

"Don't you like Monty?"

"He scares me," Salome admitted helplessly. "I've been afraid of robots since I was a child. I can't help it."

"Monty isn't a robot, he's an android. An artificial human. I understand you have a phobia, but you have to somehow overcome it because he is part of this place and you won't be able to avoid him. Grow up," Leeta's voice almost imperceptibly hardened, becoming colder. "How old are you anyway?"

"Nineteen. And a half."

"Good heavens, you're actually almost the same age as our Hallie! I don't know who signed off on your joining the police, but you're way too young for it. How on earth did you manage to get a nursing degree and do an internship?"

"I took advantage of the educational loophole," she explained. "I'm B3, but according to the regulations, I had the right to study in schools for C. If I were B2, I would no longer be eligible. This way I could easily skip several grades and enroll in nursing school at just fourteen."

"Well, well. You're a clever one," Leeta admitted. "Anyway, it doesn't matter. Monty is coming with us."

"Yes, ma'am," whispered the intern quietly, bowing her head.

The lieutenant furrowed her brow.

"Why don't you try to be a little bolder? I noticed that earlier. Such humility doesn't suit a police officer. Not even towards superiors."

Salome raised her eyes to her. Leeta smiled involuntarily. She thought it wouldn't be an easy task for her to teach this child what self-confidence and self-worth are.

"Remember, I am your supervising officer," she said, putting down the stylus. "You must listen to what I say and watch what I do." She softened her voice. "When I arrived here, I was just like you. Scott Cavanaugh showed me not just how to be a good cop, how to be a detective, but above all, he instilled in me a sense of self-worth. He taught me to walk through life with my head held high. You must learn this too, Sal.

Elvis Greyfox emerged from the archive, brushing off the dust.

"It is just as I thought," he announced. "The mayor had connections with the Lunnars before, which he did not mention and surely does not admit to at all. The name was rattling around in my mind like a broken buzzer, and I was right.

He handed Lieutenant Ankes a piece of foil submerged in plastic, with a tag attached that described the evidence. She read a few words and blushed slightly.

"What is this supposed to be?"

Elvis smiled with satisfaction at seeing this effect.

"It was a high-profile case," he explained. "Twenty-five years ago, there wasn't a regular dating center here yet, but a certain enterprising businessman set up an agency for illegal florists. He made a real fortune from it. One of the ladies of pleasure particularly caught young Kovacs' fancy, and he wrote her such... notes. He was interning on the Moon. During that time, a scandal broke out, as it turned out that women with criminal backgrounds were being recruited into the agency, who were then blackmailed, and several young girls were lured in deceitfully. An unprecedented situation, something like that hadn't happened in at least one hundred and fifty years. I was an intern detective assigned to the case and personally cataloged the evidence. I was sure they must still be here; you don't throw away such things.

"Interesting..." Leeta looked at the letter once more. It was really very bold, even vulgar. She had not thought that someone could write something like that to any woman. "But what could come of this?"

Greyfox raised his left eyebrow mockingly.

"Cherchez la femme," he declared. "This was just a prelude. Kovacs is known in politics for his highly erotic adventures. I bet if someone is hunting him today, it's more for that reason than any other."

"He must have annoyed quite a few husbands, fiancés, or fathers," Salome interjected.

The older cop laughed and ruffled her hair like a small child.

"Oh, these girls… In today's times? Be serious, Little One. We don't live in the Middle Ages for anyone to consider a wife, fiancée, or daughter as their property. No, dear, I rather think of some clever agent he could have had dealings with. We'll need to dig in that direction."

"Alright, alright… But is there anything beyond these assumptions that suggests 'looking for a woman'?" Leeta asked skeptically.

Greyfox laid a printout from the lab on the table.

"I picked this up before I went to the archive," he said. "Read the handwriting analysis."

Lieutenant Ankes took a long piece of foil in her hand. Like everything that left the small technical printers, it curled slightly, she straightened it with the fingers of her other hand. She searched for the section titled "Handwriting Analysis."

"Judging by the shape and size of the letters and the choice of words, the author of the letters is most likely a woman aged between twenty-three and a maximum of thirty years. A strong, even dominant personality. A special sign: variable pressure on the stylus suggests an untreated injury to the hand bones."

She whistled lightly. She had picked up this habit from Inspector Cavanaugh and during her short command, she had become known for reacting to revelations in this way. Rosanda Merrick even jokingly called her "whistling miss," and that term was gaining more and more popularity among Lunnar police officers.

"Of course, that doesn't mean there isn't a man behind the whole affair," she qualified. "But indeed, we have a new lead. We'll see what searching Mr. Gelbart's apartment, that malaria-infested one, will yield."

"Do you think these cases are somehow connected?" Greyfox grew serious.

"I don't know." In fact, I don't think so. However, it cannot be ruled out. In any case, not at this stage of the investigation."

The door slammed and, on command, breathless Hallie burst in, triumphantly waving the signed warrant.

"Here it is, boss! He signed it on the spot, without even checking the details on the computer."

"Very good. Also find Monty for me, it seems he went to take lunch to the detainees. I'll record where we're going on the notice board."

That was a ruthless requirement, introduced by Scott Cavanaugh – every on-duty officer had to leave on a huge board, commonly called the notice board and hung on one of the walls, the address of the place they were heading to, and this was strictly followed. In a situation where communication couldn't be fully relied upon, such an entry could save someone's life.

Fifteen minutes later, one of the police rovers left the garage, heading to the Workers' Corners, the oldest, already historic district of Lunnar. It had a bad reputation, which is why they decided to take a heavy, armored vehicle instead of a light hovercraft, although they were aware that not all rumors about the Corners were credible. The reason why better-off people kept their distance from this part of the city was not only the company but also the very buildings: dense, primitive, reminiscent of a slum from old engravings. Of course, this was only the first visual impression, as residential buildings, continuously improved, contained the same amenities as others. However, due to the appearance of the district, its poor reputation, and its distance from the center, rental prices were much lower there – half of what it was in other industrial districts and one third compared to what one had to pay in either of the two administrative districts.

The Corners were mainly inhabited by unskilled workers employed in the worst positions in mines. So why did Harry Gelbart choose to live there? The deputy vice president of the company had a well-paid and prestigious position. He could simply have such a whim. Perhaps he was morbidly frugal, if not stingy? In any case, although the fact of living below one's social standard couldn't officially be classified as suspicious, it certainly puzzled not only the police. And what did his colleagues at work think about it? They must have known where Gelbart lived; the HR department definitely knew.

The longer Leeta thought about the case, the stranger it seemed to her. No one infects someone with a long-extinct disease for fun. Such a victim is carefully chosen, according to a criterion, for a specific purpose… Or what if not? A certain thought began to knock in the policewoman's mind, still formless but slowly taking on color. She pushed it to the bottom of her consciousness, deciding to return to it after searching the apartment of the culprit.

The police-marked rover drew noticeable attention in the Workers' Corners. They were driving slowly enough to see that. Passersby, looking like members of an unidentified army, turned to look at it with clearly unfriendly expressions. It gave the impression that there was some dress code in this district – even the clothing, which was clearly "civilian," had the same gray-blue or gray-green color as the workers' attire of the miners.

"They have to wear such nastiness?" Salome finally couldn't hold back.

"No, they don't have to," replied Ted Yamato. "I mean, there are no top-down regulations on this matter. It's just that they like to know who they're dealing with. It's useful, especially when raids begin. Factory and processing workers dress in yellow and light brown. Both groups consider themselves a separate species."

"I don't understand." The Frenchwoman looked at him with her big eyes, intrigued.

The young Asian cleared his throat with satisfaction. He rarely managed to surprise anyone.

"Moon mining and processing wouldn't exist without ordinary, low-class workers," he explained. "Machines require too much energy, by could replace them here, which worked on Earth. They are aware of this and do not allow anyone to treat them condescendingly. They are proud of who they are."

"You see, Sal, once such people, uneducated and working in manual labor, were considered worse than others," Leeta interjected. "For many, many centuries, they were despised and paid just enough to keep them from starving. When the lunnar's deposits began to be exploited and it turned out that human muscle power was necessary here, they initially tried to set the arriving miners in a position where they were doing them a favor by hiring them for decent pay. They quickly put an end to that. With a single strike, they secured themselves a really high wage, dependent on the company's profit, along with many other privileges. The Lunnar Company had no choice. The CEOs of individual corporations could either agree to these demands or mine themselves. It was similar with factory workers."

"Both sides dictate the conditions here," Yamato concluded. "They also isolate themselves from the other residents of Lunnar to emphasize that they feel superior, or at least distinct. This, of course, creates certain problems, especially for us, the police. Not long ago, I came with Detective Kuncz to meet an old acquaintance. We both got a good beating, and to this day, no one knows by whom."

"What, you don't know?" Salome almost lost her breath in outrage and disbelief. Accustomed to the realities of a big city, she could not understand how anyone could commit such an act and disappear without a trace. On Earth, police officers were untouchable even by the worst criminals for a simple reason. Everyone knew that messing with one uniformed officer was like signing your own death warrant. The last recorded case of a death in the line of duty due to deliberate actions by a suspect occurred fifteen years earlier when a dealer of an illegal drug called "heavenly high" stabbed one of the patrol officers trying to arrest him in the neck. Captured the next day, the perpetrator never even made it to the precinct. The report recorded an unfortunate accident during an escape attempt, and the prosecution didn't even examine the case. The girl who hid him received twenty-five years for aiding and abetting, and even her own family did not try to defend her.

"This isn't Earth, missy. It's better not to count on social support, as you might get burned."

"That's why we have weapons with us today," Leeta said sternly. "And you must not hesitate if the situation demands it. Even before your arrival, I received permission from Earth to use extraordinary measures, right after the attack on Kuncz and Yamato. Respect for representatives of authority must be enforced. The miners know that someone among them has crossed a certain line, and that's why they are doubly hostile."

"Territory of the Comanches?" Greyfox smiled.

"Not necessarily. But we are not welcomed here, and we must keep that in mind."

The police vehicle stopped in front of one of the squat tenement houses, marked with a code number but otherwise indistinguishable from the others. As soon as they got out, an older, limping man in a dirty tracksuit with a name tag saying "Building Administrator" came out to meet them.

"What do you want?" he asked sharply.

Elvis Greyfox stepped forward.

"You say, 'How can I assist representatives of authority?'" he said calmly but emphatically.

"I'm asking what for?" the administrator did not back down. "Nothing is happening here that requires you to stick your nose in. No one invited you."

Greyfox stepped even closer and suddenly pushed the man against the wall.

"Are you dreaming of a night in a cell? Or maybe something more? From experience, I know that someone who behaves like that usually has a lot to hide." He pulled a portable scanner from his belt pocket and brought it close to the name tag. "Winston Cooper, sixty-four years old, class C1, residential building administrator license approved two years ago," he read from the miniature display. "Twenty-eight years working in the mine as a cyborg operator, five years as a supervisor. "Twice arrested for assault, ten days in the slammer for resisting arrest, well, look at that. Let me guess, you don't love the police?"

"I have no such obligation."

"Indeed not. However, you do have an obligation to follow the orders of law enforcement, like any citizen. Whether you like it or not. So please open apartment number eleven for us. This lieutenant here will show you the warrant signed by a judge."

The administrator scoffed angrily but lowered his tone.

"Eleven? What did that kid living there do?"

Greyfox turned the scanner so that the recording side was up and pressed two buttons. A holographic image appeared above the display, showing the head of Harry Gelbart.

"Is this him?"

Winston Cooper examined the head floating in the air as if it were severed, slowly rotating around its vertical axis.

"Well, I suppose it's him," he admitted reluctantly. "The calmest tenant, what do you want from him? Did he steal something?"

Leeta stepped forward, feeling it was time to take the initiative.

"We cannot disclose such matters to outsiders," she said. "However, I will bend the rules slightly to calm you: this young man is currently suspected of nothing. Quite the contrary, we are trying to help him."

"Let's say so," Cooper did not look convinced. "Maybe you could wait for him? At this time, he should already be returning from work. It's been two weeks since he went to Skalen."

"So where to?"

"Well, where do you think? You don't know yet? Skalen is ilmenite mine owned by Juvenille, the boy is a pillar miner. He's set to be promoted to foreman next year."

The police exchanged glances. They weren't going to share their information with this man, but Harry Gelbart was becoming an increasingly mysterious figure.

"Please take us to his apartment and assist with the search. According to procedures, we need an independent witness if the tenant has not been formally charged."

Leeta spoke calmly and friendly. This, combined with her charm, clearly had a soothing effect on the administrator. He even managed to muster a hint of a reluctant smile.

"Follow me. I'll just get the universal access card."

As he disappeared behind the service room door, Leeta took the moment to whisper to her companions.

"Stay on alert. Don't let yourselves be surprised."

"Maybe Yamato and your android could go with us?" suggested Greyfox quietly.

"No. They need to stay back and keep an eye on the street."

"Damn, like in a war." Elvis fell silent as Cooper just returned with a rectangular piece of plastic in hand.

"We can go."

Apartment eleven was located on the second floor of the tenement, behind the first of a series of identical doors. Cooper unlocked it with the card and pushed it open.

"You can enter," he said. "I will stay here in case any other tenants show up. It could lead to, hm, hm, misunderstanding."

"It would be better for everyone if it didn't," Greyfox muttered coldly, meaningfully tapping his hand against the holster of his service dual. After throwing the administrator one last menacing look, he stepped inside – and froze.

The girls accompanying him reacted as they had earlier.

VII
LEETA
Personal Diary

Since I became a police officer, I have learned a lot, and the sight of a corpse no longer has the shocking effect on me that it did at first. It is still, however, nothing pleasant. The woman lying on the floor, elegantly dressed, had been dead for at least a few hours, but not longer, because the blood in her straight hair, scattered around her head, had already begun to clot and darken, but her face had not yet taken on a deep blue color. The skull was shattered, and from the place where I stood, I could easily see fragments of bone and brain. The cause of death seemed clear. A heavy flashlight lay next to the deceased. The air was saturated with the heavy smell of blood and raw meat.

"We don't touch anything," I said commanding as I regained my voice. "We call in the technicians, the doctor, and Connie Benedict. Sergeant Greyfox, please take care of this. If the phones are down again, please use the pager to send the appropriate code. Mr. Cooper, do you know this woman?"

The administrator stepped closer. I noticed he had gone pale, and his face was covered in sweat. He shook his head in denial.

"I've never seen her here. I'm sure. She's not a miner."

"How do you know? Do you know each one individually?" Greyfox asked sharply, busy on the phone and listening to us at the same time. He has divided attention. "Or do you think that based on her outfit?"

"No, of course not. The dress is indeed fabulous, and the shoes are worth my salary. But so what, you can buy that online and they'll send it with the supplies. Miners earn good money. Only they all cut their hair to the length of half a matchstick, like soldiers. Besides, the hands, just look at them. Do you seriously think this poor girl ever worked physically?"

The point sounded reasonable. The deceased's hands were indeed very well-groomed, delicate, with slender fingers ending in neatly maintained, red-polished nails. Her dress was also red, tailored in the latest fashion and made of synthetic silk with a slight sheen, along with narrow high-heeled shoes. As if their owner was going to a gala, not to a working-class district. I looked at Salome. If she was to become a police detective, it was an excellent opportunity for her to start proper learning.

"You are an intern, so please: take a close look and draw some conclusions," I instructed. "Just don't touch anything."

"Yes, ma'am."

She stepped forward just enough to have a better view and leaned forward a bit. I watched her closely. I didn't know if she had participated in the examination of corpses before and I hoped she wouldn't feel faint in the presence of a civilian. However, nothing indicated that.

"It really is a person from high society," she spoke after a while. "It's not just about the clothing or the nails. She has *a very carefully done permanent makeup on her eye contours and professionally extended eyelashes. Judging by the hands, she not only did not work physically but also did not engage in any sports. The jewelry looks modest, but I bet it's of the highest quality. It's what they call 'expensive simplicity'. The skin is well-maintained and very clean. Judging by the position of her hands and head, she was taken by surprise and struck from behind, once, with great force. She definitely did not defend herself and died instantly. This flashlight... I don't know this model."*

"That's not a flashlight, it's a battery-powered spotlight," Cooper interjected. *"They use those in mines to light up the corridors."*

"That theoretically directs suspicion toward some miner," Salome continued. *"It definitely wasn't... our sick one, because he's been in the hospital since yesterday, previously we kept him at the station, and this lady was murdered relatively recently. The pathologist will comment on this, and I am not one. However, I would be cautious. Mr. Cooper, do people working in mines keep such spotlights at home?"*

"Of course. It's personal equipment, just like work clothes and many other tools."

"Exactly. The one who killed our deceased simply grabbed the first heavy object he could find. This does not, of course, rule out that the murderer was a miner, but they didn't have to be. "What else... He must have panicked because he fled and slammed the door behind him, not even trying to cover his tracks or take the murder weapon. Hence the conclusion that he did not plan what he did and is probably not a professional killer. In fact, almost certainly." She paused for

a moment and tilted her head, trying to see something. "And there's something else."

"What is it?" I asked when she fell silent.

"I think she's pregnant."

"Are you kidding?!" I gasped.

"Not at all, this is no joking matter. However, behind the victim's ear, I see... yes, it's the tip of a dosing patch. It's slightly yellowish, so it's soaked with an antiemetic drug. It's prescribed specifically to pregnant women. Unless she was suffering from Meniere's syndrome, but that will also come out in the autopsy."

"This case is getting complicated," I muttered to myself.

A pregnant woman on the Moon, that was against the law, completely unacceptable. I had to briefly outline this issue to my companions, as they might not know about it yet. The fetal protection program mandates that a pregnant woman must avoid potentially dangerous places and situations. Thus, the future mother can only travel by spaceship in one direction – from the Moon to Earth. It sometimes happens that conception occurs despite all protective measures, and then the woman is immediately sent back from Lunnar, regardless of who she is. Only at one of the planetary centers can a full, reliable assessment of the fetus and its prospects be made. Unfortunately, not all cases are detected. For a long time, we had clues that someone in Lunnar was performing illegal abortions, and so far, the investigation had not moved forward at all.

"Why do women take such risks?" Salome wondered. "After all, removing an undamaged fetus, even illegally, counts as murder. Wouldn't it be better to admit it and give birth?"

"*Logically speaking, yes,*" *I replied. "However, it has its consequences. A child conceived without a license is immediately taken away after birth and placed for adoption, and the woman has a record that can seriously harm her career. If she wants to start a family in the future, it can complicate obtaining an official certificate for the child despite established genetic suitability.*"

"*The little black one,*" *as I still referred to her in my mind, shook her head disapprovingly.*

"*I don't understand how one could even want to remove a healthy, well-developed baby. It's incomprehensible.*"

It was no surprise she didn't understand. Humanity had been struggling for so long with negative population growth – which, of course, was significantly influenced by the necessary, restrictive embryo preselection policy – that each valid pregnancy, even one for which no official permit had been issued, became an immediate treasure. The fact of that treasure's existence could be seen as an infringement on the personal freedom of the mother, hence the necessity for legal regulations protecting such a fetus arose in the first place. Humanity simply could not afford to lose valuable individuals.

"*I would like to have a child someday,*" *Cooper said nostalgically. "When my contract ends, I will return to Earth and find a wife with good genes. From the beginning, I've been saving points in the bank for that purpose. My genes were confirmed long ago as suitable for reproductive purposes.*"

"*To each their own. I prefer to be free,*" *Greyfox stated. "Besides, in the police, they look down on getting married, and in the genetic control offices, on our parenthood. Though* it's not even about chromosomes. 'Inappropriate psychological development conditions,' I believe that's how it's termed."

"Oh please. A policeman can also get a license; you just have to go through a lot of hassle," Salome protested. "It's not that bad. I also have a pretty decent genetic profile, and after joining the police, it was not removed from the register."

"So, if I understand correctly, you're interested?" Cooper gave her a half-joking, half-serious look. He seemed to like her.

I suddenly thought that this might seem strange, in the presence of the murdered woman, conducting such a conversation seems inappropriate. Is it an attempt to relieve tension? The building administrator probably did not often find mutilated corpses in apartments. He had strong nerves, but it certainly wasn't a pleasure, and he didn't want to show us that it shocked him. For the police officers, however, such an exchange of words was inappropriate, and I should have reacted somehow, but nothing came to mind. Instead, I foolishly said:

"Don't be rude."

"Why rude?" he wondered. "I'm not old yet, I have a lot of points in the bank, a house on Earth, and I guess I can still be likable."

I waved my hand at him.

The team gathered by Dr. McCave reached us before we finished discussing these matters.

"Who reported 187, what is it?" Kelley asked briskly.

I pointed to the deceased woman.

"We didn't go inside, of course," I added. "We'll check everything when you're done with your work. Just let Connie photograph everything properly first."

"Well, go have some tea or something, because this will take a while." He grumbled, hastily pulling on his gloves. Connie Benedict stepped out from behind him and, not paying attention to anyone, began taking photographic documentation.

"There's an automatic café downstairs, entrance from the side of the building," the administrator sighed. "Unfortunately, I have to stay here."

I had some doubts about whether we would be welcomed in the local café, but I decided we could go there. In broad daylight, when most regulars were probably at work, we could take the risk.

We took Yamato with us so he wouldn't feel left out, leaving Monty in the rover and instructing him to keep an eye on everything, especially the weapons. The unique property of the android, allowing him to see metal through clothing, was very useful in such circumstances.

The café was called "Friendship," but the looks shot our way from the few guests at that hour were definitely not friendly. Ignoring that, we ordered a cup of caffettino and a pastry from the machine, and took a seat by the window, where we had a good view of the street. The hot drink turned out to be better than we expected, and it was quite helpful. The thermostat in the Workers' District was set quite low; I didn't understand why, maybe it was about costs, or perhaps that was the consensus of the omni. In any case, it was definitely cold here, at least five degrees lower than the average in Lunnar.

"Terrible place," Salome muttered. "Even worse than the rest of this city."

"What do you want? This is the first settlement that was even built here. A bit of a makeshift. The next ones were considered to be nicer and more comfortable," I said, enjoying my caffettino. "Although, really, everything here is meant to be functional, and that's it. It's not a resort but an industrial city."

"Except for Selenoport," the sergeant interjected.

"Except for Selenoport," I agreed with him. "But the residents of Lunnar don't really go there, unless occasionally. At first, people rushed to explore this new Las Vegas, but you know, they checked it out and lost interest. The prices are such that it's ridiculous, and no one here works just to blow a month's salary in some snobby venue in one night."

"There's something to that," he admitted. "But maybe for some big occasion...?"

I pondered.

"It seems the presidency sometimes holds exceptionally important meetings there. A matter of prestige. Regular people... maybe they occasionally drop by for ice cream or to shoot at targets in the amusement park. Definitely nothing more."

"I could go for some ice cream..." Salome daydreamed like a child, of which she had only recently stopped being.

I wanted to tell her that maybe someday we would go to Selenoport together, where there is indeed the only real ice cream parlor on the Moon, but at that moment, one of the café guests stood up from his table and approached us. I would bet that he had drunk much more than just caffettino or tea from concentrate, as aggression and an unhealthy lev-

el of adrenaline radiated from him. He was wearing a work overall and seemed to be heading for the shift, for the second shift, because his shoes and hands were still clean. He was definitely not coming back.

"Are you in charge here, bitch?" he asked bluntly.

I frowned. Out of the corner of my eye, I noticed that Greyfox slightly reached for his service pistol and I cursed under my breath. That's exactly what I didn't need, an eager cowboy. I had to act quickly and decisively. I stood up from my chair.

"Do you have a problem, SIR?" I asked coldly.

"You are the problem! What are you doing here, damn dogs?!" the man raised his voice increasingly, while the others watched the situation develop with a certain curiosity, not revealing, however, the desire to intervene. Ted and I knew why this was happening. The newcomers – not yet.

"Please calm down immediately. We are here on official business." I tried to speak as unemotionally as possible and to influence this miner while it was still not physical.

"You were here last time too! Nobody wants you here, get out!" The miner suddenly thrust his fist under my nose. This was meant to be just a demonstration, I knew that and didn't even blink, but then something happened that I did not expect.

Salome, Forest Baby, "Little black one," sprang from the table so quickly that no one in the world could react in time. Before I could stop her, she expertly twisted the attacker's arm, kicked him behind the knee, and knocked him to the floor, where he hit his head against the ceramic tiles with a thud. He immediately lost his composure, especially since our petite intern pressed one of his thumbs straight into the radial nerve, and his knee into the left sciatic, and he could only dream of breaking free. I thought she knew anatomy well; it's no wonder she's a nurse. The sight was almost comical, as if a mouse had battered a large cat, but nobody found it funny. Only now did the other patrons of the café jump up, yet the sight of the gun aimed at them kept them in place.

"I wouldn't advise that," the sergeant said coolly. He pulled handcuffs from his pocket with his left hand. "Cuff him, Baby, and read him his rights. Charges: assault on a police officer and insult to an officer on duty."

I cursed helplessly in my mind. This was exactly what I wanted to avoid. After the events of two months ago, the peace in Lunnar was like a string pulled to its limits, and a small spark could lead to riots. This situation could easily become such a "small spark." However, I couldn't question Greyfox's actions, at least not here, in front of civilians.

"Put him in the transport with Monty," I commanded with resignation. "He won't escape. Ted, call for a prison ambulance."

"Yes, boss," replied Yamato dutifully, who was just helping Salome lift the miner off the floor. The confused man swayed on his feet and slurred some indecipherable words, glancing at his conqueror in astonishment. He probably never expected to be beaten by her, and it's no wonder. I didn't expect it either. Earlier, I had even wondered what a former nurse was doing in the police, especially one of such a slight build. Another proof that one shouldn't judge a book by its cover.

The prison ambulance arrived after several minutes, just in case accompanied by a squad of heavily armed stormtroopers under the command of Al Merino. Wilder seemed to feel that we needed additional support; someone at the *station probably made him aware of what was going on here. Or maybe he figured it out himself. He's not stupid; you can't say that about him at all.*

Al took care of interviewing the witnesses, took over the detained person, and we finished our caffettino and returned to the crime scene.

***

"You are very quick," Leeta said to Salome. "And proficient in the technique of incapacitating. It's easy to get caught by you."

Elvis Greyfox smiled proudly.

"My school, I could say. I taught her a bit. I admit, however, that our Baby has just got predispositions like few others. Show off, Sal."

The intern blushed, modestly lowering her eyes, but it was evident, she is very pleased with herself.

"For two seasons in a row, I was the national junior champion in the 100-meter race," she explained. "I also trained in high jump and placed third in the state jujitsu tournament when I was fifteen.

Lieutenant Ankes whistled in admiration.

"You have a better foundation for being a police officer than I do."

"What do you mean… I mean, you."

"Yet. I only underwent training in a special operations agency… I was almost twenty-four years old and had no sporting achievements; in fact, something like that wouldn't have crossed my mind before. I was a bookworm, until a certain accident changed everything. One day I will tell you how it happened. For now, something else is more important," Leeta became serious. "You are probably un-aware of what has just happened."

"We don't know; that's probably an exaggeration."

"No, it's no exaggeration. I should have told you ev-erything earlier, but I didn't think such a situation would arise. Two months ago, there was a chase in the Work-ers' Corners. A patrol was sent to arrest a miner, sus-pected of involvement in a fatal beating during a raid in the Factory District, Carol Masion. Such raids rare-ly end in anything more serious, but this time, after all the commotion, when we routinely checked the Fac-tory District, we found a corpse. We identified a sus-pect from the surveillance footage, and that's where the problems began."

"Why?" the sergeant wondered.

"The footage was ambiguous, meaning, what could be derived from it. We wanted to interrogate this girl for now, hoping she might shed some light on the circumstances of the crime. The thing is, she misunderstood this. She did not show up at the station after the official summons, so the patrol went to get her. She started to run, and the chase ended tragically. Carol Masion's friends tried to interfere with the arrest. Shots were fired, and Masion died on the spot. And one of those who tried to help her escape. Since that day, the situation has been very tense, and the miners treat us as you have seen."

Grayfox nodded to indicate he understood.

"Right. The person summoned to testify ignored the call, thus a patrol was sent. The suspect did not want to obey the officers' orders and started to flee. The police were attacked, defended themselves effectively, for which they deserve commendation. What's the miners' issue? After all, that woman was to blame for herself; the other one too."

Leeta sighed.

"It's hard to explain in a few words."

"I can see that. The situation is dangerous because a certain group of citizens is trying to put themselves above the law. That should never happen."

The lieutenant looked him straight in the eye.

"I know this," she said calmly and emphatically. "I had orders to defuse the situation without using the military, and I managed to do it. I met with the district council and calmly and factually explained the background of the incident. The outrage subsided enough that the miners returned to work, and until today, we have had peace. You both need to understand something: this is a very consolidated environment, and without the miners, there will be no extraction. It's not like you can just throw out the strikers and take in others from hour to hour. Recruitment, transport, training, all that takes time, and every day of downtime is measurable losses for the companies. The economy and politics are closely linked, Sergeant, and the police do not operate just because; we act on orders from above. What you think, what I think, it doesn't matter as long as we wear the uniform and the badge. We are obliged to obey our superiors, and that's exactly what we do." She softened her tone. "I know it's hard to understand all this, but on the Moon, there are simply special conditions. That's why nobody is eager to serve in Lunnar. I hope you now see how important a good dose of diplomacy and understanding of local conditions is before taking any action. You are not used to this because everything looks different on Earth;

that means, a law-abiding citizen absolutely listens to the police and wouldn't even think about resisting if they have nothing on their conscience. Yes, yes, that's how it should be here too, I agree."

Only that it isn't, and it won't be anytime soon. Yet we have to ensure order and safety despite that.

"In what way?" Greyfox wanted to ask sarcastically, but held back. He was starting to understand the heavy burden Leeta had been carrying since Inspector Cavanaugh's death and why she had so amicably welcomed her successor, without any resentment. It must have been a relief for her that someone else, not her, would be responsible for such a difficult post.

When they arrived at the crime scene, the forensic technicians under Doctor McCave's supervision were already preparing to leave.

"You can do your thing," the doctor said gruffly upon seeing them. "I'm done here."

"Any preliminary conclusions?" Leeta asked.

"Ones you probably drew as well. Without an autopsy, I won't say anything concrete. The cause of death seems clear, but... something doesn't add up. It looks like the deceased was standing like a mummy waiting for the killer to smash her head and didn't even try to look back to see who was sneaking up behind her. She must have heard something, anything, and did nothing."

"She might have known her killer," Salome interjected.

"That's a valid conclusion, though not a particularly groundbreaking thought. Ninety-five percent of victims know their attacker," the doctor observed the intern with visible sympathy. "I'll get back to you after the autopsy. For now, I'm leaving you here, and watch out for yourselves."

"A bit late for that advice," Leeta muttered sourly. "But thank you."

McCave did not delve further into the topic. He had Cooper sign the protocol for assisting the forensic team and exited, leaving the detectives with room to work.

"Alright then," Leeta sighed. "Salome the kitchen, Dakota the bathroom and bedroom, I'll take care of the living room."

The apartment consisted of those four very small rooms. It was decorated rather Spartanly, without unnecessary embellishments. The "living room," which was the main room, boasted standard furnishings: a wardrobe, a chest of drawers, a trunk, a table, and a few chairs. Leeta was immediately struck by the fact that the tenant, according to documents, had lived there for at least two years, had not attempted to personalize the room in any way—hanging pictures on the walls, curtains in the windows, anything. Not even a small vase on the dresser. She opened the wardrobe. Another surprise. It was empty. The same with the chest of drawers. None of the drawers contained even a single piece of paper. Only in the trunk did she discover something, though nothing unusual, just the standard gear of a miner: two neatly folded coveralls, a set of tools, a headlamp. Nothing more.

She took photographic documentation and closed the trunk. She felt disoriented. She sometimes dealt with obsessive neat freaks, but even among them, furniture had some contents, just cataloged and organized like in a museum. It wasn't simply empty; no one in the world could live like that.

"Did Mr. Gelbart normally come and go here?" she asked Cooper, who was leaning against the door frame with a bored look.

"Yeah, I saw him sometimes. A polite guy, calm, didn't cause any trouble."

"He didn't cause any because it seems he didn't actually live here."

"But he paid the rent regularly. And a woman visited him."

"A woman?"

"Yeah, a cutie. A girl."

"That one who was killed?" Leeta asked pointedly.

"Of course not, I've never seen her. Another one. A miner. Nothing special, like all of them. Tall, muscular, hair cut almost to the skin. I think she was Asian," he suddenly pondered. "Tanned, slanted eyes, flat nose. Not that she was ugly, but somewhat... nondescript."

Lieutenant Ankes frowned. She quickly took out the scanner and activated the display panel. She searched the device's memory for a moment, then handed it to Cooper. A hologram of a young woman formed above the screen.

"Is this her?"

He looked closely.

"Yeah, definitely."

"Oh, for God's sake."

"Is this important?" he inquired.

Leeta didn't respond. She turned off the scanner and with furrowed brows returned to work. Things were becoming increasingly complicated, and she sensed that this was not the end. And indeed, it wasn't.

The administrator, alerted by the unusual noise outside, he disappeared for a moment, then returned, clearly agitated.

"Lieutenant, you need to go downstairs," he said in a tone that alarmed Leeta that the situation was serious.

"Cease the search and follow me!" she shouted.

Together they rushed down the stairs, not waiting for the elevator. Through the armored glass of the main door, they saw an unusual scene.

A sizable crowd had gathered in front of the apartment building. Judging by the hostile shouts, they wanted to get inside, but Monty and Officer Yamato blocked their way, trying to calm the assailants with verbal commands. The miners, however, had no intention of backing down. Rocks were thrown. One hit Yamato in the head, while several others flew at Monty, who shielded the young officer. His visible insensitivity to the hard projectiles astonished the miners, who hesitated for a moment. Leeta took advantage of this.

"Monty, inside!" she shouted, yanking the door open. "Take Ted!"

The android picked up the crouching Yamato and took refuge in the apartment hall with him. Lieutenant Ankes quickly slammed the door shut just in time as more rocks immediately struck it. Cooper used his card to lock the door.

"This is exactly what I feared," he said grimly.

"No one asked for your opinion," Greyfox snarled. "Lieutenant, any orders?"

Leeta did not respond, busy tending to the semi-conscious Yamato, whom Monty had laid on the floor. It wasn't until she applied a makeshift bandage that she stood up from her knees.

"Salome, keep an eye on him," she instructed. "He may have a concussion. Mr. Cooper, do you have a landline phone here?"

"What? Yes, I have one in the duty room, over there," the administrator struggled to tear his gaze away from the thickening crowd visible behind the armored glass. "What the hell has gotten into them?"

"Watch your language, there are women here!" the sergeant sharply reprimanded him.

Leeta darted in the indicated direction, and after a moment, they heard her voice from the duty room.

"Hello! Who am I speaking with? Oh, it's you, Mabel. Tell the boss we urgently need support. Worker's District, block three, house number sixty-five. Code red."

Winston Cooper swore again. Not at the sound of those words, but at the sight of what was happening behind the door's glass.

"Great, now they probably think I'm a collaborator."

"What kind of collaborator?" Greyfox shouted angrily. "Watch your words! Do you have the police as your enemies? What the hell is going on here?"

"Calm down, sergeant," Leeta stepped out of the duty room, wrinkling her brow in displeasure. "He's new here, Mr. Cooper. He hasn't fully grasped everything yet." She looked through the glass. "It seems, however, that we cannot maintain the status quo any longer."

"Do they want to lynch us?" Salome asked fearfully.

"I don't know. It has become dangerous. Is there anyone in the neighborhood who might be deliberately inciting them?" the lieutenant addressed the administrator. "Think carefully about your answer."

The man wiped his sweaty forehead with his sleeve.

"I don't know," he mumbled.

"Are you sure? Please think."

"Well, I don't know! I swear! Now that you've asked, I can see it would make sense. People have been terribly worked up for some time now. I hadn't concerned myself with it until now, thinking it was none of my business. I'm supposed to manage the building, and that's it."

Cooper seemed as sincere as he was terrified, but Leeta detected a barely noticeable note of falsehood in his voice. He definitely wasn't telling the whole truth. He knew something and had a good reason to hide it. In these circumstances, it was better not to delve deeper into the topic, so she turned to Greyfox.

"If things get really hot, shoot both of you for real. Salome, as a trainee, still doesn't have service weaponry, so let her take the dual from Yamato. He just picked it up, and I know he hasn't personalized it yet, luckily. Salome knows how to shoot, I hope?"

"Oh yes, I taught her myself."

"That's good. I hope it doesn't come to that, but if it does, it will be 'us or them'. Don't hesitate."

"There's no worry, lieutenant." Elvis knelt down and drew the service weapon from the holster of the injured colleague. He examined it closely and slid the safety off. The indicator light turned green, which meant that Yamato indeed had not yet completed the mandatory registration for uniformed personnel, which involves calibrating the dual weapon's sensor to their biological signature. This procedure ensured that the weapon could only be used by its owner, but it could only be done by a technician from the command arsenal. The fact that Yamato had not done this yet constituted a serious violation of regulations, yet there was a mitigating circumstance – the officer had lost his previous weapon due to mechanical damage, and he had only received a new one that morning when the technician had not yet come to work.

"Hold this," the sergeant handed the dual weapon to the intern. "If they break down the door, shoot as much as you can and don't think."

The girl accepted the weapon handed to her. Watching her from the corner of her eye, Leeta noted with satisfaction that Salome's hands were steady, and more color was returning to her face. "She's tough," she thought with admiration.

"Fucking hell…" Cooper grunted in disbelief at the sight of the ready weapon and hid in his duty room.

"What manners," Salome grimaced in displeasure upon hearing that unparliamentary expression.

"Miners rarely have mouths full of violets," Lieutenant Ankes smiled faintly. "At first, I had a problem with this too, but over time, one gets used to strong language and stops paying attention to it. Although, of course, one shouldn't use it themselves, regardless of the circumstances. Especially on duty."

"I have no intention of doing so. I wasn't raised that way."

"Neither was I. My foster mother didn't allow the use of strong language. For a simple 'damn', one would get grounded for a week," Leeta interrupted, perking up her ears. "Warning, I hear a wail. The cavalry might be coming."

Indeed, from afar, a mournful, modulated voice of a siren approached. The crowd shifted restlessly, hostile shouts turned into warning calls. From three sides, heavy military vehicles rolled into the street, from which soldiers armed with long-barreled vibrational weapons, intended for suppressing riots, spilled out.

VIII
CLINT WILDER
Personal Diary

Lieutenant Ankes' report deeply troubled me, especially when combined with the concise message from Colonel Sirtis. As an addition to it, she brought in the detainees – several miners and the entire council of the Workers' Angles district. In exchange, she left a unit of her soldiers at the town hall and also sent additional reinforcements to ensure order on the streets. The military took control of the district, and I was presented with a fait accompli. Although theoretically I could have protested, I already knew enough about Lunnar to avoid doing so. Of course, I wouldn't say anything in front of the detainees. During training, we were strongly reminded that uniformed services should always support each other and never stand against one another in front of civilians, but of course, a private argument is another matter. Lois Ann Sirtis probably preferred to preempt situations and as soon as the doors to the office closed behind us, she said:

"It had to be done, Clint. This isn't the first incident like this. Someone is setting the miners not so much against the police as against authority in general." She opened the bar without asking and poured herself some gin, still from In-

spector Cavanaugh's stock. With a glass in hand, she settled into an armchair.

"What does this someone want?" I asked, approaching my own chair. On the desk, a mug of caffettino was steaming, placed there by someone unknown. One of the new subordinates must have thought of me when I was taking over the detainees. "Secession of the Moon, like in the movies?"

Sirtis laughed hoarsely.

"No, of course not, that would be childish; even they know that," she waved her hand. "Interrupting supplies from Earth would end such a silly rebellion in a week. No, they probably just want to gain representation in the city authorities and some additional privileges. They've got their heads turned around, and maybe..."

"Maybe what?" "Maybe there is something we don't know. It has always been easy to push workers into ignorance, and as I said, someone is intentionally inciting them with some personal political or economic goal, who knows." She took a sip in thought. "Or maybe a personal one...?"

"Whatever the reason, it needs to be stopped," I noted. "My people could have died. If it weren't for you... I don't even want to think about it."

Sirtis poured me more gin into my caffettino.

"Take a sip," she advised. "The matter is even more complicated than you think, because I'd bet it has something to do with the new governor. I have no idea what yet, but I can feel it in my bones."

"You don't like him, do you?" I guessed.

"You'll understand once you meet him." She replied briefly.

I took a sip of the fortified caffettino; it was quite good. I wasn't sure if the alcohol consumption on duty was within regulations, but in this situation, it seemed to be the least important thing. The situation was on a knife's edge, heading who knows where. Everything indicated that, whatever happened, I definitely wouldn't be bored here.

The speaker crackled, and Leeta asked, "Can I come in?"

"Come on in!" I called out.

My deputy entered, carrying several printouts.

"Here you go," she said, laying them on the desk. "List of detainees along with their short profiles, medical certificate for Ted Yamato's hospitalization, testimony from Winston Cooper, preliminary results of the search of apartment number eleven in building sixty-five, third quarter of the Workers' Angles district, my assessment of the first field case with officers Greyfox and Delaforette, and the deceased's report. We were able to identify her based on DNA. That's Annabelle Banks, a graduate of the hospitality department, licensed VIP assistant, employed at the 'Parish' hotel in downtown Selenoport, twenty-six years old, class B2, no criminal record."

I picked up the printout, which was adorned with a holographic photo of an attractive brunette with a captivating smile.

"Absurd," I muttered. "What was she doing in the workers' district?"

"I have no idea," Leeta pulled a chair closer. "A girl from a good family, excellent academic results, valued at work for professionalism, you could say a gem. She moved in good company," she pondered. "I checked information about her in the virtual world. Not much, but it's all positive. I can't

imagine what she was doing at Gelbart's miner's apartment, but Gelbart, the vice president of a corporation, is something else."

"Are you sure it's the same person?" I expressed cautious doubt. There was some fiction in this that I couldn't wrap my head around.

"I'm not sure for now," she replied honestly. "However, since I've dealt with the clones of Leon Hampton, nothing surprises me anymore. Winston Cooper, the administrator, swears that Gelbart is a pillar miner. The mine supervisor, Huang Wei, recognized him in a photo, gave me a confirmed schedule of his shifts and surveillance recordings. I sent Kuncz in civilian clothes, with discreet security, to talk to Gelbart's colleagues. In two hours, I have a meeting with President Juvenille myself. We need to compare work hours. We obviously rule out bilocation, so if the schedules of the miner and the vice president coincide, we are dealing with two different people, undoubtedly somehow related."

"What's going on with those clones?" I asked a bit confused.

Leeta briefly explained what she meant – how a very wealthy businessman tried to persuade various scientists to create a new body for him and what resulted from that.

"Here, I think we might be dealing with doppelgangers," she concluded her story. "Just in case, I sent two officers to the hospital to keep an eye on Gelbart. He's still very sick; I don't want to interrogate him in that condition, but we can't allow him to slip away either. We still don't know if we are dealing with a victim or someone who is consciously participating in a criminal conspiracy."

"When will he be in suitable condition?" I wanted to know. She shrugged.

"There are three doctors working in the hospital today," she replied. "Each of them has a different vision. From a week to three. For now, they are getting medication that disturbs their consciousness, and the illness itself is also doing its part."

"What a pity," I muttered. I knew that the longer the interrogation of the suspect was delayed, the more variables could disrupt the investigator's plans. "What about the autopsy?"

Leeta looked at her watch. "Kelley will be here in no more than ten minutes," she said. "He warned me that he would come as soon as he finishes and that it will be quick."

"I hope he found out something."

"Definitely," she assured me. "Kelley is an excellent pathologist. You didn't like him, did you?"

"No," I admitted. "I just can't manage it. I always feel like he looks down on me."

She chuckled. "Now that would be an achievement," she measured me with her eyes. "He'd probably have to get on a ladder. But seriously, give yourself a little time on this matter. It's hard not to like our doctor, even when he initially makes a bad impression. He's a good professional and a very nice person, even though he has his quirks."

"And who doesn't? Lunnar is the biggest madhouse in the world," Sirtis said with a laugh.

I cleared my throat and changed the subject. "Anyway, we need to talk to the miners. For some reason, they have started treating the authorities as enemies, and we need to stop that as soon as possible before it leads to a tragedy."

Leeta grew serious. "To be honest, a tragedy has already happened. However, we should indeed stop this while there is still a real chance to cool the tempers. Moreover, conducting an investigation in the face of hostility from the miners will be very difficult. We need to change that into a willingness to cooperate and restore these people's trust in the uniform," she rubbed her forehead with her hand, clearly pondering something. "Let's think. The miners are mostly representatives of the lowest C or even D class, for whom coming here is their only chance at a career. Simple people with intelligence at the edge of acceptable minimum, with only basic education. However, that doesn't mean they are, colloquially speaking, some social pathology..."

She stopped, searching for the right words. I understood her well because I was sometimes troubled by this issue too. The matter of intelligence is very sensitive these days, to the point that it has become almost taboo, and it is rarely mentioned in everyday conversation. This topic is meticulously avoided in social discussions, and a jab at someone's class is considered the worst kind of rudeness. However, that does not change the facts – different classifications exist and determine human life, which in itself is not necessarily a bad thing. As I see it, it cannot be otherwise, and the equivalent of this mechanism also functioned at times when there were no officially approved assignments to this or that IQ class. Today, it is even easier than before. A person has their place in society, and the employment office they turn to will always find them a suitable job. From an early age in guidance classes, we are taught that everyone deserves respect as long as society benefits from them, and yet almost everyone dreams of being classified higher than what they have been assigned. I don't, but for example, Anna was ready to do anything just to change that label on her forehead. Those who cannot count on that sometimes fall into the other extreme, closing themselves off socially within their own circle, and among workers, it is quite common. Such individuals carefully nurture pride in the fact that without them, the global economy would collapse, and they can be very arrogant towards representatives of higher classes. I was very afraid that we were dealing with such people now.

"I know what you mean," I decided to help Leeta. "Someone could have guided their minds in such a way that they immediately assumed that someone from a higher class than theirs looks down on them, does not consider them equal partners for conversation, and from the very beginning positions themselves in a dominant role."

Let's discard conventions and speak openly.

"Exactly, it will be easier," she nodded with relief. "From their point of view, you may belong to the opposing camp, although much less than I do. Among the miners, there is probably not a single B. We have C officials, but they may now be perceived as 'collaborators.' And someone needs to speak to the workers and explain to them that they are mistaken. They won't listen to me, I'm too high up. However, you…"

I nodded my head.

"I'm just B3. Just one rank above."

"No offense," she stipulated.

"Relax, I'm not ashamed of my classification. You won't offend me bringing it up. I think you're right; we need to talk to them. Not with one, two, five, but with the largest possible number. Lois Ann," I turned to Colonel Sirtis, "you need to help me with this."

She shrugged.

"Sure. What do you need?"

"Have your people gather the residents of the district tomorrow morning in the square in front of the town hall. They probably won't want to listen, but they need to be there. Also, have them set up sound equipment for me so I don't have to strain my voice."

Colonel Sirtis looked at me closely.

"I hope you know what you're doing. This is no joke; your people were almost lynched."

"That's exactly why I have to do something about it before..." I was interrupted by a vigorous knocking at the door. Some did not recognize microphones. "Come in!"

Kelley McCave entered and immediately, without asking anyone anything, poured himself a shot of gin from the bar. People drank here much more than in an average place. With a glass in hand, the doctor sat in the armchair standing in the corner.

"And we have quite a mess," he announced gloomily, then sipped with pleasure.

I frowned.

"I request a report," I demanded, trying to maintain a reasonably neutral tone. I try not to show our pathologist that I dislike him, but it's not easy, especially since he already knows that.

McCave looked at the ceiling as if expecting to read something off it.

"Well, Leeta has probably already provided the details of the deceased, which she found simply in the virtual. We know who she is and where she worked. We have a rough idea of

her life path, that is, the official data. The autopsy revealed that not everything matches here."

"And 'not everything' means?" I asked.

"Almost nothing."

"What do you mean?"

McCave smiled in his nasty way, which indicated that he considered the interlocutor a fool, or at best, a complete ignoramus.

"It's true that she worked at the 'Parish' hotel as a VIP assistant; I know because I checked it myself. As for the rest… Maybe I should start from the beginning. In a situation where we have any data about the deceased, I verify it in real-time. One thing jumped out at me immediately: the class mark on her forehead was formatted. As I established, at about seventeen years old. That intrigued me. Based on mitochondrial DNA analysis, I determined that the girl came from a forbidden relationship, from a class mesalliance. A detailed analysis of her teeth, bones, and hair revealed that she could not have been raised in a so-called 'good family'; on the contrary. As a child, she often went hungry, and her daily food lacked essential nutrients. In short, no one took care of her. Everything changed when she turned twelve. I asked Sue Herefort to check it; she knows how to obtain classified and even erased information. In any case, something happened then that changed the fate of the deceased, as she started receiving nutritious food. Five years later, she was reclassified. There must have been strong grounds for that because such a thing rarely happens before a citizen reaches adulthood."

"Okay, and what about the cause of death?" I asked.

"And here we have another mystery. Her skull was smashed with a mining flashlight, and there is no doubt about that.

Only she was already dead by then. She died about ten or maybe fifteen hours before that act of aggression, but the murderer... well, one can call him that, although from a legal standpoint, we were dealing more with desecration of the corpse... may not have been aware of it."

"Are you kidding me?" This was completely nonsensical.

"I wish." McCave tossed a miniature object onto my desk. "Have you ever heard of a zombie?"

I searched my memory and shook my head.

"That's a pity."

***

In the New Era, horror as a literary and cinematic genre has long been forgotten. Global interest in it faded during the Ecological Catastrophe when harsh reality became horror. Only experts in popular culture, out of obligation, familiarized themselves with the most characteristic works of this genre. Certain concepts in everyday language nearly disappeared. Words like "vampire," "devil," or "zombie" fell out of use, and almost no one understood them anymore. However, they survived in some of the least obvious fields – in technology.

"There is a special method that allows for a spectacular 'revival of corpses,' as long as it has not been more than twenty-four hours since death," Dr. McCave explained. "A cocktail of heparin and several other substances is injected, and then a device that generates strong electrical impulses with a specific rhythm is placed, most often in the throat. They act on the peripheral nervous system of the corpse... it's like the wiring of our body. This causes tonic tension in all muscles and mechanical movements of the limbs, which can be remotely controlled as long as the nerves have not yet perished. The precise control used in the case of our deceased lady, of course, requires additional implants. It is technically called galvanization of the corpse, less technically – zombification."

"Alright, but what is all this for?" Leeta spoke up after a moment.

The doctor shrugged.

"Basically, for nothing. Sometimes it is useful for certain research, and also in the education process in medical fields. As you can see, it has also served a crime now."

"How did she die?" Wilder asked matter-of-factly.

"She was poisoned with a mixture of botulinum toxin and synthetic opium, administered orally, in rum cream that she had for dessert after lunch. Someone knew exactly what they were doing. The dose was precisely measured, like in a pharmacy. A side note: opium was not necessary; botulinum kills without fail, like an arrow shot from a bow. Someone clearly wanted to ensure the girl didn't suffer."

"Could she have suffered?" the captain raised his eyebrows. He had limited knowledge of toxicology.

"Suffocating with paralyzed lungs while fully aware is hard to consider comfortable. The murderer spared her that, although from the point of view of effectiveness, they didn't have to."

Leeta quickly wrote something in her notebook on the new device, known as a POD – short for "personal objective document." It replaced the previously used PADDs, and the officers quickly became accustomed to them.

"Is it true that she was pregnant, as Salome claims?" she asked.

McCave nodded.

"Ten weeks. I isolated the embryo; we will try to identify the father later, although I don't think it will be significant. It wasn't an accident; besides, in today's times, accidental insemination is truly a rarity. Judging by the hormone levels, the deceased was using professional supplementation, so she wanted to maintain this pregnancy."

"On the Moon?" Wilder frowned. "That seems against regulations; they should have sent her back to Earth."

"That may have been in the plans."

"Hands?" Leeta asked again. The doctor shook his head.

"Completely fine. She didn't write the letter to the mayor."

"It's getting more and more interesting," the lieutenant murmured. "It's a pity we lack a profiler. We have to handle this work ourselves and pretend we know what we're doing."

"You're doing well on your own, princess," the doctor laughed. "What have you come up with?"

The girl lifted her head and looked at Wilder. She could see that he was irritated by the coroner's nonchalant behavior and tone, although he was trying to hide it. McCave knew very well that the new superior disliked him and deliberately provoked the captain. He could afford it; he was essential at the station and had no fear of being fired or transferred to another position.

Wilder urged her with an impatient nod, so she cleared her throat and began:

"My preliminary conclusions are as follows: whoever smashed the head of our deceased,"earlier he poisoned her and made sure she was dead. They probably had lunch together, maybe a date, because the girl dressed up and did her makeup quite provocatively. It definitely wasn't her work uniform; I know how hostesses dress. Someone staged the body and delivered it to Gelbart's apartment to scare the perpetrator. A theatrical move, but effective, because thanks to that we have enough gathered evidence to nail the murderer in court. The scene looked, I think, like this: our suspect was rummaging through the apartment, and when he turned around, he saw the corpse standing behind him. His nerves failed him, so he smashed her head with the first object that came to hand and fled, not thinking about covering his tracks. So: they knew each other well. She learned something or even collaborated with the murderer; in any case, she began to threaten his plans. He decided to get rid of her in the mildest way possible." She paused for a moment. "He cared about her, and he only had botulinum at hand. What is botulinum actually used for?"

McCave furrowed his brow.

"Actually, yes," he replied. "It's an ingredient in various medications, including facial rejuvenation treatments. Of course, it's used in minimal doses, and really this so-called rejuvenation involves paralyzing the muscles responsible for wrinkle formation… Personally, I am against it, but compared to other methods, it is a quick and very cheap way, so it is still used, although it has been around for about three hundred years. As a poison, it has the added advantage that it sometimes appears in poorly stored food. Do you understand? Accidental poisoning from a contaminated can, it's not hard to stage something like that."

"In Lunnar, we have a cosmetics factory, and in Sele-noport, there is a professional SPA center combined with a cosmetic medicine clinic," Colonel Sirtis interjected. "In both of those places, this filth could be found if it's as you say. There's also Medfarm."

"Let me finish." Leeta looked at the pad screen. "The dead girl was found by someone who knows everything and also knew who killed her. They didn't call the police for reasons known to them; instead, they decided to act unconventionally. They staged the corpse to scare the mur-derer and provoke them to make a mistake, not necessarily like this one. So, we're looking at two individuals, at least two, that we need to find. Plus the one we basically already have because I will never believe that all this happened in Gelbart's apartment by mere chance. That's all for now."

The captain rubbed his forehead. He expected various problems on the Moon, but not such a complicated crimi-nal puzzle right from the start.

"Anyway, first we need to calm this boiling pot in the Workers' Corners," he spoke up after a moment. "At least part of the investigation will take place there, so it's a prior-ity. We need to convince the miners that we're not their en-emies and that they've been misled. After all, they are nei-ther lunatics nor disabled individuals; they'll understand."

"Do you think?" Colonel Sirtis looked at him doubtfully.

He shrugged.

"We have to take a risk. Leeta, have the detainees from the district council brought to the interrogation room. I need to talk to them first; after all, they are representatives of the residents and enjoy their trust."

"That's why they're acting all tough," Sirtis scoffed. "They need to be taken down a notch."

"Especially if I can convince them; others will probably follow. The miners should cool down, and then the investigation will be easier."

"Definitely," Lieutenant Ankes agreed with Wilder, standing up from her chair. She smiled. "I'll organize a normal interrogation for them; let them not feel too confident. They need to know they're in a position of suspicion and could end up in prison. Then they'll humble themselves and be more willing to accept your proposal.

Doctor McCave raised his thumb up.

"Good idea," he praised her. "I recently charged the sprayers; turn them on."A little bit of truth serum in the air won't hurt, just make sure to take a blocker before going in there. Better that it doesn't work on you, or you might blurt out something you shouldn't.

IX
LEETA
Personal Diary

I don't like conducting interrogations. It always involves a certain psychological violence, and one has to know how to dominate the person being interrogated, which I am not good at. I have always been compliant and accommodating, which are not good traits for a detective. This time, however, I wasn't going to face criminals, but rather a few officials, none of whom had ever faced any charges and, frankly speaking, hadn't done anything wrong. So far... I had to consider all possible scenarios.

"Monty, you're coming with me," I said. "You'll act as the recorder."

There is no obligation to create a written record in cases like this one; a simple recording would suffice, but I preferred having Monty at my side. He guaranteed my safety, much more discreetly than a guard with a gun in a holster. If any of the advisors wanted to physically attack me, they would probably feel much less inhibited by the presence of an unarmed recorder. Particularly if they were counting on the support of the others.

My android has, among other advantages, the fact that he doesn't look intimidating. He is tall and well-built, it's true, but he has a gentle face, innocent eyes, and very calm, even slow movements. Anyone who doesn't know him would certainly not be frightened by him. They wouldn't perceive him as a threat. It's a different matter with an armed police officer. Did I want to provoke the detainees? Not necessarily, but I took the possibility of such a scenario into account. I preferred to have the sweet assurance that there was someone beside me who could take them all down in a couple of seconds, without causing excessive harm, rather than knowing that in the event of some unforeseen action, it could lead to a massacre.

There were three detainees in the interrogation room, and I assessed them immediately. They had all previously worked in the mines. Thanks to the election to the district council, they had become public officials, which was a significant social advancement, but it didn't add to their intelligence. You could tell just by the way they looked at me - like I was an enemy. Not because they were prisoners and I was a police officer, but because of the symbols on our foreheads. I had to deal with this before I started the actual interrogation.

"Gentlemen," I began, sitting across from them. "My name is Juliette Ankes, and I am a lieutenant of the lunnar's police, and this is Monty Romain, police assistant and recorder. I have the impression that for some reason we have entered a warpath, and it needs to be stopped immediately. Such an attitude serves neither public order nor you personally. Speak up clearly about what you want."

For a moment, they glanced at each other, nudging one another with their elbows, and finally one of them, a stocky brunette with Asian features, decided to speak.

"This is not about you at all. Dogs, I mean. Sorry, the police," he added hastily.

"Oh really?" I asked politely, feigning surprise.

"Everyone knows you're in with the corps. You can't help it. It's your job."

"Corps," that's how the workers refer to corporations, I recalled with some effort. Slang shortens what is not replaced with a mask-word. Sometimes it's hard to understand what those people are even talking about, but the officer has to.

"You are mistaken," I said calmly. "The state police serve society, not its specific component. If it were as you say, the previous governor wouldn't have been executed as a result of our investigation. By the way, several important officials of the Lunnar Company lost their heads over it. And how does that relate to your theory?"

He shrugged.

"I don't know. It must have served those pigs at the very top somehow."

"No. It didn't serve anyone. Not even the new governor, for whom this position is a demotion from the previous one, which everyone knows." I paused for a moment to let that sink in. "Dear ones, so far we've all managed to live in harmony. Something very bad has been happening for some time now."

"And it is happening, it is happening!" the second, tall, muscular redhead interjected passionately. "You have unleashed the military on the people!"

"In your opinion, what were we supposed to do, sir…"

"Clarence Hardy."

"…Mr. Hardy?" I continued. "We were attacked in an unprecedented manner while fulfilling our official duties. Your sentiments were so hostile that the district had to be secured. Please believe me, I was not pleased with such a solution. I have always believed that people should talk to each other; however, at that time, no one wanted to talk. And I would like to find out why."

My calm voice clearly influenced the detainees in a way they did not expect. They probably anticipated shouting and pressure, prepared for a fight, and now they were not quite sure what to do. They glanced at each other with questioning looks, and none wanted to speak first. I waited, observing how their confidence waned, not rushing them.

"You killed Carol Masion," the Asian finally mumbled. "What did she ever do to you?"

"Sir…"

"Ray Jackson."

"Mr. Jackson, had that lady followed the commands of the uniformed services, she would be alive today. Her death was a regrettable accident, not the result of intention. The question is, who and for what purpose frightened her so much that instead of clarifying the suspicions surrounding her, she preferred to run away."

"What suspicions?" wondered the third advisor. So, they knew nothing.

"And you are…?" I asked.

"Ariel Kaminsky, chairman of the District Council. I have not heard of any suspicions regarding Carrie."

"The police do not summon anyone just for fun," I said reproachfully, noting in my mind that the tone of this man's voice and referring to the deceased with a diminutive name indicated personal involvement. "And when you take the Citizens' Rights and Duties Charter in hand, you will easily find paragraph twenty-eight, which clearly states that a person summoned to testify is obligated to appear at the designated police station. Ms. Masion disregarded the official letter from the command, and when a patrol was sent for her, she began to flee. Random passersby intervened in her defense, not even knowing what was going on. Someone drew an illegally possessed weapon, shots were fired, our officers had to defend themselves, and disaster struck. Blaming the police for this is a gross misunderstanding."

"If you hadn't chased her, nothing would have happened, miss." Jackson snarled.

"Please be reasonable and do not demand something that is contrary to logic," I requested coolly. "No one is above the law, and no one can place themselves in such a position. Regardless of the situation. The uniformed services exist to ensure the enforcement of laws, and that cannot be done by remaining passive. It cannot be the case that those who want to listen to police orders do so, and those who do not want to disregard them, feeling certain that there are no consequences."

As I spoke, I observed the faces of the men sitting across from me. I could see that they were slowly beginning to understand the meaning of my words and were starting to consider what they were actually participating in. It looked like sobering up after involuntarily being intoxicated by something strong. And in a sense, that is exactly what it was.

"In my opinion, someone is sowing discord among the miners," I continued after a moment. "They are turning them against the legitimate authority and convincing them that they are victims of some oppression. The effect is that there *was almost a lynch, and prior to that, two officers were beaten. Further escalation of violence could lead to the government deciding to impose military oversight in working-class districts, along with all its consequences: for example, a curfew and checks at every street corner. Is that really what you want?"*

They shook their heads almost simultaneously. I was starting to gain the upper hand over them, and it needed to be used quickly.

"Someone, I do not know who, is clearly spreading planned disinformation," I continued. "No one is against you, and no one treats you as second-class citizens."

Everything is happening only in your imagination. It is serious enough that it has already cost one person their life, and it might not end there. Do you have any suspicions about who might have an interest in disrupting public order and inciting riots?

Ray Jackson definitely shook his head.

"None of us know that, ma'am. I mean, lieutenant. No one came to us and started blabbing. We just listen to people when we go for a beer, to a dance, or to some meeting. And people gossip..."

Ariel Kaminsky raised his hand, interrupting him. His face showed that he was thinking hard, which for someone of his social standing is a considerable effort.

"If you say so, then indeed," he finally said. "I mean, it's strange, and it hasn't happened before. Suddenly, various information, suspicions, assumptions started circulating among people. As if someone was whispering in their ears. You know, teaching kids, they go and repeat what they hear,

and it all started in the pubs. There, first they were telling various gossip..."

"What kind?" I asked.

"Well, supposedly the police got directives from above to extract confessions in case of any trouble. That it doesn't matter who is truly guilty, what matters is to put someone from our side in jail, the rest will be scared. And then Carrie came back from the raid on Factory district all shaken..." he paused, as if he felt he had said too much.

"Please continue," I encouraged him. "I am also interested in explaining how this woman died and who had something to gain from it."

"Someone must have had something to gain? After all, you said it was an accident."

"Yes," I admitted. "That is how it is presented in the report. However, there are still many question marks. Carol Masion was killed by a bullet from an unregistered gun that someone used during the shooting. In the Workers' Corners, it circulated that it was a shot from police weapons, but that is not true, because none of the officers shot at her. It never even crossed their minds. They were defending themselves from attacking passersby, and Miss Masion was several blocks away by then. However, since at least five different people were shooting, and bullets were flying in various directions, it was initially assumed that she was hit by accident. She had no enemies, no one wished her harm. Personally, however, I believe, in light of recent events, that her death could have benefited someone."

Kaminski furrowed his brow.

"She was very scared," he said after a moment. "She kept saying that they wanted to frame her. She was planning to flee to Earth, but she didn't make it."

"Who could have wanted to frame her? For what?"

"She didn't say. She was acting strange after that raid. Who could have wanted her dead?"

"I can bet it was the same person who is turning the miners against law enforcement," speaking, I watched the subtle reactions of my conversation partners and noted the emotions reflected on their faces. "During that raid, a man, a factory worker, a simple laborer, was killed. He was stabbed... Miss Masion was supposed to be interrogated in connection with his death, as she could have been the perpetrator or a witness. In any case, she was at the crime scene."

"Carrie would have killed someone?! Nonsense!" shouted Kaminsky. A pulsating vein appeared on his forehead, distorting the sign C1.

"Please calm down," I mitigated him. "I shouldn't reveal this, as the investigation is still ongoing, but ultimately we ruled out her direct involvement in the murder. However, she might have seen something, known something. As you said yourself, she was scared. It's a pity she couldn't trust the police, she might still be alive."

Ray Jackson cleared his throat.

"Maybe that's exactly the point, so she couldn't trust," he said. "Neither she nor anyone else. I have a feeling things are becoming clearer in my head. I'm starting to figure something out. Lieutenant, what was the name of that stabbed man?"

"Jeff Cormack."

Jackson was silent for a longer moment.

"*I know that name. It's a link to the top brass,*" he finally muttered.

"*What do you mean?*" I was surprised. He shrugged.

"*Well, supposedly those at the top. They spy on us to know what we think. In the Corners, there's Harry Gelbart. And on Przywarsztatowa, there's Shansha Rock. Everyone knows that. We do nothing about it.*" bo a better snitch, whom we already know, than an unknown one. They could turn out to be craftier and better at disguising themselves, and then someone might slip something about them unintentionally, and it would be a disaster."

"*A better old devil than a new broom,*" Hardy added with a contemptuous twist of his lips.

I made sure they didn't realize that they had accidentally provided me with very important information. A multitude of questions pressed at my lips, but asking them now would be a tactical mistake. I had managed to establish a fragile thread of communication with these people, and it needed to be maintained at all costs.

"*The police are conducting an investigation into his case,*" I said. "*We are also trying to determine who is truly responsible for the death of Carol Masion. You can be sure that we take both matters very seriously. Unfortunately, such cases are multiplying. Perhaps you might be able to tell me something about the third victim. Officer Romain, please provide me with the image emitter.*"

Monty handed me the requested object. The interrogated individuals didn't even glance at it, focused on me, which was very advantageous for me. Ignoring the presence of the recorder, they had no chance to notice that something was off with it. I activated the emitter, and a hologram of Annabelle Banks appeared above the table.

"Do you know this girl? Have you ever seen her? Take a good look."

They looked on with a certain surprise, which was easy to understand. They probably rarely saw women like that, elegant, polished, as if from a fairy tale.

"I wouldn't throw her out of bed," Jackson finally mumbled, almost licking his lips. Hardy jabbed him in the ribs with his elbow, and when his colleague looked at him, he pointedly tapped his forehead. "But I haven't seen her. Definitely."

The others nodded in agreement. They were likely telling the truth.

"Well, too bad," I turned off the projection. "Then maybe Mr. Jackson could clarify something else for me. For some reason, you asked me about the name of the killed worker. Why did you think that I would know who it was?"

The councilman cleared his throat and averted his gaze.

"Well, because..." he started hesitantly. "That..."

"Spit it out!" Kaminsky suddenly got angry. "Don't make a fool of yourself; now's not the time for that. We're all knee-deep in this mess; there's no point in pretending!"

He added a few epithets and fell silent only when Hardy cuffed him on the back of the neck.

"Ray was scouting before the raid." He addressed me in a tone as if this fact explained everything.

"What scout mission?" I asked.

"Well, before every raid, the terrain needs to be checked," Jackson explained to me. "It's to make sure that you can ac-

tually go into battle. It could be that there was a serious accident in some factory or processing plant, there are injuries, or someone has kicked the bucket and there's a mourning period. Then, you can't raid, right? That would be a bastard move, not a game."

"Raids are a game for you? Interesting."

"To each their own, lady. So, I went to Factory district"

"Doesn't matter. I have a buddy there, so I always drop by his place, bring a half-liter, and I find out everything right away. I don't have to wander around various shady joints to get the scoop."

"And?" I encouraged him gently.

"And Sheldon was terribly morose. The boss had kicked out several of his buddies on the spot because he got some tip-off. He muttered that they wanted to get to that snitch before leaving. I didn't pay too much attention to it at the time; I was interested in something else, and besides, I was already a bit tipsy. I mean, I had drunk a bit."

I rubbed my forehead with my hand. Something didn't add up.

"Wait a second, wait a second. A tip-off is one thing, but what did it contain since those people were fired? And effectively? Nowadays, no one could do that for just any reason, like cursing a superior while drunk or sneaking off work five minutes early. The allegations must have been serious and, additionally, confirmed."

Once again, there were faces full of disbelief and uncertainty. It was clear that this perspective had not occurred to the councilors; they were focused on their anger towards the informant.

"And are you absolutely sure that Cormack was the one who tipped off?" I added.

They shrugged almost simultaneously.

"That's not our business," Jackson replied to me. "Our business is Gelbart. But for now no one has squealed... I'm sorry, I mean no one has ratted anyone out. It's a calm informant. They told him to do it, so he is, and that's that. A quiet guy, not overzealous. We haven't been interested in anyone else. But I think to myself that if Cormack was killed, they must have had a good reason."

"It's more complicated," I muttered sadly. I had no intention of explaining that the deceased was first severely beaten, and only then someone stabbed him in the heart. And while Masion could have participated in the beating, though the reason for it was unknown, she certainly didn't use a knife. She was left-handed, and the fatal blow was undoubtedly dealt by someone right-handed."

"Alright," I finally decided. "Gentlemen, sign the interrogation protocol. Captain Wilder will be coming to you shortly with a certain proposal, and I advise you to take it very seriously."

***

The speech of the new commander of the lunnar's police was concise, substantive, almost military. In a few words, he explained to the gathered residents of the Workers' Corner that they had fallen victim to manipulation, which could have ended fatally. One of the steps being considered by the heads of the mining companies was the forced relocation of all district residents back to Earth and bringing in new workers from there. This would, of course, involve huge costs, not only operational but primarily downtime costs.

However, there was a special, secret target fund established by the Lunnar Company specifically for such an eventuality – a rebellion from some part of the workers. The Company's management simply had to have such a safety valve, although everyone hoped it would never have to be used. The fact that the captain was supported by official representatives of the district, meaning "their own," certainly influenced the miners to listen carefully, and something started to get through to them. After the meeting, they dispersed in silence, heads down, clearly detonated.

"Now everything depends on you," Wilder addressed the advisors as the market was almost empty. "Get hold of them some way, let them stop listening to rumors and start thinking for themselves. And above all, let them not treat the uniformed services like invaders from another planet. Such an attitude is detrimental not only to us but primarily to their own disadvantage.

"That's probably true," Ariel Kaminsky reluctantly agreed with him. "That makes sense. Somebody here has to be doing dirty work, and it hasn't been recent. Thinking back, maybe for half a year..."

"Miners are cool guys, sincere," Jackson supported him. "We've never had any major crimes here, we're like family, at most they fought when drunk. The uniformed officers came, conducted an investigation, sometimes someone paid a fine, sometimes served two months. Nothing major. There was no reason before to clash with the dogs, I mean, with the police. And for the past few months, the fellas have started to downright hate anyone in uniform and treat them as enemies right from the start."

"We need to put an end to that." The captain shook his head. "I hope your people understood well what I was talking about. Under normal circumstances, I would ask you to contact us if you find out anything about the identity of the 'gossiper,' that is, the person behind these troubles, but I don't want to put you in an even more difficult situation. One that could undermine the miners' trust in you. Just focus on calming things down and restoring order, and we'll do the rest."

He turned around and was about to leave when Kaminsky grabbed his hand.

"Captain, do…" he hesitated, "do you promise that you will find Carrie's murderer?"

The officer looked at him sympathetically. Already several people had asked him a similar question, and he always felt an unpleasant cramp in his abdomen at such moments.

"We are working on it all the time," he assured. "We will not give up. For us your friend is just as important as anyone else who has fallen victim to a crime, whether it's a sweeper or a corporation president, it doesn't matter."

"You say that because you have to," Hardy interjected venomously. "And it's still clear that the rich are always more important. A poor person can be ignored, what's the difference if someone is dead? A small loss, a short sorrow."

Wilder frowned. Such suspicions always hurt him, and they weren't exactly rare.

"Please listen: I grew up in a very poor neighborhood, my father was killed in duty, and my mother was so ill that it was hard for her to earn a living for us. Sometimes we simply went hungry, often we didn't have enough to eat. We were dressed by social services and they paid the rent for our sleeping corner. I worked after school since I was twelve. My younger sister died because we couldn't afford expensive treatment. The police fund paid for my college, which I will repay over the next ten years. I am the last person who would 'neglect' any crime victim, even if it was a homeless derelict whose only dream is another bottle of cheap gin."

There was a moment of awkward silence.

"I'm sorry," Hardy finally whispered, feeling regret.

The captain forced himself to smile, although he felt very down. He didn't like recalling his difficult childhood, let alone playing that card on others' emotions, but sometimes, in a situation like this, it could help. He was sure that because of it he gained favor in the eyes of the advisors, who – he felt – would not keep such information to themselves and news would spread through the Working Corners, and likely beyond, that "the new commander is basically one of us." Priceless in such circumstances.

"It's not your fault, after all. Such things have always happened and will continue to happen. As long as there are people in the world, there will be poor and rich. However, not everyone prays to money, and certainly, someone who serves the law should not do so. And do not assume in advance that everyone does. That can be hurtful."

"We will remember that," Kaminsky assured him warmly. He turned around and, lowering his voice, added questioningly, "Your bodyguard is a bit strange. Does he always stay so silent?"

Wilder looked at Monty, who had stood behind him during the entire meeting with the miners, carefully observing everyone and everything. "Trust him," Leeta had said when they spoke before he headed to the Working Corners. "He's worth more than a whole squad of storm-troopers... whose presence in the eyes of the miners would signify that you're afraid of them." He trusted her judgment but could not bring himself to treat the machine as a person. The android probably didn't care about that either. It had been given the order to protect the health and life of the commander at all costs, and it was likely ready for that. Salome, although reluctant towards the "artificial cop," objectively acknowledged in her report on the incident in the Working Corners that it was very effective. Wilder was glad, however, that there had been no opportunity for him to witness it firsthand. No one attempted to attack him, the mood among the miners had calmed. Of course, an attacker could appear in the market who was not from their environment, for instance, someone who killed Jeff Cormack, Carol Masion, and Annabelle Banks – he assumed it could have been one person. However, that opportunity was not taken, or maybe they were simply not interested in eliminating the police commander. Because, logically, why would they? Such an action would raise alarms with the authorities and could have serious consequences, and that certainly wasn't the goal. Thus, Monty had no chance to show what he was worth, and Clint was pleased about that – he did not fully trust the android's capabilities.

"He never speaks without a significant need," he said evasively, turning away. "Don't pay attention to him."

He had to return now. He had plenty of overdue documents to fill out, not to mention a report to write. He caught himself thinking absurdly that it was a pity he couldn't assign that work to Monty. Suddenly, he was curious if the android could do something like drafting a report from a police operation or incident.

"Monty," he began when they got into the rover, "tell me something. Can you… write? By hand?"

The android looked at him with its usual cold calm.

"Yes, sir," it replied.

"But by yourself? I mean, when no one is dictating to you, just describe an event in your own words?"

"In my own words," Monty repeated. "I have no 'own words'. I was taught them in the necessary range for me."

"Alright," the captain started the engine and drove off. "But if you had to use those words you were taught to create something like a report? Let's say, if I ordered you, 'Monty, describe what happened today at the Workers' Angles market'?"

"You cannot order me to do anything. My owner is Juliette Ankes, not you. She gives me commands."

Wilder felt his patience slipping away. He had the impression that in the driver's seat – he had decided to drive himself today, not wanting to risk an additional subordinate in case something went wrong – there was not a robot, a machine as he perceived Monty, but a particularly malicious human being trying to throw him off balance. He knew it was absurd, but that's how he felt.

"Monty, I'm asking about something else: would you be able to do that?" he clarified after a moment. "Please answer me clearly, yes or no."

"Yes," the android replied. "And no."

"What?!"

The vehicle swayed, and the lights on the dashboard flickered. Monty pointed at them with his finger.

"Please turn off the automatic assistance. Now."

Surprising himself, Wilder complied. Driving the car without automatic assistance was frowned upon by the earthly road authorities, but he obviously knew how to do it. The android did not stop at one suggestion.

"Please pull over and stop the vehicle."

"As soon as you say 'a'..." the captain muttered doubtfully and turned, wondering casually what was going on.

Barely had he managed to brake when Monty released the door lock, grabbed Wilder by the neck, and with childlike ease dragged him outside, moving with almost incomprehensible speed. In less than three seconds, they were several dozen meters away from the car. And that saved them.

The explosion was not loud. It resembled more of an implosion, after which the car's body collapsed inward like a cardboard box, and just afterward literally shattered into pieces as if a second charge had been detonated inside. The hot blast knocked the officers off their feet, even though they were already quite far away. Clint hit his back and the back of his head on the surface so hard that he was momentarily dazed. When he opened his eyes, he realized he was lying on his back, and Monty, supporting himself on the ground with the tips of his hands and feet, was creating a shield above him. He saw Monty's immobile face right in front of his eyes, pale, regular, and expressionless. The air was thick with hot smoke, and tiny particles of heated metal were still flying around.

"What was that?" Wilder groaned.

"A thermal charge," the android replied in his even, calm voice. "Please do not move yet."

"How did you know?"

"The car computer transmitted it."

"I didn't hear anything."

"His voice function was blocked. He was flashing lights. I understand technical language. Unauthorized physical manipulation, unauthorized controllable objects in the engine compartment." Monty looked around. "You can get up now, captain."

He helped Wilder up. The latter took it after a slight hesitation and stood up, involuntarily groaning with pain. From a distance, a wailing sound of a siren approached – one of the drivers, though he himself didn't stop, must have reported to the appropriate services.

"There won't be much left to investigate. Bad luck," Clint muttered, looking at the still-burning wreckage of the car.

"Thermal charges are calculated for maximum destruction of the object, captain."

Wilder looked at Monty.

"I owe you, my life."

"That's my role. I was to protect you."

"I have to ask. If you hadn't received such a command from Leety, would you have reacted differently?"

The android turned his incredible silver eyes on him.

"Then I would not have accompanied you."

"But if you had accompanied me and something had threatened me…" he pressed, to no avail. He had the impression that for some reason Monty was avoiding a clear answer again – like a person, not a machine. He did not understand this.

A fire truck stopped beside them with a piercing screech of tires. Four uniformed officers jumped out from inside. They paused at the sight of the two police officers. One of them, a woman, pushed back the visor of her helmet.

"I'm Zara Tagliani... Oh, it's you, Commander. Is anyone hurt?"

Wilder grimaced painfully, rubbing his neck with his hand.

"Let's just say," he replied. "I feel every bone, but if it weren't for Monty, I'd be a charred toast right now."

An ambulance pulled up next to the fire truck, and one of the paramedics peeked out.

"Do we need to be here?"

The captain waved his hand impatiently.

"No, you can go back. This time there were no casualties."

"Are you sure?" The medic studied him with a knowing expression. "You look like you've just lost a fight with a wall. The other one looks better, but his outfit doesn't."

Wilder glanced at Monty. Indeed, his uniform bore signs of mechanical damage and contact with burning metal fragments. Bernit, which had recently been used to make police uniforms, was an exceptionally durable material, but like everything in the world, it had its limitations. Not everything could withstand everything all the time.

"Yes, that's true," the captain admitted. "But it's nothing. We took a bit of a beating, just a bit, don't worry about it. You should head back."

"As you wish."

The firefighters, ignoring this conversation, were extinguishing the remains of the rover and looking for places where a fire could have been started. Having found two such spots, they secured them before returning to the police officers.

"I'm leaving one person here to guard the ruins," Tagliani said. "You'll probably send technicians and detectives here, but for now, you should head back to the station. We'll give you and that android a ride."

Zara already knew Monty as Leety's assistant, but like many others, she simply saw him as a robot, devoid of personality and independent judgment. She paid him as much attention as a chair, so now she wasn't even looking at him. For reasons unbeknownst to him, this struck the captain in an unpleasant way, even though it didn't differ much from his own attitude.

"Alright, give us a ride," he agreed dryly, emphasizing the word "us." "It's really the best solution. But please leave two people behind. And they should be armed."

"Why?" the firefighter asked in surprise.

"Because it wasn't an accident, but an attack, and someone might want to cover their tracks… although of course, there aren't many left."

Zara nodded, not commenting on this revelation. She opened a compartment in the wall of the vehicle and took out two small rifles.

"Milo, join Fred," she instructed one of her subordinates, handing him both. "Give him the gun and let him fire without warning if anyone comes at you. You too, of course. I'm not ready to lose people due to someone's whims."

X
CLINT WILDER
Personal Diary

Someone wanted to take me out. That in itself might not be all that surprising, but the circumstances were quite strange. The explosive device wasn't planted in the station's garage, I was sure of that from the start, and the internal monitoring ruled it out. The perpetrator could have only done it in one place – where I left it when I arrived in Workers' Angles. And now the question is whether they took advantage of the soldiers' inattention, their carelessness or lack of knowledge, or whether they were in cahoots with one of them.

Someone would say I should share these suspicions with Colonel Sirtis. The thing is, I'd end up getting a good slap in the face from her, and that would be the end of it. She wouldn't believe me without hard evidence that one of her subordinates was involved in something so nasty. She stands behind them like a wall. And I can't even blame her for that.

I still can't get my bearings. Every bone aches, even the ones I didn't know I had, and my head hurts. But I'm alive, and that's what matters. I owe it to Leety's android, who – I would swear in court – doesn't like me. Can a machine dislike someone? Impossible. Conclusion: he is not a machine.

Did I really write this? Yes. After this hellish day, I am convinced. Monty is not a machine; he is a being. It doesn't matter what he is made of. So what now? How should I treat him? It's too much for my poor brain. Only now do I see how lacking my education is, supposedly normal for someone like me, but now it is weighing on me. The Moon is probably the only place where it is better to be more... versatile than to confine oneself to one's own specialty.

Salome, who has taken care of me as tenderly as a sister – four days after the attack I had to lie down, the damn doctor suspected I had some internal injuries, I was dizzy and nauseous, I needed to be looked after like a child – is still afraid of Monty and would never, for any treasure, be left alone with him. It's not just about him, really. She is just mortally afraid of artificial intelligence in any form. Nowadays, it's not only peculiar, but it also complicates life to some extent. Probably deciding to travel to Lunnar, which has a reputation as a primitive place, she hoped it would be easier for her here, if only because the houses here are not equipped with smart systems. But here, surprise.

Leeta, of course, is a completely different type. I have the impression that she prefers the company of her android to any human, which is a pity because she is a very beautiful and worthwhile girl. She might be a technophile, though... I don't even know. After all, her romance with the previous commander is an open secret. I sometimes wonder if their relationship was somehow fueled by the fact that he had an old-type visor replacing his lost eyes due to an accident. I've seen photos; it's horrendous. How can someone wear such a contraption on their face permanently? Leaving aside aesthetic matters, it must be terribly uncomfortable. There have been better solutions for a long time.

My head hurts again. I knocked it against the surface quite nicely. My skull held up; I just have a bump like a duck's egg and "small hemorrhages on the surface of the brain tissue in the right occipital lobe." Whatever that means. Only reading the scan result did I learn that the human brain has some lobes. Maybe also lobules, like a flower? What am I thinking?

Leeta currently has supervision over the investigation, and Kendra Maru and Salome are helping her as a detective intern. A truly feminist trio. Maybe deep down, I'm a caveman, but I've never been fond of women in the police. They are physically weaker and less resilient than men (I'm not holding this against them; it's simply biology), they have trouble making controversial decisions quickly. They are also generally much more defensive than offensive, which can be undesirable in police work. Still, they manage, which has always filled me with amazement. I have to admit that. Not only in the police; for example, Colonel Sirtis...

Recently, she sent her orderly to me (I don't know if this title has a feminine form) because she couldn't visit me herself. She has some issues in the garrison, and she wanted to emphasize that she thinks of me and considers me a friend. That orderly... I have never in my entire life seen such a beautiful, charming, graceful person. How did she end up in the military? She is incredible, perfect in every way despite her buzz-cut hair, not to mention the uniform. I was left speechless at the sight of her and probably ultimately considered me a brute and a fool because I responded to her mainly with monosyllables and not coherently. Since that day, I can't shake thoughts of her, and yet I don't have time for that, meaning for silly dreams fit for a teenager. An investigation is ongoing, or rather several parallel investigations, and I am responsible for this mess before my superiors.

Before the doctor allowed me to return to work, Harry Gelbart had recovered, and at least he could finally be interrogated. I decided to do it personally, thereby getting involved in the investigation and pressing the guy against the wall. However, it was strange. Gelbart turned out to be completely unresponsive. Regardless of that, I pressed hard, and he responded indifferently and evasively, as if my questions, the crimes that had occurred, or his own situation did not concern him. It threw me off balance because I had never encountered anything like it before. In the end, I decided to do something that wasn't entirely in accordance with the rules: I took the recording of the interrogation to the direct superior of that poor fellow. Or rather, her superior.

The vice president of Juvenille, Olivia Grander, immediately sang a whole litany of praises for her deputy and complaints against the police, who harassed such a crystal-clear person under any pretext. I finally had to interrupt her and explain that I wasn't accusing him of anything specific. After all, he was also a victim, and he couldn't be directly linked to any of the murders, to any of the attacks. And indirectly? That was what I had to uncover.

"Alright," she said with visible relief. "What can I do for you, Captain?"

I set up the projector on the table and started the recording.

"Please take a look at this and listen carefully," I requested. "What is your impression? Is this normal behavior for Mr. Gelbart?"

Ms. Grander watched intently, and I observed her face. She seemed quite young, but I noticed subtle signs indicating a rather late middle age, something between forty-five and fifty years. Gelbart was twenty-two. The woman's strong re-action indicated personal involvement. Maternal feelings or an office romance were at play, nothing unusual. A large age difference is not a problem, of course, one could question how sincere the feelings were, at least from Gelbart's side.

I pondered this while Grander focused on the recording.

"This is not Harry," she finally said firmly.

"What do you mean?" I was surprised. "Impossible."

"It's not him."

"We tested the DNA."

"Forget the DNA! Harry doesn't talk like this or behave like that! What's going on?!"

Her fierce reaction seemed to confirm my suspicions. It was just that I was certain about Gelbart's identity. They even performed the Akharonov-Brown test, which allows distinguishing a clone from the original – and nothing.

"Are you sure?" I asked cautiously.

"Absolutely!"

I may not have an A-class mind, but the conclusions came to me easily. Something must have changed this man's behav-ior pattern so much that a very close person mistook him for a stranger.

"Thank you," I said, standing up and taking the projector off the table. "You've been very helpful. If I have new infor-mation, I'll notify you."

Olivia Grander also stood up. Her lips were trembling.

"Will Harry ever come back?" she blurted out. "Will you find him?"

"We'll do what we can." I promised and left, closing the door behind me so I wouldn't see the silent pleading in her eyes.

The vice president of Juvenille was truly convinced that I was interrogating a fraud, a doppelgänger, maybe a clone, but not her deputy. I knew how things were, but I didn't want to convince her. It was better this way. A person tends to live in hope, and one should never take that away from them. That is the first lesson a rookie cop learns. I felt sympathy for that woman. I didn't know if she was losing a semblance of a son or a young lover; either way, she must have been suffering.

My next steps had to be directed towards McCave. I still couldn't warm up to that doctor, the little smart-aleck, but we had to work together. And I was increasingly convinced of how competent he was, which is what matters most, not just in police work and medicine.

I found him in the morgue, examining some samples while vigorously chewing a large piece of tobacco gum. He loved it and spent a lot on this treat. Upon seeing me, he pushed the gum between his cheek and jaw with his tongue so it wouldn't interfere with our conversation.

"What's up, Chief?" he asked cheerfully, almost not tearing his eyes away from the microscope's monitor.

I can't stand his style of being. "Can a person's character and way of reacting change to such an extent that their loved ones will consider them a doppelganger, and a rather unconvincing one at that?" I asked directly, not bothering with preliminary niceties.

"There is such a possibility," he replied. "Why do you ask?"

"*Because it seems important.*" I snapped involuntarily, more sharply than I intended.

He did not appear offended. He has thick skin; I had noticed that long ago.

"*There are various ways to change someone's personality, but to say something more precise, I would need to know who it is about.*"

Whether I wanted to or not, I laid out the crux of the matter for him. He looked intrigued.

"*Is it that serious? Well, it didn't jump out at us. We didn't know the individual until he showed up at the station.*"

"*The problem is that it's definitely Harry Gelbart. The original. There's no room for error. And yet Ms. Grander insists firmly that it's not him.*"

McCave fell into thought.

"*There was a book 'Invasion of the Body Snatchers.' An old sci-fi story. To be honest, it has been adapted into film several times,*" he mumbled after a moment. "*The phenomenon itself is described in medical textbooks. The catch is that such a thing occurs as a result of mechanical damage or serious brain disease, not just like that.*"

"*And what about malaria?*" I tried. He waved his hand dismissively.

"*Not an option. Unless,*" he suddenly perked up, "*we accept far-reaching manipulation. I need to get back to the secured samples, or rather to the preparations I made from them.*"

"*What are you thinking about?*"

McCave turned to the console and fiddled with the switches. An image appeared on the screen, depicting an unpleasant-looking, wriggling creature.

"Plasmodium falciparum," he explained, noticing my expression. *"Like any organism, it has its secret weapon, which is its genome. The cycle looks like this: The sporozoites of the parasite enter the bloodstream. Some of them are destroyed by leukocytes, but many, with the flow of blood, reach the liver. Within about 30 minutes, sporozoites disappear from the blood. In liver cells, over the course of seven to twenty-one days, something occurs that we call the extraerythrocytic developmental phase. The sporozoites change their shape, forming schizont forms. They divide multiple times, transform, and ultimately burst, releasing anywhere from a few to several tens of thousands of merozoites, which enter the blood and attack its red cells. Now you pay attention, Wilder. Merozoites can be reprogrammed so that instead of destroying red blood cells, they transmit various DNA sequences and, more importantly, RNA. That is exactly why parasite samples have been preserved in government laboratories. I haven't dealt with this branch of medicine, so my knowledge is just general, but this way, it was possible to develop innovative therapies for various serious diseases."*

I shook my head and grimaced, as it started to ache again.

"I understand DNA, but what about the other one?"

"RNA is… broadly speaking, something that is the matrix of life. The most primitive genetic material. It can modify, create, and repair DNA. This opens up unlimited possibilities, but let's not dwell on that now. From our point of view, only one aspect is important. This method can provide human brain cells with information that will change neural connections. Consequently, although theoretically a person will be the same as before, will have the same body and the same memories or knowledge, they will become someone completely different."

This was understandable even for someone like me, without a specialized education.

"But that means we are dealing with something worse than we initially thought," I said after a moment.

"Indeed," McCave nodded. "Manipulations of the human brain were forbidden as soon as such a possibility arose. However, that doesn't mean that attempts have stopped. And we can take it for granted that no one is doing this just to annoy some bureaucrat."

***

Leeta returned from the city very tired and very discouraged.

"I think there are better ways for a person to earn those few thousand points a month," she complained, sitting at her desk and entering information into the computer from the report. "And competitions where no one lets you know that you are imposing on them."

On her own initiative, she took it upon herself to interview Harry Gelbart's superiors, Shansha Rock and Jeff Cormack, operating under the assumption that understanding their motives might shed some light on the death of three people and the strange illness of a fourth. Unfortunately, she learned very little. She did, however, get the undeniable impression that she was an unwanted person, for whom time was wasted.

Her furious muttering was heard by passing Elvis, who turned back to sit in the chair next to Leeta's desk.

"What's bugging you?" he asked. "Confide in an old soldier."

"Soldier?"

"Well, kind of a soldier. I started in the army. Why do you have such a sour face? Did Tomcat bother you?"

Leeta smiled involuntarily, as always when she heard that nickname. She still didn't know why the new commander was called that, as he hadn't told her, and she felt awkward asking his friends. They might think she was being nosy, and she didn't want that.

"No. I talked to people who sent so-called informants to the working-class districts," she replied. "They all made it clear to me that I was wasting their time and that since they hadn't committed any wrongdoing, they had nothing to say to me."

"Aha," Elvis scratched his ear thoughtfully. "Did it ever occur to you that those people are just afraid?"

Lieutenant Ankes raised her eyebrows.

"Afraid?" she repeated. "I know someone scared the miners, but the executives?"

"That stick can have two ends, my beautiful. We already know that the miners, and perhaps other workers, have been subjected to a kind of brainwashing. And what if the one behind this is acting on multiple fronts at the same time? They sent informants, right? Why? That's not standard procedure. Don't you think that the management of the companies has suddenly started to fear the lowest-level employees, or rather what they might do in a fit of madness? Maybe someone has convinced those guys in suits too."

Leeta looked at him with wide-open eyes.

"Wow," she said slowly, after digesting what she'd heard. "You might be right, Dakota. There's a lot to support that. I can't believe I didn't think of it myself…"

"You're still very young." Elvis patted her on the shoulder.

Monty approached the desk, carrying a steaming box with the bistro "Favorite" logo.

"Your order," he said, placing it on the countertop. He turned his eyes to her conversation partner. "Good evening, Sergeant."

"Hey, Monty." Elvis smiled broadly. Unlike Salome, he liked the "synthetic," generally seen as Leeta's shadow and almost nothing more. Few looked at him differently than as a mechaloid, a robot sometimes purchased by wealthy individuals who, for various reasons, didn't want to hire traditional service. Greyfox realized Monty's uniqueness from the very beginning. Lacking technical knowledge, he prided himself on his highly developed intuition, and thus, instead of ignoring the android or – like Salome – being afraid of him, he formed a closer acquaintance with him on only the second day of his work at the station. Initially, he had the impression that Leeta's synthetic assistant didn't trust him, but not easily discouraged, Elvis quickly broke down that distance.

"Would you also like me to bring you something from the bistro?" asked the android and added. "The drone delivery operator has a malfunction, and fixing it will take a few more hours."

Greyfox looked at Leeta.

"May I take advantage of your assistant's kindness?"

"Since he offered it himself…" she smiled.

"Then bring me spicy roast with fries, Thai soup, and a portion of rum cake. They have my card number on record; just give them my name and service code."

Monty glanced at Leeta, who confirmed the order with a nod, turned around, and walked away, treading silently as usual.

"How quietly he walks… And yet he must weigh something," noted Elvis. "Matter of size, less than a human," Lieutenant Ankes replied. "But indeed, his footsteps are basically never heard. Some find it disconcerting. I've gotten used to it."

The android returned to "Favorite" in just under ten minutes. He could have gotten there even faster, but he tried to match his stride to the average walking speed of people on the sidewalk. According to what he had been taught, he aimed not to stand out in the crowd and he succeeded so well that no one on the street realized his true identity. It was made easier by the fact that humanoid robots could sometimes be found in Lunnar, but none of them were as deceptive as he was. They looked like metal dummies or, at best, moving mannequins, and no one would mistake one for a living person, even, as Dr. McCave jokingly said, "at night, at midnight, in thick fog." Monty was a whole class above the best of them, and so far, no civilian had known that an android worked at the police station. Representatives of Romain Corp, entangled in the Laboratory F case, could say something about it, but everyone was convinced that the artificial human created by engineer Karpinsky was taken along with his creator to Earth and was probably dismantled there. Surely no one would believe that he wore a police assistant's uniform and participated as support in operational activities.

Upon entering the bistro, he immediately noticed Salome, waiting for her order. The girl saw him too, and a certain nervousness reflected on her face. She still feared him and tried to keep her distance. Monty stood at the end of the line, not attempting to approach the intern. He was aware of her attitude towards him and accepted it not as something offensive or unpleasant, but as a natural thing. One of his traits that distinguished him from humans was perceiving such matters in strictly logical terms. He did not have the most human of traits – imagination, so for him, there was only what was, and he saw no reason for it to appear any differently. Since these new police officer did not accept him, it had to be so in his eyes, and that was the end of it. He did not fight against it or impose himself on her, so as not to put the girl in unnecessary embarrassment. However, he was committed to fulfilling the sergeant's order, so he could not just leave.

At last, Salome received her lunch box, paid, and with poorly concealed relief dashed out onto the street. Monty was already second in line at the order panel when his super-sensitive hearing caught a distant, faint scream and the sounds of a scuffle. He made the decision in a split second – if human life was at stake, matters of provisioning had to take a back seat.

A human would have trouble determining where the scream had come from, if they had heard it at all. Monty located the source of each sound with flawless accuracy, and he could get there faster than any human. And press his hand, appropriately positioned under the collarbone, against the prostrate Salome, constricting the torn artery. All of this happened in such a short time that witnesses stood frozen, unable to react. They were in shock, perhaps more astonished than terrified. An attack on an officer in broad daylight, in the middle of the city, something like that hadn't happened in a very long time, and no one expected it. They did not know what to do, or perhaps they were afraid to do anything.

Monty reached into his pocket for the biper and selected two codes on it, 0 and 2 – injured officer, needed support. Salome opened her eyes and groaned.

"Please don't move," he warned her. "I've called for support."

"It hurts. Take your hand away..."

"I must refuse. If I comply, you will bleed to death in no more than two minutes."

"Me...?" the girl half-conscious lifted her head, looked at her arm and the blood-soaked sidewalk. "That man who hit me... he must have had a knife?"

"Please don't say anything." A woman shook off the shock and began to scream hysterically. After a moment, others joined her. Clint Wilder rushed in from the command post, followed by Leeta and Sergeant Greyfox. A pursuit vehicle with a team of stormtroopers skidded to a stop at the curb.

"Calm down!" shouted the captain. The screams and wails fell silent. "Don't disperse, we will need statements! Did someone call an ambulance?"

"I did," stated one of the witnesses, a trembling man in a sanitation worker's jumpsuit.

"Good." Wilder knelt beside Salome. "The medics will be here soon. What happened, Baby?"

"I-I don't really know," she stammered. "I was coming back from 'Favorite' when he bumped into me. He grabbed me, I tried to push him away, I think I screamed. Then I felt a hit and fell, I couldn't catch my breath, for a moment everything blurred before my eyes. I was jolted awake by the awful pain when he... It still hurts... A lot. Please, make him stop."

Wilder looked at the relentlessly calm, as always, face of the android.

"Why are you hurting her?" he asked.

"Miss Delaforette has a severed subclavian artery," Monty replied. "I'm blocking the bleeding. First aid, lesson three."

"You have to hold on," the captain told Salome. "Clench your teeth and focus. Would you recognize this man?"

The girl looked at him with her big, black eyes, sharply contrasting with her pale face, struggling to catch her breath through parted lips.

"Yes," she whispered barely audibly. "It's the miner I arrested... in Workers' Angles."

"Oh fuck," Wilder muttered.

Neil Slavik had informed him just two hours earlier that the arrested individual named Ogden Fierce had been released due to a lawyer intervention with the judge, representing the company he worked for. The reason was that he was being treated for mild emotional disorders that had worsened due to medication withdrawal. Slavik seemed worried, even suggesting that the commander should use extraordinary powers to keep the hotheaded miner in custody, and the captain could not forgive himself for not having listened to him.

He stood up and grabbed Leeta's arm, who, along with Greyfox, was taking "on the spot" testimonies from witnesses.

"Take care of securing the surveillance footage," he ordered. "Issue a wanted notice for Ogden Fierce and send Hallie with it to the judge, have him sign it immediately."

"Is it him?!"

"It looks like it. The situation is getting complicated. We'll talk later."

An ambulance arrived with the siren wailing and braked at the curb. The paramedics jumped out, unfolded a stretcher, and one of them knelt beside Salome, taking out some device from a bag.

"I'll secure this, and then you can take your hand away," he addressed Monty. "Please wait until I give clear instructions. And you, don't move a muscle."

He skillfully applied the clamp and then offered the injured person a pain relief medication.

"There's no time, you were in a hurry!" Wilder barked.

"There was an accident at the granules factory. We came from the other side of the city." The man rose from his knees and turned to his colleagues. "Get the injured person on the stretcher and let's go to the hospital with sirens on. Critical condition, immediate to the operating room."

"Will she survive?"

"How would I know? I'm not a fortune teller. Get out of the way, man."

The medic pushed the captain aside, disregarding the authority of his uniform. He could afford to do that since the medical branch, part of the existing division of power, didn't have to consider Wilder's orders. The ambulance drove away as the captain watched with concern. He still couldn't forgive himself for not taking Slavik's words seriously, though on the other hand – what basis did he have to question the judge's opinion? That was not what he was trained for.

"Do you have anything?" he turned to Leeta and Greyfox to stop thinking about it.

"Not much, but we took the names and addresses of the witnesses," the sergeant replied. "Everyone will receive a summons. The stormtroopers are searching the entire block. Tomcat," he hesitated, "what about Baby?"

"They took her to the hospital. Let's hope they make it in time. If she survives, we'll owe it to Monty and his skills. Solely."

"I'll go to the hospital," Leeta offered. "I'll wait there until I receive some news."

"Are they going to let you in?" Elvis asked skeptically. He had tried visiting injured colleagues on duty more than once and had had bad experiences with hospital staff. For many people from lower classes, getting into the medical field—which was very difficult—was a unique opportunity to gain some power over others, and they exploited it shamelessly.

"I have a friend there. They'll let me in. Don't worry, Dakota. We'll stay in touch, you'll get all the news firsthand. Hey, where are you going?!"

These last words were directed at Monty, who had just turned and started to leave. Leeta's voice stopped him.

"Mr. Greyfox wanted lunch."

"Are you crazy? Come back! In this state, you want to show up at 'The Favorite'? People will faint at the sight of you." Lieutenant Ankes grabbed him by the arm.

"Why?"

"You're all covered in blood! Good heavens, I still sometimes forget that he doesn't understand certain things."

"You're going back to the station," the sergeant supported Leeta. "You need to change, and I've completely lost my appetite anyway. Go to the hospital, girl, and let me know as soon as you can."

XI
LEETA
PERSONAL DIARY

The Salome operation lasted long enough for me to sweat nervously. Jeanne McCave let me into the doctor's lounge so I wouldn't have to keep answering nurses' and attendants' questions about what I was doing in the hallway, and offered me tea. She herself didn't participate in the operation as she is an internist, not a surgeon, but she promised me news first-hand. We became friends when she tried to save Scott's life, and it stayed that way.

When I thought I couldn't handle the tension any longer, Jeanne returned.

"You can go home now," she said. "Your friend is alive; the operation was successful."

"Was it tough?" I asked.

"Very. They had to do a complicated reconstruction of the blood vessels. Dr. Navrotzky said the artery was not so much cut as torn. It wasn't a knife, but some other tool. If it weren't for your assistant... It was a close call."

"Can I see her?"

"No way! No visits until her condition stabilizes. I will keep you updated, but for now, don't come here until there is official permission to contact anyone from outside. I'll let you out through the emergency hallway so that no one reports you to management."

I was truly grateful to her and understood that for now, there was nothing more she could do for me. The new hospital director had instituted very strict rules. The previous one didn't pay much attention to regulations or anything at all. That was why he was eventually dismissed.

Returning to the station, I reported to the captain and Dakota what I had learned. We had to wait, but not idly. First of all, we issued a wanted notice for the culprit of the whole misfortune and began working on what we already had.

Whoever was behind the events of the past weeks began to emerge as an extraordinarily dangerous opponent. They knew how to choose their people and steer them towards specific behaviors, while remaining in the shadows themselves. Who were they and what were they after? Initially, we considered a certain Winston Cooper, who publicly threatened Wilder, but timing was against that theory. The problems started even before the appointment of the new commander, from pranks aimed at the new mayor Lunnar and letters written to him. There was no reason to believe that these two matters were not connected, so Winston Cooper was out of the picture.

I took the mechanisms removed by Kelley from Annabelle Banks' body out of the evidence locker and brought them to Chris. None of our technicians could perform such a thorough analysis as he could, and besides, I hoped it would give him pleasure. He still couldn't wait for his new assignment, and I knew he wouldn't want to stay on the Moon as the chief conservator of the machinery of Selenoport, a position he currently held.

I had a good idea. Chris brightened up at the sight of the implants I brought and immediately got to work, while I peeked into the kitchen and decided to make us some snack. It reminded me of the old times. I always cooked for us, because although Chris had a better hand for it, he wasn't keen on that kind of work. And I, being naturally accommodating, couldn't force him to follow the division of household chores. How distant...and beautiful those times seemed now. You have to lose something to truly appreciate it.

I managed to make dough with flour substitute, powdered cream, and various additives, and I fried pancakes before Chris finished his work. As soon as he came out of his workshop, he pounced on them as if he hadn't eaten in a week. "Delicious, no one can make pancakes like you," he declared with a full mouth. "I was so hungry."

"Why don't you move in with me and Sue?" I asked. "You'd always have meals on time, clean and ironed clothes, care in case of any illness."

"Thank you, Goose Mama, but no. I like being independent, and as for clothes, that combo is destroyed. I'm waiting for a new programmer and signal box to fix it." He smiled at me the way only he can, with his mouth, eyes, and whole face.

"Alright, fix it and do whatever you want," I agreed with resignation. "But tell me, what about those implants?"

He swallowed the rest of the pancake. "These are specialized mechanisms," he replied. "I don't know if you know, but they are illegal in private hands. Only medical departments have the right to possess them for demonstration purposes. The only thing is, what you brought was made here, on the Moon."

"How do you know?" I was astonished. I knew Chris was a great professional, but to that extent?

"It would take a while to explain," he replied. "It's not as difficult as it seems. Sven could manage such work during lunch break, and I'm not even sure if he didn't have a hand in it."

"You've got to be kidding," I muttered. Is it possible that Thorvald got himself involved in something? How and why? He always shied away from trouble. Chris noticed that I had become gloomy and added, "I'm sure he didn't want to break the law or harm anyone. However, you should talk to him. If you wait a bit, I will give you the technical documentation of those mechanisms. It won't tell you anything, but he'll just take a look and know what it's about."

He was right in saying that his documentation wouldn't tell me anything. A lot of numbers and technical jargon, he might as well have written it in Chinese. However, Sven, being an electronics engineer, understood the notation immediately. "Indeed, I've installed a few circuits that match this diagram," he said right away. "But that was about three years ago. What's it about?"

"Who gave you the order?" I asked. He hesitated, so I added, "Sven, this is very serious. A murder, and not just one, but probably a conspiracy as well."

"Anti-government?"

"I have no idea. Honestly, this case doesn't make sense, and I don't know what to think about it. Who did you make those parts for?"

He scratched his head.

"For the Medfarm laboratory," he said gloomily. "The order was signed by the director of one of the departments, I think… yes, it was definitely the endocrinology department. I remember it well because they paid me so much that I could pay off my debts, and I was in a really terrible situation at the time. Listen, Leeta, I signed a confidentiality statement…"

"No one will find out that you spilled the beans," I assured him solemnly. "We are friends, Sven. No one will even find out that we talked here. Not even Commander Wilder. You have my word. Just tell me everything you remember. You don't have to give me what you signed. You must have a copy, but never mind that. I won't mention your name in the report."

I hoped he believed me. I didn't want to jeopardize our friendship, although for the sake of the investigation, I would have gone that far. Monty, Mabel, and I owed this man a lot, but now the situation might require me to forget that. I would have preferred it not to be so, but… well, exactly. Life is not always how we want it to be. Especially when working in the police.

"Sue, find me everything you can about Medfarm," I requested when I got home. "I mean, not about the company itself, but about the people who work at the lunnar's branch."

"As I understand it, by yesterday?" Sue looked at me from beneath her falling curls. She had lost weight recently, but her friendly, girl-next-door face still remained nearly as round as before. She hadn't changed her messy hairstyle either; I must admit it suited her beauty the best.

"Well, as soon as possible."

"Alright. Official order or a favor request?"

I nearly laughed. Virtualists are often seen as people completely disconnected from everyday life - quite wrongly. In reality, they are sober and very grounded, especially when they start negotiating their fees for their efforts.

"Official. Don't worry; you'll get the usual rate. When I'm at the station, I'll write what needs to be done. For now, focus on who might have any connection to Kovacs and the Moon Company."

She nodded and immediately sat down at her computer. I'll admit that although I'm quite good as an amateur IT person (necessary for a librarian), and Sue has taught me a lot, I wouldn't be able to handle her personal equipment. Each virtualist's specialized computer is "custom-made," and the user constantly upgrades it according to their preferences, so, in reality, there are no two identical ones in the world. Yet their capabilities exceed all imagination.

I added some water to Sid's bowl, gave him some food, scratched his back, and left Sue with her work. I had my own tasks to return to.

***

"Explosion in an underground crossing, perpetrator unknown."

"Mannequin with an explosive mechanism, installer unknown."

"Letters to the mayor, author unknown."

"Jeff Cormack, killed during a raid, perpetrator unknown."

"Carol Masion, killed during an arrest attempt, perpetrator unknown."

"Annabelle Banks, poisoned, perpetrator unknown. Head smashed post-mortem, perpetrator unknown."

"Harry Gelbart, infected with malaria, perpetrator unknown."

"Attempt to incite workers against business managers, perpetrator unknown."

"Attempt to discredit law enforcement agencies, perpetrator unknown, motive - unknown."

"Role of Juvenille company in all this."

Leeta was looking at her board in deep thought. After a moment, she wrote: "Attempted murder of Salome Delaforette, perpetrator Ogden Fierce, motive unknown."

"I don't understand any of this," she muttered to herself.

"Me neither." Rosanda Merrick approached her unnoticed until the girl flinched at the sound of her voice. "I can bet, just like me, you know where to look for the solution now."

Lieutenant Ankes glanced back at her. The head of the economic department watched her with her round, brown eyes, the only pretty accent on her rugged face, not so much questioning as with the certainty of a seasoned investigator.

"I know," Leeta sighed. "In Selenoport. If someone lets me in there. All the clues lead right there, but you know that based on the agreement signed somewhere higher only the commander is supposed to contact the authorities of Selenoport. It's basically an automatic city."

"A greenhouse playroom for the wealthy," Merrick scoffed. "Even their internal police is from the upper class, did you know that? For sure. Where would they allow the plebs to stick their dirty noses into fancy salons."

"Now they will have to allow it," a voice behind her spoke up, that of Wilder. Both women turned around. The commander stood behind them, looking grimly at the board. "The truck from that mannequin was registered to the 'Ambassador' restaurant in Selenoport. The technical department managed to recover not only the removed engine numbers but also found fragments of fingerprints. That's the leverage we needed to issue a legal warrant. Come to my office."

"There's going to be trouble," Leeta warned him. He shrugged his powerful shoulders.

"Let it be. You know where I have the whims of those important people? It won't be easy for them with me."

"Great." Merrick nodded in appreciation. Selenoport had been her thorn in the side from the beginning, as guided by the instinct of a seasoned police officer, she suspected there were numerous scams and cases for which she could hold the people governing that place accountable. Meanwhile, she was not allowed to handle any cases related to that place, although she had her informants who reported various strange incidents to her.

"Rosie, will you do something for me?" Lieutenant Ankes asked.

"Sure."

"Have your people check the local Medfarm branch. The laboratory and drug production… That ought to fall under your purview."

Merrick thoughtfully scratched her chin.

"Of course… But I've never had any troubling reports from there, and I have two contacts there."

Clint Wilder, who had already turned around, looked at her in astonishment.

"Seriously?!"

"Piranha" smiled with clear satisfaction, seeing that she had made an impression on the new commander.

"Yes. I have people everywhere. Discreet eyes and ears. Did you really think I only had officially employed officers at my disposal?"

The captain did not respond to this provocative question. Until now, he had not had any contact with the economic crime department and had not been interested in how it operated. It seemed he would have to now.

"That's too much for me to handle," he thought, but of course, he didn't say that out loud. Leeta followed Wilder to his office (for her, it was still "Scott's office," and entering it brought a slight sadness to her heart) and carefully closed the door behind her.

"Did they really read those numbers?" she asked with a touch of disbelief. She knew that all parts of the van and the mannequin itself had been examined using the latest methods, trying to find even the smallest clue, and so far, she had not heard of any success.

"Really. I got the message half an hour ago." Wilder handed her the lab prints. "The technicians used some new method that allows for obtaining a 'deep molecular fingerprint,' whatever that means. In any case, evidence obtained this way is admissible in court. As soon as the judge signs the warrant, we're heading to Selenoport."

"They're going to be furious there."

"Let them be furious. I have no intention of caring about the whims of the upper class. As long as it was about petty thefts, card scams, or two guys beating each other up, one could somewhat respect... a division of competencies. But not anymore." The captain spoke quietly, but decisively and with a threatening tone in his voice."At least three murders have taken place, two attempted murders, an attack on law enforcement, incitement of a crowd, creating a public threat, and an attempt to assassinate the mayor. I don't understand why the governor is silent, but that's his business. I plan to make use of special powers."

"Ouch." slipped out of Leeta.

Special powers, if the commander of the lunnar's police decided to exercise them, would allow them to bypass the official channels and effectively declare a state of emergency on their own, with the local garrison obliged to assist them. This carried significant risks, as under the provision, Wilder would become personally responsible for anything that might arise from that move.

"What do you mean by 'ouch'? Someone must do it. Regardless of the risk. Though not just yet. We'll see how the investigation goes in this damn city of sin." They hesitated for a moment. "I don't want to criticize you, but you shouldn't have signed as acting commander under the governor's agreement with the Selenoport management. That was a serious tactical mistake, not to mention that it completely contradicts the applicable law."

The girl didn't seem offended.

"You're not entirely right," she replied with a heavy sigh. "What do you actually know about the real owner of Selenoport and Governor Stanton?"

Wilder furrowed their brow.

"Owner? Selenoport is managed by the GEB company, Government Entertainment Corporations…"

"Officially, it's registered as an association, not a company. However, there is something resembling a private owner: an investor who covered most of the construction costs and now holds actual control over the city through their proxies."

"Do you know who this person is?" that question hung in the air like a dot over an "i."

Leeta raised her eyes to them. It seemed she was hesitating to reveal the information she possessed. She was clearly torn between loyalty to her new superior and former commitments; her pretty face, marked by several golden freckles, tightened and paled. The captain waited, not rushing her.

"They call him Citizen Hakat," she finally said. "Former Chief of Arms. What I am about to say cannot leave this office."

"I can't promise that. It may be relevant to the investigation."

"And it is. Still, no one besides you is allowed to find out about this, and you'll soon understand why. Citizen Hakat lost his position due to internal strife in the government and a wide-ranging conspiracy that he could not prevent. It was not due to ineptitude, incompetence, or malice on his part; he was simply unfortunate. Everything was taken from him; he managed to keep only what he acquired privately and invested all his resources that did not come from political activities. The controlling stake in Selenoport that he received in exchange for stockcoins contributed to the construction."

"Stockcoins?"

"Yes. They are like investment money, a virtual exchange of food and industrial points. Trading in them facilitates the functioning of the economy; counting everything in two types of points would be unnecessarily cumbersome. Have you never heard of stock market operations?"

"I've heard of them, but I know nothing about it."

"You don't need to. I didn't need to either, but some time ago, I had to delve into a few issues in that area and picked up some knowledge. In any case, from the perspective of private ownership law, Selenoport belongs to Citizen Hakat."

The captain nodded.

"I understand," they said. "The guy may have lost his position; he may have lost his material possessions apart from those shares, but he still has political connections."

Leeta sighed despairingly.

"That's not the point. He doesn't need connections; he always manages on his own. What's important is something else. I'm one of perhaps three or four people who knew from the very beginning to whom the lunnar's entertainment capital actually belongs."

"And that's why you signed that agreement? I don't understand. What does Citizen Hakat have to do with the governor? Is he getting a cut? And that didn't bother you?"

"Clint!" Leeta shouted angrily. "Who do you think I am?! I'm trying to tell you something crucial. Citizen Hakat and

Karl Stanton are the same person. I know this today, along with someone else. And now you too."

Wilder didn't expect this. He looked at his deputy with his mouth open, unable to find words. Meanwhile, Leeta continued speaking.

"The agreement practically meant that the only real jurisdiction in Selenoport belongs to Karl Stanton, and he decides everything that happens there. At least, that was the intention. I'm afraid someone wants to, using the slang of the criminal underworld, 'squeeze him out of the business.' It wouldn't bother us either way if it weren't for the fact that it involved outright breaking the law. The only thing I don't understand in this matter is what Victor Kovacs has to do with it. Somehow he's connected, but I still can't grasp how."

"Maybe he's just behind it?"

"That's not out of the question, though there's no evidence or trace. He is either devilishly clever or truly innocent. Maru is still figuring him out, but even Sue hasn't managed to dig up anything in the virtual world beyond what we already have. And she is a first-class professional."

Wilder nervously ran his hand over his closely cropped hair.

"Alright," he said after a moment. "You know about paperwork, sit down and write the application. We need to have open access to Selenoport and all its facilities for the time being."

The girl obediently sat at the desk and began filling out forms. A deep furrow crossed her forehead. She would give a lot right now to be able to talk to Citizen Hakat... I mean, Karl Stanton, because that's what he was really called. Sue's uncle, for whom being a governor was a social demotion and exile. She was seriously worried that Wilder's determination, clearly fueled by the attack on Salome, could lead him into a blind alley. And she had already gotten to know him well and even liked him. She had no idea how to stop him, though she felt she should before it led to disaster.

The speaker by the door clicked and Chris Nikanov's voice came through.

"Is anyone there?"

The captain pressed the button, releasing the door lock, and the young engineer walked in.

"Do you have something?" Wilder asked him. Chris shrugged.

"Yes and no," he replied reluctantly, which unpleasantly reminded Wilder of his conversation with Monty. "There is indeed something going on, although I hadn't paid attention to it until now. I manage the engineering department, and I haven't had much to do with management because there's no need. Only after you brought it to my attention did I start discreetly sniffing around."

Leeta lifted her head.

"Why are you involving my brother?" she asked sharply.

"Because it seems I must," replied the captain, and turned back to Chris. "Continue."

"The main manager is Symeon Lange, an exceptional scoundrel, as his colleagues say. I would say he is a tough boss and a very ambitious person. He treats Selenoport a bit like his private kingdom. He manages it very efficiently, but I wouldn't expect him to cooperate with the 'external police.' It will be very difficult to get anything from him. That's one thing. The second is worse. He might have some private income from the operations of certain institutions in Selenoport. According to the people I contacted, his bank account is much fatter than it should be, and it was already that way when he managed Las Vegas. It's safe to assume he moved his operations to the Moon. I'll say right away that they won't talk to you. None of them know that my sister is a police officer, which is why I could talk to them."

"Interesting, but that's more of a matter for Merrick than us. Although, of course, motives could be sought there." Wilder pondered. "I'll check this lead. Anything else?"

Chris hesitated, then reached into his pocket.

"I broke into Annabel Banks' apartment," he said. "I can open any electronic lock; of course, I don't do that on a daily basis. I found this, hidden under the seat of one of the chairs."

He handed the commander the 'S' card. A mandatory health document for every citizen of Earth. Wilder furrowed his brow with some discontent. It was clear he was hesitating whether to reprimand the engineer for acting in a way that clearly broke the law – he should perhaps even arrest him – or to let it pass in silence. In the end, he slid the card into the reader. Above the desk, a hologram of a girl formed, whose body was now lying in the police morgue, and next to it a series of letters formed into personal data. At least theoretically.

"XXXX? What is this supposed to be?" he exclaimed in astonishment.

"This is the so-called 'imposter'. That's what similar cards are commonly called," Chris explained to him. "They belong to strictly controlled identifiers available only to government agencies. With a simple manipulation, any data can be entered on them. And this is her official card," he handed Wilder a second, actually identical item. "Please... or no, I will do it, it will be faster."

He changed the cards in the reader's slot. Above the desk, the same image appeared, this time accompanied by a legible description. Chris began to quickly type something on the device's keyboard. Leeta and Wilder watched him with growing curiosity. They both knew that the "S" cards had securities that prevented manipulation of once-entered personal data, and so they were extremely astonished when the text hanging next to the woman's hologram began to change. Not only that.

"Here you go," Nikanov finally said. "Melinda Crawford, born in New York, registration district Bronx, citizen category Sigma Plus."

Leeta whistled through her teeth.

"Oh crap..." she added.

Besides the social class markings, already established at the maternity ward, there existed, in the legal order, a classification based on the social position of the newborn's parents. The Sigma Plus category meant "family under special supervision," threatened with having their children taken away due to suspicion of pathology, but not yet fully qualifying for state intervention. Intervention could happen in the future, and this meant that children who had already been under the care of parents for some time would be taken away. In practice, intervention occurred very rarely, and not at all because these children did not need help. The new social care system stood in the way, where practically no institution like an orphanage existed. It was replaced by foster families, and so-called "shelters" were only temporary holding places, where, according to law, a child could not stay longer than two months. And therein lay the catch. Very few foster families wanted to commit to raising a child from a pathological environment, and the child could not be taken away until someone was willing to take responsibility for it. This explained the signs of malnutrition discovered by McCave in early childhood. However, Leeta's reaction was caused by something else.

It was the personal details she recognized. Not only her, in fact. Although the information reaching the public underwent careful selection to ensure that nothing would cause social unrest, there were occasional leaks. And such a leak occurred regarding Melinda Crawford, shocking public opinion. The girl, raised by a well-known and respected family of local politicians named Collins, officially accused her social father of rape and his wife of inciting to rape. The man admitted to an affair but maintained that it occurred with mutual consent, and his social daughter was in fact the initiator of the relationship. Family police, which is the department established to resolve such matters, has established beyond any doubt that the basis of the accusation was plain extortion. Of course, Mr. Collins's career collapsed due to his sexual exploitation of a girl under his roof, but he did not face criminal responsibility for that. The situation was worse for Melinda, who – after the case was dropped – added an attempt to murder the Collinses to the accusations made against her. Since her sanity was in question according to the experts, she was placed in a closed facility, from which she soon disappeared under mysterious circumstances. Despite extensive searches, no trace of her was found.

"In order to function in our society, the girl must have stolen someone's identity," Chris explained. "However, this required not only cunning and ruthlessness, but also skills she did not possess. A name is one thing, a face can also be changed, but the biometric data on the card must match. It is more than certain that she made contact with someone who helped her with this. Under her already changed name, she completed her studies, so this was not a 'temporary' acquaintance; it is safe to assume she was sponsored."

"Surely you are not an undercover agent sent from Earth? Because you reason like a real cop," Wilder asked half-mockingly and then became serious. "This information is invaluable. Please continue your work and be careful that no one connects you with us. Surely no one in Selenoport knows you have a sister in the police?"

"Definitely. It's not mentioned in the records, and no one from there even shows up in Lunnar, for what purpose? I also did not provide the fact that I have a rented apartment here. My team thinks I live like other technicians on the outskirts of Selenoport, where quarters have been built for support staff, you know, for waitresses, cleaners, cooks, technicians, maids…"

"Sure, the help lives far from the high and mighty so as not to stink up the place." The captain scoffed with disdain. "And everyone is satisfied."

"Don't be so bitter," Chris smiled with involuntary sympathy. He was starting to like Clint, although he didn't want to. "That's how the world works, and it has always been that way. And people like you, living on minimum wage, save the behinds of those who spend the equivalent of it on one breakfast. If that doesn't suit you, why did you join the police?"

"To ensure everyone is equal before the law," Wilder said seriously. "So that the wealthy who break the law end up in the same cell as the similarly behaving poor. And so that even Number One himself cannot wriggle out of an eventual arrest with a bribe or connections."

"Let me guess: is that why you are here?" the engineer winked at him and, without waiting for an answer, left the office.

"He's quite cheeky," the captain muttered to himself and partly to Leety. "Did you write that?"

"Yes, yes. It just needs your signature and we can send it to the judge."

XII
CLINT WILDER
Personal Diary

Obtaining a warrant and getting into Selenoport are two different things, as I discovered after a rather brief conversation with the city management president. It was almost entirely impossible to do politely, despite the documents presented. I had to strike hard right away. Before Mr. Lange realized what was happening, I twisted his arms behind his back, put on the handcuffs, and recited his rights to him.

"Lieutenant, please call for the prison ambulance," I addressed Leety. "Charge: refusal to comply with a court order."

"Sir, are you out of your mind?!" Lange yelled, purple with rage, trying to free himself. "Do you know who I am?!"

"And resisting arrest," I added with satisfaction. "Do you have anything else to add?"

"You'll regret this, fascists in uniforms!"

"Please add insulting a public officer in service, lieutenant." Three men in internal police uniforms entered the office and stopped uncertainly as Monty blocked their way. I had already noticed earlier that his immobile face and precise, calculated movements instilled involuntary respect

tinged with fear in many people, even though they had no idea he was an android and could snap any of their necks more easily than they could break a drinking straw.

"Apparently, there was a gang robbery here..." one of the guards (I hesitated to call them policemen) said, looking around the office.

My eyebrows shot up. A gang robbery, how delightful.

"Is this what you call legal operational activities here?" I asked with the utmost sarcasm I could muster, glancing at my apprehender's attractive and very nervous secretary, who was trying to hide behind the door.

"We have a signed agreement with the authorities!" she squeaked defensively. "Selenoport is extraterritorial!"

"You might be mistaken, but I don't have time to explain obvious things to you," I announced. "In short: Selenoport could rely on its own police until there was suspicion that a murderer of three people and their sponsor was hiding within its walls. It is now under the jurisdiction of the head-quarters and will remain so until we resolve the case."

"You are finished, curbside," hissed Symeon Lange. "I will see to that, I swear."

"And please add criminal threats to the indictment, Lieu-tenant Ankes. Altogether it will amount to a nice sentence," I smiled sweetly at the man, who was as red as a beet. "Oh, did I hear a siren?"

Indeed, the wail of a prison ambulance sounded outside, and moments later, stormtroopers under the command of Corporal Matt Norris entered the office. The internal police guards quickly stepped aside, letting them pass. Lange, in contrast, turned pale, as it probably finally dawned on him that I was not joking and that he was not dealing with an attempt to intimidate or extort a bribe.

"I think that..." he stammered, "...that this could some-how be settled."

"No, it can't," I cut him off. "Boys, take care of this gentleman and transport him to the precinct. Lieutenant Ankes will provide you with a list of his offenses. Notify Slavik immediately so he can handle it legally."

"Yes, sir," replied Matt Norris dutifully. His eyes behind the visor of his helmet sparkled with satisfaction. Like many people from the lower classes, he hated officials and generally well-off individuals, and I could bet he was enjoying himself right now. Leeta handed him a printout from her "poda," containing a list of charges. By the way, if these devices could be connected to more efficient mini-printers, they would be truly universal. They are already much more convenient to use than traditional paddies and have excellent security. It's good they were introduced as police equipment.

"Go now with Monty to Annabelle Banks' apartment and conduct an official search there," I addressed Ankes. "Send me Officer Fillert from downstairs. I'll finish up here, and then the two of us will visit whom we need."

I preferred not to say out loud that I was heading to the "Ambassador." For now, I had to sign the protocol and officially hand over the office keys to Lange's deputy, who had not yet appeared.

Having dealt with the bureaucratic nonsense, I set off with the officer to the upscale establishment. People turned to look at us on the street with clear surprise, but we didn't pay it any mind. Nat Fillert discreetly surveyed the area, curious about the place; I wasn't as interested. It simply reminded me *of... Las Vegas, where I had been transferred for two weeks (as a substitute for a colleague). Yes, this is Las Vegas–part two, only on the Moon, and therefore under a dome. Another thing is that if I didn't know where I was, I might not have realized it because that dome perfectly imitates the earthly sky. The joints between the individual panels are not visible at all, and the colors and intensity of light are perfectly matched. I decided to take the opportunity to congratulate Chris on the achievements of his team. As soon as we crossed the threshold of the "Ambassador," we immediately drew widespread attention. Like by the touch of a magic wand, the murmur of conversations quieted down, and the room manager appeared from literally nowhere. I nearly doubled over at the sight of him; black tailcoat, red bow tie, white gloves, he looked just like a maitre d'hotel from a cheap operetta, I don't know how I managed to stifle my laughter. A circus on wheels.*

"Excuse me, gentlemen," he said in a voice that could have frozen the air, "but only guests in formal attire are allowed in an establishment of this class. Suit and tie."

"How about the ladies?" Nat Fillert asked sarcastically. I gave him a light jab in the side to bring him to his senses and turned to the penguin, who stood in his place with the demeanor of a mortally offended maiden.

"Lead me to the manager of this pigsty."

The stiffened stiffened even more.

"Please leave immediately," he hissed through clenched teeth.

"And why is that?" I asked.

"Security!" he yelled, turning toward the back door. It opened, and two muscle-bound goons sprang out from be-

hind it. Fillert immediately reached for his silencer—he doesn't yet have the right to a dual—and he was right to do so because the two security guards, paying no attention to the police uniforms, hurled themselves at us with the momentum of people with zero imagination. Nat fired two shots, and both collapsed to the floor before they could reach us. A few women screamed in horror; one even fainted, I think. I had no desire to check.

"Don't worry, they are just tranquilizer darts," I said loudly. "They'll sleep it off, and perhaps they'll get smarter when they're summoned to court. You won't escape this either," I turned to the standing room manager, who was as stiff as a board. "I could arrest you immediately, but who would take care of this fine company."

I took out a DNA sampler from my pocket, broke the seal, and, grabbing the manager's hand, pulled off his glove. Then I pricked his finger with the probe needle, put on the cover, and placed the whole thing into a disposable bag, which I labeled with a code and put away. I repeated this procedure with both unconscious security guards. There was no point in calling a prison ambulance for them or even preparing a protocol. It's good that the samples taken constitute a sufficient reservoir of information; nowadays, they are much better than writing down from a document, it saves a lot of time.

The restaurant director, a guy as plump as they come and polished up for a diplomatic reception, was waiting for us in the doorway of his office, informed by the staff.

"I am Sergio Tocopoulos. I just want to say that the right people will hear about this high-handedness." He spoke coldly at the sight of me.

"Please do," I replied. "You can even write to your mommy about it. I have no objections to that. Now please provide me with a list of employees and call them here one by one."

The director lifted his nose and tried to sidestep me, so I pushed him into the office.

"I advise you not to resist, because I'll put the handcuffs on," I said sharply. "The CEO of Selenoport is already sitting in jail for pretending to be tough. Do you want to be next? Officer, please pull the employee list from the computer."

Nat obediently positioned himself behind the director's desk and began searching the computer's memory, while the pallid with anger Tocopoulos sat in an armchair, huffing, trying to regain his composure. "There's quite a lack of order in this entertainment city, no doubt," I thought. What law is being followed here? If the governor has spoiled them all this much, then my congratulations. I will have to have a chat with him, and I will do so regardless of whom he is or who he thinks he is. He won't have it as easy with me as with Leeta. She is indeed too soft to establish any semblance of order here.

"Well?" I urged Nat. "Come on, give me that list. We need to interrogate the entire company, and we need to take fingerprints and DNA samples from everyone. Did you bring the fingerprinting kit as I instructed?"

The packets of registration film, which replaced the traditional ink pads, had only arrived at Lunnar last week. Interesting, that only recently someone thought of producing them, but better late than never. We immediately started calling them "pressers" and that's how it stayed.

"Of course I took it," Fillert replied, staring at the screen. "Captain... could you come here for a moment? I think you should see this."

Intrigued, I approached and looked over his shoulder.

"Annabelle Banks!" I exclaimed in astonishment. There was no mistaking it; next to the personal data was a photo. "She worked for you?" I asked the director. He stopped panting and turned his fish-like eyes toward me.

"What do you mean 'worked'? She still works. Unless I'm missing something."

"Well, you don't know," I admitted without going into details. "It's just that Miss Banks is also listed as a VIP assistant at the 'Parish' hotel. How is that possible?"

He shrugged his shoulders.

"And what do I care?" he threw back reluctantly. "I don't get involved in other people's private affairs. She works for me part-time as a showgirl and as long as she's doing well..."

"Did," I clarified. "You can remove her from the list."

"Is she sitting? What did you arrest her for?"

"That's not your concern. Now please take the microphone and call people from the list one by one."

***

While Captain Wilder was conducting difficult interrogations in Selenoport, Leeta and Monty had long finished searching the deceased woman's apartment and returned to the station.

"Do you have anything?" Kendra Maru asked, lifting her head from the hastily eaten stew.

"Nothing special," Leeta replied with frustration. "It's as if she never lived there. I mean, she definitely lived there, her things are there, but everything looks staged and left behind. It's spotless, no normal signs of use in the bathroom and kitchen area. This is the second such case; Gelbart's apartment looked the same. And you? Do you have anything on Kovacs?"

Kendra nodded while chewing industriously.

"I'm terribly hungry," she explained with some embarrassment. "I've been wandering around civilian style in the center since four in the morning. I managed to reach people who have various information about what's happening in city hall, but most of them don't want to talk to the police right now. I worked so hard to get something out of them. I had to take two of them for vodka... I usually don't drink, but those two had the juiciest information and I had to make a sacrifice," she grimaced, "and endure their compliments."

"Was it worth it?" Leeta pulled her chair closer and sat across from her colleague.

"Oh yes. I have a lot of recordings, I've already handed them over to the technicians, you know, it's hard for me to remember everything. However, I remember the most important things." Kendra scraped the last remnants of the stew from the box and licked the spoon. "So, Victor Kovacs is bankrupt. He's not just a drunk; he also compulsively plays poker. He's a frequent visitor to Selenoport, where he loses everything. Despite that, he has some means for everyday functioning; no one could tell me where it comes from. He doesn't steal from the city funds, besides he wouldn't be able to. According to my informants' observations, he makes normal purchases and it seems like he's not lacking anything. One thing doesn't quite add up with the other, but I'll try to figure it out somehow."

"And women? Does he have any?" Leeta asked.

Monty, who had stepped away a few minutes earlier, returned carrying two cups of caffetino. He set them on the desk and took a step back. Kendra put the spoon back in the box and opened the bag with dessert. She took a knife from the drawer and methodically divided the doughy cake into two equal parts. She pushed one toward Leeta and stuffed the other into her mouth.

"At least two were visiting him, supposedly very attractive, but about a month ago those visits stopped abruptly," she replied after a moment. "It's not just about the women. The mayor practically stopped receiving anyone in his private apartment. One woman, who cleans occasionally, Mirla Bailey, told me she had never seen such a dirty and cluttered apartment in her life."

"Did she clean it at least?"

"No, she came to offer her services, but the mayor told her to get out and only asked: who even let her into the building?"

Lieutenant Ankes snorted with laughter, but quickly grew serious.

"Indeed, who let her in…"

"Administrator," Maru replied calmly. "He knows her well. Mirla is valued by people who don't like to clean up themselves. She used to be a clerk, but she became an alcoholic and ended up on the street. Supposedly she doesn't drink anymore, but honestly, no one cares. She earns a living by cleaning and is a good informant."

"Yours, I take it?"

"Now she is." Kendra's expression darkened. "Previously, Silvana was paying her, then it was Scott. After his death, she came to me and offered her services. I asked why she didn't approach you, and she said you somehow intimidate her. You're A3."

"Scott was also A."

"Yes, but she didn't know that. The visor covered his class sign, after all. She thought he was at best B, like her."

Leeta popped a piece of cake into her mouth and chewed it slowly.

"In a nutshell, something happened in our mayor's life," she finally summarized. "Previously, women visited him, so he somewhat took care of his place. A man usually doesn't put his lover in a pile of trash unless he wants to lose her. Since that event, he stopped taking care of his apartment, so he probably does not expect any visitors and is sinking into neglect."

"That's not all." Kendra took a sip of caffettino from her mug and swallowed a pill. "One of those I drank vodka with works for the city hall as a driver. By the way, he also works part-time, getting paid per ride, which is alarming because according to the law, he should be on a full-time contract. He told me something interesting. Right after the Selenoport started operating, the city hall signed a supply contract with the management of that establishment, supposedly to ensure transparency in procurement. To avoid any skimming. However, a little later, the rules were changed for a mundane reason: the city hall does not have a fleet, while the Selenoport institutions have had it from the start. To keep the wolf fed and the virgin saved, it was established that the delivery trucks would belong to the Selenoport entities, but their drivers must be ordered from the city hall. Their duties include not only delivering the cargo but also checking it and creating a delivery protocol. Recently, my interlocutor lost one such ride, but he didn't make a fuss about it because he was paid more than the contract was worth."

Leeta whistled briefly.

"The pieces are starting to fall into place. Does the guy know who set him up?"

"That's the most interesting part." Kendra raised a finger, like a teacher in class. "Unofficially, he found out, from a third or fourth hand, that they are testing a new way of remote control that would work on the Moon. This obviously frightened him because it would mean the fall of the entire profession, so he began to dig deeper. Nobody confirmed these revelations to him; he just heard from some buddy that supposedly... supposedly... there was a trial, but it ended in failure. He didn't know the details."

"Our mannequin. Wilder had a nose for taking him," Lieutenant Ankes nodded. "By the way, where's Dakota?"

"In the technical department. I told him right away what I just told you, and he dashed off there."

"Then I'll go too," Leeta stood up. "What are you swallowing again?"

"Neutralizer. I can't sit in the station as an officer 'under the influence.' I feel awful."

Her colleague patted her reassuringly on the shoulder and went to the technical department. However, she didn't get there. Halfway there, her beeper buzzed, so she headed to the videophone. After selecting the call number, she saw Jennie McCave's face on the screen.

"Miss Delaforette's condition has stabilized. She's no longer in danger and is conscious. You can visit her, but briefly," the doctor said. She nervously glanced behind her. "You need to hurry before the director and the chief return from their requested lunch. Go to the back door just in case."

"I'm on my way."

Leeta quickly scribbled on the official board where she was headed, called Monty, and together they went down to the garage, where several sleek gliders were parked, meant for less significant and less dangerous tasks.

Jeannie was waiting for the officer in front of the entrance for hospital staff.

"Let him stay here," she motioned her head towards Monty. "I can explain your presence if needed. You have special authorization."

"You've been terrorized by that new boss."

"Oh, don't even mention it."

She led Leeta to the ICU and opened the door with a personalized access card.

"Don't stress her out. She's on strong painkillers. I'll be in the hallway."

Salome lay under the monitor, where the graphs of vital functions pulsed lazily. She was very pale and exhausted, but at the sight of Leeta, she managed to muster a faint smile.

"Lieutenant..." she whispered.

"How many times do I have to repeat? My name is Juliette." Leeta sat next to her and gently squeezed one of the girl's hands lying on the hospital blanket. "How are you feeling?"

"Not great, but I'm alive. The doctors say they lost hope at one point."

"You're stronger than you look, Little One."

"Did you catch him?"

Lieutenant Ankes' expression darkened.

"Unfortunately, he disappeared without a trace. The search is ongoing, and you can be sure we won't give up."

Salome closed her eyes for a moment.

"What did he do to me…?" she asked after a while. "It wasn't a knife."

"The tip of a drill for placing explosives. He had it on him at the time of arrest, and when he was leaving, they handed it back to him because such tools are not classified as weapons. Who could have guessed he would do something like that."

For a moment, they both fell silent.

"If it weren't for your android, I would already be lying in the morgue." Salome finally spoke. There was remorse and guilt in her voice. "I… I have always been rude to him."

Leeta squeezed her delicate, slender hand again, which hardly seemed fitting for a police officer.

"He doesn't perceive your behavior as rude," she comforted the girl. "He is very intelligent, but he doesn't read emotions because he doesn't have them. Not in the human sense." She pondered. "It's hard to articulate something that hasn't been studied yet. One could risk saying that he has his feelings, but they are very difficult to define. He doesn't understand human emotions at all."

"He can't be offended?" Salome asked, lifting her unusually beautiful eyes at her, which were enhanced by a rare anomaly: a double row of eyelashes. Leeta only noticed it now.

"I don't think so," she assured warmly. "I know you're afraid of him, and he knows it too, but that doesn't bother him at all. He thinks it's natural for it to be that way, since he exists."

"I can't help that everything mechanical, that thinks for itself, or even pretends to think, evokes irrational fear in me. I was even afraid of the automatic vacuum cleaner as a child. I don't run away screaming, of course, but I avoid it as much as I can."

"Any reason?"

"I have no idea. I've felt this way forever, and as far back as I can remember, nothing has happened that could explain it. No therapy has helped." The injured officer suddenly sniffed; tears flowed down her cheeks. "Will Tomcat come to visit me too?"

"Oh, Sal…" Leeta looked at her with compassion. "There are no visits here. I shouldn't be here either, but I have my connections. The captain is currently in the field, interrogating the necessary people. Tell me, you love him, right?"

Salome broke down in tears. She tried to stifle her sobs, but a concerned Jeannie immediately peeked into the room.

"What's going on?"

"Nothing, nothing," the girl collected herself with effort. "It's the medication, doctor. I'm fine."

The doctor didn't seem convinced, but returned to her post.

"I'm sorry." Salome wiped her tears. "Give me a tissue, please. Yes, you're right, but he doesn't pay attention to me. As a woman, I don't exist for him."

"I think he sees you as a sister, but that could easily change. Don't lose hope and above all, don't cry. Don't waste your strength on tears, darling."

"And... you?"

"What about me?"

"I had the impression that you liked him and were trying... to somehow... get closer to him?"

Leeta laughed despite herself.

"Oh, my dear! You're mistaken. Yes, he's a very attractive man, I won't deny that. But first of all, he's completely not my type, and secondly, I'm not available."

"Do you have someone?"

"Yes. Someone I am very close to and whom I don't intend to replace with another model. You can be absolutely at ease; you are not in danger from my side."

Salome clearly breathed a sigh of relief and wiped her nose.

"I'm an idiot."

"Not at all. Think positively about yourself." Leeta wanted to continue speaking, but Jeanne peeked into the room again.

"You have to go now. The management is coming back."

The policewoman hurriedly kissed her colleague and ran after Doctor McCave.

Elvis Greyfox was waiting for Lieutenant Ankes, sitting at her desk with his hands clasped behind his head and his legs casually stretched out on another chair. At the sight of the girl, he hurriedly dropped them to the floor.

"Good that you're here," he said. "I have something interesting."

"Then go ahead."

The sergeant laid a stack of printouts on the desk.

"I asked the techs to compare the implants removed from Annabelle Banks's body with the mannequin's mechanism. According to them, everything came from the same manufacturer. You understand, not from a certified factory, but from some little workshop. They managed to obtain fragments of fingerprints from various components and sent them to the evaluation department. And now, pay attention: the fragments on the implants and those from the mannequin's mechanism belong to two different people, but both of them touched both the one and the other. Maya Burns will bet her head on that. She's currently working on the reconstruction; she said she could definitely present a complete profile of the fingerprints of both these people, along with the information about which finger belongs to which hand."

Leeta started looking through the printouts. Maya Burns's testimony carried weight. The retired evidence assessment specialist, who was almost a legend in her hometown of Sydney, was one of the few volunteers at the precinct. She moved to the Moon of her own accord and, of her own initiative, buried herself in the evidence department, hardly ever coming out from there. She was not much different from the archetypical virtualist. She was a true enthusiast of her work, while at the same time an introvert so unsociable that she had no contacts outside of her professional life. To the extent that new employees at the lunnar's precinct usually found out about her existence only after several months.

"These are very important pieces of evidence for further proceedings. Were you able to collect any biological traces?" Leeta asked after a moment.

Elvis cleared his throat.

"Not from the mannequin, no. However, it's a different story with the implants. The technicians are still trying to extract something from the blood on them. As they told me, there are many indications that besides the DNA of the deceased, there are fragments of the DNA of the person who did the implants, but finding them takes time. It's some intricate work, you understand. What interests me right now is something else."

"What?"

The sergeant glanced away. He was silent for a moment, then gathered his courage and looked his colleague straight in the eyes.

"You were at the hospital with Baby. What about her?" His voice unexpectedly trembled.

"Better. Much better. She'll get through this." She reassured him.

"That's good. For me, Tomcat is like a younger sister. You see... it worries me that the patrols and stormtroopers still haven't found Ogden Fierce. Not only because, in a human way, I would love to beat him up until he remembers his great-great-grandmother. And don't say anything, I'll do it even if it means I'll be demoted to a constable afterward. If Baby died, I would dedicate the rest of my life to finding that bastard and chopping off his head. I would do it, you can believe me, regardless of the consequences."

"I believe you," Leeta replied seriously. She had gotten to know Elvis enough by now not to doubt his words. He had a primal sense of justice and honor, like some "masked avenger" from a young adult novel.

"However, there's another side to this coin. Where did he disappear to?" Yes, that was a good question. The attack on the cop was a rarity in public opinion. It was also commonly regarded as a typical casus bello – all cops participated with the same commitment in the search for the aggressor, who curiously always ended up not in custody but in the morgue. Not that the higher-ups condoned such practices. On the contrary, proven involvement in the vendetta carried severe penalties, but capturing and convicting the guilty happened very rarely. Usually, the code of silence made it impossible to identify the perpetrators, and the investigation stalled at a standstill. This attitude quickly led to even the toughest criminals avoiding attacks on police officers. The law, after all, offered some chance of saving one's skin, especially since their verdict had to be approved by a licensed judge made of flesh and blood. Solidarity among the police – almost never.

The awareness of the risk not only caused lawbreakers to avoid attacking the uniformed officers. It also made it so that if they dared to do so, they became outcasts even in the criminal underworld and could not expect support. This made the disappearance of the hot-headed miner all the stranger. Few would risk giving him shelter after what he had done. Yet Fierce disappeared, and despite the most diligent searches, he could not be found. The whole story had one positive aspect – miners and other workers, among whom rebellious sentiments had been brewing for some time, now fell silent, sobered up. Perhaps they finally realized how absurd and how dangerously perilous the situation they had gotten into was, as well as how much they could lose if they did not wise up. They would hardly harbor such a dangerous person as Fierce turned out to be. And yet he remained elusive.

"He won't hide forever. There is relatively little space on the Moon, though it raises the question of who is hiding him and why," Leeta lightly squeezed Greyfox's arm, sensing the tense muscles. "Calm down. We will catch him. He won't escape. No one from airport security will risk smuggling him onto the shuttle; they are seasoned people."

XIII
LEETA
Personal Diary

When I got home, Sue was sitting at the computer and didn't even turn her head at my greeting. Sid, who was sleeping on her lap, sighed contentedly in his sleep, and only mumbled when I scratched his back. Ever since I asked my friend to look for news about Medfarm, she had hardly left her equipment and was working like crazy, neglecting everything else. Knowing her qualifications, this meant one thing: that the task turned out to be extraordinarily difficult. Like every virtualist, Sue did not tolerate failures and did not give up until she had exhausted all possibilities. And there were countless possibilities in the virtual world, according to the principles of string theory. The quantum computer that my friend was using had been designed specifically to fully leverage the capabilities that this theory offered, but to use it, one had to be a genius like Sue. I had seen her more than once in a state described by the virtualist community as "jazz" – completely immersed in work, day and night. Sometimes this was required by some exceptionally complicated assignment. But now she looked so exhausted that I was genuinely startled.

"Slow down, Sue!" I called out. "Take a break; you'll overload yourself."

She waved at me with her hand armed with a switch-scraper, not taking her bloodshot eyes off the holographic screen.

"Later. I finally found a lead. Don't bother me."

There was no point in trying to convince her.

"Make our bed," I turned to Monty. "I'll just eat something, take a sonic shower, and I'll be right back."

I made a whole plate of sandwiches, ate two myself, and brought the rest to Sue, adding a pot of fortified caffetino. Judging by the state of the pantry supplies, she hadn't eaten anything during my absence, as she always did when she fell into "jazz." I was right, as she immediately reached greedily for one of the sandwiches and nearly stuffed the whole thing into her mouth without interrupting work. I left it and went to the bathroom. Monty was waiting for me, lying in our shared bed. I had become so accustomed to his presence at my side that I couldn't imagine falling asleep alone now. The possibility of cuddling up to his muscular, smooth body was invaluable. I felt safer then than ever and anywhere. Scott was slowly becoming just a distant memory for me; after all, I didn't know what I truly was to him even to this day, and Monty remained by my side unyieldingly, like a rock supporting someone's home. It wasn't that he considered himself my property. Indeed, he did think that way, but his unwavering loyalty did not derive from that. Neither did his care for me. Honesty, truthfulness, and the absence of human flaws resulted from the nature of AI. However, Monty's attitude towards me went far beyond the general theory of artificial brains. "You won't understand everything," Dr. Karpinsky warned me in one of his letters. "Even I wouldn't be able to answer the question of how androids think and what they feel. You have noticed that they have a certain equivalent of human emotions, something that, given the current state of knowledge, would be difficult to name and properly define. I believe Monty will surprise you many more times."

The greatest surprise, without a doubt, was that after Scott's death, and moreover, after discovering that he never truly cared for me, I began to treat the android differently than before. However one might explain it, I was important to him, the most important person in the world. To him alone. The moment I understood this, it became clear to me that I didn't need another partner in my life. Someone might think that in this kind of "relationship" it was only about sex, and they would be completely mistaken. Of course, the fact that thanks to him I didn't have to have regular visits to the Dating Center was a relief for me. I had never liked that institution, but if I wanted to have a doctor-stamped "S" card, I had to either go there once a month or find myself a steady partner. Alternatively, I could purchase a sexbot, which had always seemed to me an act of desperation, something I rebelled against with all my heart. I thought it was good for very old people, for exceptionally unattractive individuals, or perhaps for finished oddballs—in a word, for resigned people. I couldn't imagine myself in such a situation. Meanwhile, I accepted Monty without difficulty. Odd? Perhaps. But one would need to know him to understand it, to know that he was not a machine but a sentient being with a free mind. Few could do that. Maybe in a hundred years, or maybe in two hundred, people will be ready for it. Today, we are still far from that.

I slipped under the duvet and embraced my companion in a motion I had gotten used to. Next to my head, on the *pillow, Sid settled in and began to purr contentedly, so theoretically I should have fallen asleep almost immediately. However, despite this, I struggled for a long time before finally succumbing to a light, restless sleep. I've had this problem for a while now, and nothing helps. In the early morning, I was awakened by a piercing scream that sounded like an explosion. I sat up in bed, frightened, immediately reaching for my sidearm, convinced that someone had broken into our apartment. Sid hissed, jumped off the bed, and hid in a corner. Just then, Sue burst into my room, dancing and shouting triumphantly like an operetta Indian on the warpath. "I got it, I got it!" she cried. "I did it! Long live me!" I lowered my weapon with a mix of relief and anger. "I could have shot you, you maniac! Why are you screaming like a drunk homeless person?" "I found the Medfarm database! Not only did I find it, I opened it! I had already lost hope... They camouflaged it with interference patterns so that everything bounced off them. They didn't just mask it; they locked it in a quantum loop so damn complicated that it must have been created by some genius. But once I located it, I knew I would crack its algorithm, even if I had to burst." "Something doesn't add up," I thought. "Medfarm is not some secret base, a pharmaceutical laboratory. What could that possibly hide?"*

"Ah, that's your business to find out." She pressed a small device into my hand. "I've downloaded all the possible data, and my role ends here." She yawned widely. "I'm going to bed. Adios muchachos. Have a nice day."

Monty, still stretched out lazily on the bed, waved her hand. Unlike me, he didn't panic, first because he couldn't succumb to panic, and second – he immediately knew that Sue was yelling and that it was out of joy, not for any other reason. He not only had a far better sense of hearing but also an extraordinary analytical ability, unavailable to humans.

"Get up, we're going to work," I ordered him.

I got dressed in a hurry. By the time I finished buttoning my uniform jacket, Monty was already ready and handed me a hot caffetino. It's interesting how a being that doesn't need an external energy source understands the needs of someone built according to evolutionary standards so well. He made sure I ate regularly and always prepared caffetino with toast for me in the morning, and interestingly, he also sprinkled a portion of food into Sid's bowl. My cat eventually accepted him, likely just as a distributor of tasty pellets and stopped running away from him.

Now I had the most thankless job I know ahead of me – digging through decoded documents and extracting what's important for us.

***

The briefing in the commander's office was set for three in the afternoon. The captain wanted his subordinates to have time to eat lunch because then instead of thinking that they were hungry, they would focus entirely on the matters being discussed. And there were quite a few.

First of all, the results of the parallel investigations needed to be discussed, so a long session was anticipated. Everyone prudently brought along a cup with their favorite drink and a bottle of something cold. Currently, they were studying the topics written on the board in the office:

– Explosion in the tunnel under downtown

– Assault on Officer Yamato and Detective Kuncz in the Workers' Angles district (Wilder decided that this couldn't be overlooked)

– Truck with a mannequin controller and its target

– The case of Harry Gelbart

– Murder of Jeff Cormack

– Murder of Carol Masion

– Murder of Annabelle Banks aka Melinda Crawford

– Case of explosive materials in the police vehicle, i.e., an attack on officers

– Acquired evidence and information, analysis

– Where is Ogden Fierce?

– Victor Kovacs – what is his role?

– Juvenile company – does it have anything to do with anything?

"That means we have a lot of work," said Rosanda Merrick after reading all of this.

"That's true, we've accumulated quite a bit," Feri Kuncz agreed. "I don't remember it ever being like this, and I've been on the Moon for ten damn years."

"Even for Bogotá, that would be a lot. I know what I'm talking about.

The capital of Colombia was widely regarded as an informal hub of crime in Latin America, and Merrick was gaining police experience right there."

Lieutenant Ankes tapped her spoon against her cup. This was the agreed signal that she wanted to say something important or ask a question.

"Before we start, may I say something?" she asked, looking around at those present and checking with her eyes if everyone was there.

"Speak," the captain allowed her.

"I have a suggestion: let's start from the tail end."

"I don't understand."

"Everyone will understand soon. Everything indicates that Victor Kovacs is the driving force behind the recent events. Not in the sense of direct culpability. He is, in his own way, an honest person, meaning he doesn't cross certain boundaries. I carefully traced his professional career and personal life. He has never directly broken the law. He knows how to use it, bend it, even evade it, but so skillfully that he couldn't be charged with any statute. However, all the actions our opponent takes seem to be aimed precisely at Kovacs. I would risk saying that someone wants to force him to resign from his position. And this brings us to the heart of the matter. – Leeta showed the device she received from Sue. – The data obtained by Miss Herefort contains very interesting information. Namely, if Kovacs resigns... not when he dies, because then there will be an investigation and according to the regulations, a successor will be chosen in a competition... but when he voluntarily steps down, his place will be taken by the so-called Second. Homo Secundus, as the city statute of Lunnar refers to him. Do you know who that is?

"How are we supposed to know?" The captain shrugged. "What kind of guy is he?"

"Actually, not a guy. It's a woman, Yolande von Stolp, note: owner of Medfarm. By the way, a nasty piece of work. She also applied for the position of mayor, and with the governor's support, but Kovacs had, to put it bluntly, much better backing."

Wilder cursed before he could stop himself.

"Indeed, a bombshell – he said after a moment. – That lady has good reason to harbor a grudge against Kovacs, but can this be linked to the attacks? One thing I know for sure is about that malaria with which Gelbart was infected."

Kuncz tapped his spoon against his cup and everyone looked at him.

"Gelbart has been transferred to the recovery ward. I was allowed to interrogate him," he said. "I know you've already done that, captain, but since I was the one investigating Medfarm, you understand. According to the testimonies of the employees I interviewed, no one there had ever heard of Gelbart or seen him in person. Meanwhile, my informant with the codename Coati pried information from a drifter named Dobbs, who participated voluntarily in tests conducted by one of the company's laboratories. This bum identified Gelbart as one of the testers from a collage of photos shown to him. That surprised me, so I dug deeper."

"You should have reported this to me," Leeta muttered discontentedly. "Sue would have taken care of it; she's a professional."

"Not only Herefort knows how to find something in virtual, I can too," the detective refused to be thrown off balance. "And I found it. Harry Gelbart has a diploma as a medical technician, yet has never worked in the profession. I also tracked a request for certified malaria parasite culture made a year ago by Medfarm. Since Dobbs had a slight cold and was coughing terribly, Coati treated him to a private doctor's visit as payment for his information, where blood was drawn before administering any medications. In such cases, one of the samples is usually given to the patient as protection against fraud. Coati brought me that sample, and I gave it to McCave for analysis."

"Why?" Kendra Maru asked, surprised.

"I thought that if that unfortunate derailleur participated in any tests, we would find out which ones specifically," he explained to her. "People like him sign up for all kinds of experiments just to have money for another bottle or a hit of cocaine. It's morally disgusting to exploit them, but legally, there's nothing to complain about, and scientists rarely have any scruples."

"So what?" the captain pressed him.

"Well, the genetic memory of white blood cells contains traces of toxins secreted by malaria parasites and the substances used to treat symptoms. However, what's very interesting is that there were no traces of the parasite's DNA found. Someone must have checked whether it's possible to induce malaria symptoms without the parasite."

Wilder bit his lower lip with his fingers.

"Are those kinds of studies not prohibited?" he asked.

"Of course they are. What's the point of placing laboratories on the Moon? The ethics committee oversight doesn't check here, and if they do, it's already known several days in advance that inspectors are coming. It can't be hidden."

"Alright, but what's all this for?"

"Dumb question," the doctor's voice sounded at the threshold. As usual, he had to emphasize his independence by arriving late for the briefing, to which, by the way, he hadn't been invited at all. Wilder frowned in displeasure and pressed the button that locked the door. "What does the entire pharmaceutical industry base its existence on?

On diseases. Now the plague is new profits. It's just about having the remedy before the epidemic starts. It can simply be convinced to people, like restless leg syndrome or something like that. However, the wiser ones will not fall for it. Therefore, it is more effective to cause some real global disease. As long as it doesn't kill on a mass scale, it will be good for us. That's why toxins themselves are good. They will cause symptoms that will be easy to manage with medications, without additional surprises."

"How do you do that?" Maru scoffed. She still harbored some resentment towards the doctor for their breakup, because although she was the one to initiate it, she believed he was to blame for everything.

"Oh, it's the simplest thing in the world. What are external vaccine diffusers for?"

"Doctor, those are very serious accusations," the captain said slowly.

"Because I am a very serious person." Kelley McCave walked over and pulled up a chair. "Unfortunately, I cannot prove my theory for now, but I swear it's correct. Go on, Feri."

"Talking to Gelbart, I already knew where I stood and made that clear to him," the detective continued, encouraged this way. "The guy is really down about what happened, especially the death of Annabelle Banks. He was hopelessly in love with her, as he confessed to me."

"And how did he know?"

"From me. I showed him her holopic and he nearly fainted."

"According to his supervisor, he is a different person than before," the captain interrupted him. "I'm sorry, please continue."

Kuncz nodded.

"That would explain a lot. The doctors want to send him back to Earth due to abnormal reactions. They even suggest a mild mental illness, although they are not certain. This raises a problem because his testimony could be dismissed in court on that basis. Nevertheless, I learned some interesting things. I have everything recorded, but it's probably a waste of time for us to watch it together right now. In short: Gelbart met Annabelle at Medfarm, where he was doing some side work, mainly as a scout. He was looking for people who are able to do anything for a few points on their card, so those misfits like Dobbs, a former bartender by the way. As such, he has wide connections in various circles, especially the very low ones. So, Coati clung to him as a drinking buddy. That might come in handy later. Returning to Gelbart, as a trained medical technician, he not only knew who to look for certain tests but could also be helpful during their execution. Initially, he saw his involvement in the experiments as an opportunity for extra earnings, but at one point he realized that it was a beneficial way for Medfarm to keep him quiet, really worth those few pennies. Drifting in his affairs, he couldn't just go to the police when he found out the direction it was heading. Still, he wanted to do something… That's why they injected him with sporozoites."

Leeta tapped her spoon against her cup and the detective paused, looking at her.

"Why sporozoites?" she asked. "Wouldn't toxins be enough since they have them?"

"Because they wanted to have serum," he explained. "It's quite foolish to trigger an epidemic or something that will mimic it, and not have a vaccine for themselves and their closest collaborators. The doctor spoke wisely, but he doesn't know something. The scientists at Medfarm don't want to spray toxins with vaccine diffusers; the question is whether they would have access to them. They have another plan. They want to cultivate viruses from the DNA of malaria sporozoites, which would eliminate the role of intermediate hosts, that is, mosquitoes and the parasite itself, which would become unnecessary in the infection process. As I understood, the viruses would be easier to infect and easier to combat with medications, produced of course by Medfarm, which would have exclusivity over them."

"Oh fuck..." slipped out of Wilder's mouth.

The picture emerging from Kuncz's words could terrify even in ancient times, and it was truly apocalyptic in a world almost free of infectious diseases due to scientific advancement.

Kelley McCave meditated for a moment on what he had heard, then spoke again.

"That makes sense. To obtain a full-quality serum, they needed a healthy individual, with a well-functioning liver and other organs. The wanderers are usually too weakened by addictions and poor nutrition, and they won't find other volunteers for medical experiments here, even for a hefty payment. Especially for such ones. As I understood correctly, Gelbart wanted to withdraw from the whole business and maybe even report it to the proper authorities, so he became something like a reluctant volunteer. Am I figuring this out right?"

Kuncz nodded.

"In a way, yes," he admitted. "Although it didn't come across that smoothly during our conversation. If someone wants, they can listen to the recording in their free time, and they'll understand for themselves. Gelbart speaks chaotically, unevenly; sometimes you have to guess what he actually wants to say. In any case, he managed to escape from the isolation cell where he was locked up. That's why I mentioned earlier that his testimony is worthless to the court... Exactly for that reason. Someone who runs the experiments allowed for the possibility of such an escape at any point during the serum acquisition process. This is undoubtedly a very intelligent person, and they must have considered something like this. Something was done to him, I don't know what, but they secured themselves against potential troubles from that side."

"Yes. I think I know," the doctor looked at Wilder. "You once asked me, Captain, whether malaria can change a person's character, and I then gave you a lecture on microbiology, genetic engineering, and brain functions. Do you remember?"

"I remember. I didn't understand everything back then, but you wanted to tell me that a parasite can be used as a carrier of mind-altering information."

"In short, that's how it looks. I wondered then why on earth someone would go through so much trouble to change a nice guy into a disturbed sad sack without resorting to surgical intervention. Now we know."

Silence fell. Everything was starting to come together into a whole that couldn't please the officers.

"Since when has the Medfarm branch been operating here?" Sergeant Greyfox finally asked.

"For six months," Rosanda Merrick replied. "When they started working on Selenoport, the construction crew first built a center for that company. It was said that the owner has some connections with the promoter of the construction."

"And that means the then Chief of Arms, and the current governor," Leeta added. "Damn it, all the clues indirectly lead to him!"

Captain Wilder looked at her thoughtfully.

"You probably know him best. What do you think about it?" he asked.

She grimaced reluctantly.

"He is not a man prone to scruples," she admitted hesitantly. "He can be cruel and ruthless; he pursues his goals at any cost. However, I don't think he would get involved in something like this. Too thick a matter. He definitely has some connections with Yolande von Schtolp, after all, he supported her in the mayoral race for Lunnar. He is surely a protector of Symeon Lange, hence his confidence. Overall, since he took office, nothing important happens without his consent and approval. That's all I know. The rest is speculation."

"If that's the case, then why is he not reacting to open acts of terror?" Kendra Maru asked skeptically. "He doesn't even speak up."

"Good question," the captain supported her. "We'll have to talk to the governor, like it or not. Now, let's move on to discussing the investigation results regarding the attacks… Firstly, the van loaded with explosives, one belonging to the Hirschfeld restaurant chain, which has exclusivity on Selenoport and is registered to 'The Ambassador.' It turned out that a team of three mechanics responsible for servicing the vehicles disappeared without a trace as soon as we came into action. We have their details; the only question is whether they're not fake…"

A sudden noise erupted in the corridor behind the doors, followed by Hallie's desperate scream.

"You can't! You must not go in there! I won't let you! I'm not allowing it!"

"What is going on there?" Leeta jumped up from her seat.

Someone kicked the door with force, the magnetic mechanism released, and it opened with a bang. Hallie, with the determination of a doomed person, tried to block the entrance with her body but was unceremoniously shoved aside. "Get out of my way, brat, or I'll kick your ass and plant some beets." The authoritative voice rang out. Colonel Sirtis entered the office accompanied by two armed privates and a corporal. She stopped at the sight of the two guns aimed at her – Wilder's and Greyfox's. The rest did not react.

"Calm down," she said with pity. "Do you think I came here to stage a coup? You're still new on the Moon, so this time I'll let you off the hook, just put away those toys before someone gets hurt."

The captain laid his gun on the desk.

"Sorry, Lois Ann, but you entered here uninvited, and in a rather unusual way. You're damn lucky I didn't shoot your head off right away," he said stiffly.

Sirtis shrugged it off. Her entire demeanor and the tension in her facial features told observers that she was literally seething with anger.

"Don't be so sensitive," she shot back. "I have a good reason to be here."

She grabbed the corporal and shoved him violently toward Greyfox. It was only then that everyone noticed that the young man's hands were cuffed. Elvis instinctively grabbed him by the shoulder and looked at Colonel Sirtis questioningly.

"This bastard confessed to planting explosives in a police vehicle during the operation in the Workers' Angles," she explained, pointing at the corporal with crushing contempt. "Jason Wang, promoted personally by me last year. We took him alive. His accomplice, senior private James Curtis, was getting smart and had to be shot on the spot. When I found out about your suspicions," she turned to Wilder, "I was initially furious. I wanted to come here right away and sock you in the face so that the dentist would have work for the whole day. But then I decided, I admit under the influence of my orderly, to first check my people so I wouldn't look foolish. I scrutinized their finances and connections, and tracked down the scumbag."

In a fit of rage, she kicked the prisoner hard on the shin with her heavy, reinforced boot, causing him to yowl and shrink in pain, but he didn't muster a word of protest. Wilder furrowed his brow in dissatisfaction.

"Calm down, please," he said coldly. "Go on."

"I'm done. The rest is up to you and your people; you should know how to extract information from detainees. Just sign this for me when you're done." She placed a sheet of information foil on the desk.

"What's this? Ah, a request for demotion and disciplinary discharge from the military; I have to confirm the charges. Of course, I'll put my signature here as soon as my people investigate this matter." Wilder stood up, stepped out from behind the desk, and placed his hand on Colonel Sirtis's shoulder. "Just relax. I know this is hard for you to swallow, but a rotten apple can be found anywhere. Even in uniformed services, which should indeed be beyond suspicion. Don't torment yourself."

She impatiently shrugged off his hand. He suddenly understood that she was not only angry but also felt utterly humiliated by what she had discovered. Like almost every senior officer, she trusted her people, and while she was a strict commander, she stood behind them in every situation. The fact that one of them turned out to be untrustworthy was taken as a personal insult.

"I'll handle this. You do your job, and I'll do mine. I have quite a bit of work left. Even if I have to drop dead doing this job, I'll check each of my people back three generations to make sure that this bastard didn't have any additional accomplices in the garrison."

XIV
CLINT WILDER
Personal Diary

So, Mabel took advantage of what I hinted to her during our meeting at the "Chez Paul" pastry shop. By the way, they would have dug up pastry experts outside the door on Earth if they started serving guests something like this, but it only takes a few weeks in Lunnaria to learn to appreciate these flavors.

Mabel Frost, Colonel Sirtis's orderly, to my utmost astonishment, agreed to clandestine meetings on the condition that I wouldn't put any pressure on her.

Taka beauty and an ordinary policeman... Once every two weeks she had a so-called release from the garrison and could spend about an hour or so of her free time with me. We would then go to the walking yard and stroll hand in hand amidst the wide-plastic landscapes, or to one of those places like "Chez Paul" for terrible pastries and equally bad coffee. For both of us, it was a moment of respite, giving nearly the illusion that we were ordinary people, without traumatic experiences, without burdens. I know my own, but hers – I can hardly guess. I only know she has been through some really tough times and the military became a kind of last resort for her. I didn't ask for details, assuming that when she is ready, she will tell me herself.

At our last meeting, I hinted at my suspicions, and Mabel seized on that. No, I don't blame her for it. I understand that she is loyal to her commander, to her protector, and perhaps, in a way, to a friend, more than to me, whom she barely knows. And yet, it hurt me a bit. Another thing is that it turned out to be effective. Lois Ann, "Tiger Lily," as they call her those who have been on the Moon longer than I, conducted her own investigation. As a result, she dragged to me by the neck a man who could have become my killer if it weren't for Monty.

I entrusted the investigation regarding Corporal Wang to Kuncz, his intern, and Dakota. Kendra Maru is just about to take the detective license exam, and Leeta is too delicate to conduct effective interrogations in really tough cases. Here, it was necessary to press the guy hard. I didn't want to do it myself. After all, I am the commander. No need to beat around the bush: obtaining testimony sometimes requires a bit of creativity in choosing means of persuasion. If someone doesn't want to talk, they need to be convinced, and when serious crime is at stake, no one really keeps an eye on the interrogator. The thing is, someone who commands a given facility, in my opinion, should not legitimize certain means of coercion with their presence.

I just read what I wrote a moment ago. It reeks of hypocrisy for a mile. However, the world is not perfect. On the contrary, it is damn imperfect.

We continued the meeting with five of us – me, Leeta, Maru, Merrick, and the doctor, who had no intention of leaving our company. The matter interested him more because of *its medical aspects than its criminal ones. He actually had a lot to say, as it turned out.*

"Before we go further, I would like to say something," he began as I temporarily closed the door damaged by Sirtis (what a hellion she is, by the way).

"Go ahead," I allowed. "As long as it relates to our investigations..."

"Yes," he assured. "First, I will say that the malaria parasites that pleased Gelbart indeed contained modified DNA that could have damaged his brain. But the second issue is more interesting. I examined the embryo removed from Annabelle Banks's body closely and compared the resulting DNA profile with the database. Very interesting things came to light. The father is Victor Kovacs."

"Well, that's explosive!" I interrupted him. "We have a perpetrator!"

He shook his head.

"I don't think so," he said. "Kovacs is someone who is called a putative father, but the embryo also contains chromosomes from the biological father. We are dealing with something called procreative triolism, used to obtain an embryo with maximum genetic value. Generally speaking, every one of us has some flaws in our DNA, some shortcomings, but each one is different. To somehow patch them up, it is necessary to use different DNA. The procedure is extremely costly and complicated, applied so far only a few times in a ethically questionable attempt to create a superhuman. I will add that in every case, the researchers' hopes were disappointed because the child born this way turned out to be the most ordinary in the world, which can be successfully achieved in a traditional way and without such costs. In only one case

could such a poor creature turn out to be invaluable: if it naturally produced in its blood a protein that is a component of IVI, the integrated shock vaccine.

"Is that possible?" Leeta asked, clearly shocked.

"Theoretically, yes. IVI has been in development for a long time, without much effect. It is not currently necessary on Earth, but it may become essential if humanity travels to the stars or even to the moons of outer planets. And there are such plans."

"And that embryo..."

"At this stage of development, no final conclusions can be drawn yet, but in my opinion, the matter was on the right track."

Rosanda Merrick scoffed disdainfully.

"Nice things. Do you know how much such a brat would be worth on the black market?"

"One can guess," I replied. "And multiply by a hundred, then we might get close to a range of value."

"In that case, killing her represents a measurable loss."

"Not quite." McCave shook his head. "They certainly have a backup."

"So?"

"Oh, because I haven't mentioned something yet. Victor Kovacs is undoubtedly the biological father of the embryo, and someone else, I don't yet know who, is the father of descent. But Miss Banks was not the mother. The egg donor was another woman; Annabelle was merely the incubator."

Leeta whistled in admiration.

"That really changes the situation," she said.

"And you should know it. We are dealing not only with genome manipulation but also with in vitro fertilization. In such a procedure, several embryos are created, most of which end up in the freezer. They have something to work with, they just need a new carrier."

Leeta looked at me.

"I request permission to present a theory," she said in an official tone.

"Don't be silly, just speak," I grumbled. Her servility sometimes gets on my nerves.

"In my opinion, the sequence of events was as follows. Annabelle Banks, alias Melinda Crawfor, was a very greedy person for additional income. She probably sought out Kovacs' genetic material herself, being attractive and sexy enough, as he likes women. Then she agreed to have the embryo implanted. Once all tests indicated that the pregnancy had taken and the embryo was developing as planned, demands began. Perhaps she was accommodated for some time, but that had to end. One day, Mrs. von Stolp appeared and explained to Annabelle in short terms that she was just a hired womb and had no right to place any conditions on the owner of the company. The ambitious girl must have been offended. Using her charms, she forged a conspiracy to extract as much money as possible from Medfarm. She recruited at least two men to it, besides Gelbart, one of whom turned out to be the boss's mole, that is, a rat. First, he had him imprisoned in the laboratory and treated him like a guinea pig. However, Annabelle turned out to be smarter than he thought; she figured everything out, may have also obtained evidence, and began to openly blackmail him. When the mole realized how ruthless and dangerous the "carrier" was... she definitely ob-

tained information that could seriously harm the company and had no qualms... he decided to poison her, possibly on the direct order of Yolande von Stolp. It was better to lose a promising fetus than everything she had achieved. The next day, only then, because at night even a card couldn't open the apartment building door on one's own and he certainly didn't want to attract the administrator's attention, the mole went to Gelbart's apartment. He reasoned correctly that he would likely find stolen data with him rather than with her. The girl surely did not have full access, while he might have."

"I wonder if he found it," Maru pondered.

"I don't know. In any case, the third participant in the conspiracy at that time fabricated Annabelle's corpse and made it appear in the apartment rented by Gelbart. The mole panicked; most likely that was the intention. I suspect that although he poisoned the girl, he did it cleverly enough so he couldn't be linked to it. And he won't escape from smashing her head."

It made sense. It sounded like a soap opera, but everything could have unfolded this way. While interrogating the employees of "Ambasador," I learned, among other things, that Annabelle, who worked there part-time as a showgirl, was widely regarded as extremely selfish, unsociable, and devoid of any empathy. She was only interested in material benefits. Inevitably, men sought some justification for her flaws because they simply liked her; women were more critical. A clever, intelligent girl without reservations, determined to extract as much as possible from life, could indeed have concocted a plot to blackmail the owner of Medfarm. However, finding evidence for that will be quite difficult.

Although...

***

Symeon Lange, sitting in police custody, lost a lot of his bravado. Initially, he probably counted on being released at any moment, but days passed and nothing happened. No one was causing a commotion at the headquarters, no one showed up with a release order signed by the governor, and every lawyer he called from his limited call allowance said briefly that they were too busy. Meanwhile, he had to adjust to the rhythm of prison days, listen without complaint to the guards' orders on even the smallest issues, change his sweat-soaked expensive clothing for an orange jumpsuit made of drill, and eat not what he had previously ordered at an exclusive restaurant, but what was served to him as part of the police menu. It was a painful awakening for him from a dream of power. Therefore, seeing Captain Wilder, he got up from the bunk without a trace of his earlier arrogance, trying only to maintain a shred of dignity.

"Have you cooled down a bit?" Wilder asked rhetorically. "Yes? Well, let's talk."

"About what? I didn't do anything wrong. I don't even know what I'm repenting for."

"Oh, you know very well. For not being able to behave like a citizen, but acting like a damned petty tyrant towards the representatives of the uniformed services." The captain sat on a prison stool, bolted to the floor of the cell. "But let's forget about good manners. I looked over your file, not concerning your education, career, and so on, because I care the least about that. I was interested in your character. You have your flaws. You are pathetically ambitious, rude to subordinates, and arrogant towards equals. Fine. Independent opinions about you, however, say that despite everything, you are an honest official and a decent person in your private life. That's why I have a certain proposal for you."

"What proposal?" Lange asked, suddenly filled with hope. His eyes gleamed, which the captain noted with some satisfaction.

"If you help us with the investigation, the police will not file charges. Let me be clear: we are dealing with subversion aimed at social order. Someone, whether an individual or an organization, is consciously provoking chaos. In Selenoport, you do not feel this for now because, shall we say, the organism is comfortably separated from Lunnar and its offshoots, but if the situation slips out of our hands, you too will suffer from it."

"I don't quite understand how I could help."

"All you need to do is cooperate. Some leads lead to Selenoport. To help you understand the seriousness of the situation, I will add that we already have at least two terrorist attacks, three corpses, and an attempted murder of a police officer, so this is really no joke."

The CEO paled slightly under the stubble that had covered his face since the day before. He probably hadn't realized until now that the whole matter, including his arrest, does not revolve around him, but has much deeper roots.

"I thought that…" he began. "For some time I've heard rumors that someone might want to replace me. In a sneaky way, meaning sabotaging my actions or 'setting me up'. I had no idea that something was happening beyond that."

Clint raised his left eyebrow mockingly.

"If you had let me speak back then, I would have explained everything to you on the spot and we could have avoided this arrest," he stated. "But fine, let's move on. If you agree to cooperate, you will be conditionally released from custody and will return to your nice air-conditioned office, with a bar and a charming secretary, incidentally very loyal to her boss. I have not squeezed anything out of her, on the contrary, she took a call against us with security. I could even arrest her for that, but I settled for a warning. You will say what you want, that for example you got away with a fine, apologies, and a promise to improve. And immediately, I emphasize, immediately you will start acting. I am giving you this chance because, first of all, I am convinced that apart from unnecessary bravado, you haven't done anything wrong. And secondly, what is happening now may threaten the institution you supervise in the future. This pastoral town."

Lange nodded somberly.

"I understand," he said slowly. "However, it will be hard for me to help since I don't really know what I should be paying attention to."

"You will receive as much information about the investigation as I can provide. I assure you it will be enough." Wilder got up from the stool and extended his hand. "Have we come to an agreement?"

The detainee hesitated for a fraction of a second, then shook the offered hand.

"I will help," he promised solemnly. "If I can, I will help."

The captain responded with a smile and warmly shook his hand.

"Please take a shower, shave, change your clothes, and I invite you to my office. We'll discuss the details."

An hour later, Symeon Lange, refreshed and in his own suit (which to his pleasant surprise not only had been stored in police custody but was also carefully washed and ironed), pressed the doorbell to the commander's office.

"Please come in, the lock is broken anyway." A voice came from the speaker.

The door indeed moved with a pendulum motion at the first touch. The magnetic lock had been forced open and hung forlornly at the joints.

"Do you have a problem with the technical staff?" Lange asked, looking at him with some surprise.

"What? Oh, that." Wilder waved his hand dismissively. "I haven't called anyone yet. Please have a seat. We will write an official agreement, I will bring you up to speed on some aspects of the investigation and show you some photos."

At the same time, Leeta and Kendra Maru were working on another report, based on the results of the tests provided by the doctor. Both genuinely hated "paperwork" – it was still called that, although for a long time no one had been preparing documents on paper – but they could not avoid it. As the popular saying in the police went, "the work of a detective is five percent operations in the field and ninety-five percent sitting on your backside in front of a computer." It may have been a bit exaggerated, but nevertheless, it well reflected the reality of their profession. That's just creepy," Kendra said, throwing another slide onto the screen. "I had no idea that a child could have two fathers and, effectively, no mother at all."

"Come on, let's not exaggerate. Someone had to be the egg donor; otherwise, this wouldn't have worked," Leeta replied, looking at the lab chart. "There was a time when this kind of genetic engineering was considered the future of humanity. You know, children without congenital defects, programmed right from fertilization to be healthier, stronger, smarter, and more beautiful…"

"And so? Why didn't it work?"

"The costs were disproportionate to the outcomes. It turned out that nature is unpredictable and can play some tricks. As the doctor said, from procedures worth a fortune, ordinary babies were born, just like the hundreds you can find in any working-class neighborhood. Sometimes experiments are done when some wealthy person gets a notion and wants a tailor-made offspring… But even in such cases, they mostly pay for illusions and that's all there is to it. Even a clone, though it has identical genetic material, is not anyone's perfect copy, but a distinct human being."

"This is all terribly complicated," Maru sighed. "Not my cup of tea. Wait, we also got reconstructed fingerprints from the evidence department, from Maja. She issued them a certificate with an eighty-seven percent probability."

"That's high. Any court will accept it. If only we had something to match it to," Leeta lifted her head from her desk. "Upload it to the database. Maybe we'll get a match."

"I've already done that. The result should be coming in soon. In the meantime, let's finish this case with the embryo. How about: 'identifying the stepfather and the egg donor is currently not possible due to the lack of matching results in the available DNA database'?" Kendra changed the slide. "In the case of the stepfather, that's not entirely true, but indeed the results are currently so doubtful that it's better not to mention them."

Leeta remained silent. She returned her thoughts to her conversation with John Collins yesterday when she brought him lunch. The old policeman listened to her story and summed it up with a brief remark:

"If you eliminate the impossible, whatever remains, no matter how improbable, must be the answer."

That ailing, resigned man, waiting in a rented apartment for death, had pointed her to the right solution more than once with his experience. However, she didn't understand this statement right away. How could something remain when you reject the obvious absurdity and what doesn't match the results in any way, when the DNA obtained simply wasn't in any of the databases?

The answer exploded in her skull like a firecracker. She almost dropped the pod on the floor. She struggled to suppress the urge to rush to Sue immediately, who was the only one who could confirm her discovery... apart from someone else.

"I need to talk to him!"

Kendra didn't pay attention to her exclamation. She was staring at the computer screen with her mouth half-open.

"You won't like this, boss," Leeta finally said.

"What?" Lieutenant Ankes looked at her semi-conscious.

Maru pointed at the screen. The words "Positive Match" appeared on it.

Fingerprints of Sven Thorvald were found on the implants removed from the body of Annabelle Banks. The DNA fragments in her blood also matched the engineer's profile.

"Oh hell!"

She had been pushing that thought away from the very beginning. The implants, stimulating the nervous system of the corpse, were an extremely precise mechanism, and someone who not only had them but also knew how to use them had to have microelectronics down to a fine art. Such people were valued more than gold, rather than platinum, and they simply didn't exist in Lunnar. Even Chris was not in the picture, as, being a cosmic electronics engineer, he dealt only with macro-scale electronics. Only Sven possessed the necessary knowledge and skills, along with, thanks to his small business, the materials and tools. Leeta didn't want to admit this to herself, hoping that perhaps she could track down another implant specialist, preferably one connected to Medfarm. In the company's database obtained from Sue, she did not find the name Thorvald, and it relieved her immensely. He himself convincingly denied everything. Now, however…

"So he's involved in this. Either I'm very wrong, or we have a father descendant," she said after a moment. "We need to file for an arrest warrant. Where's the captain?"

"I don't know. Do you think…?"

"It would make sense. Sven must be knee-deep in this mess; otherwise, why would he be making this circus with the corpses?"

Kendra rewound the image.

"The other one is still quite mysterious. I'll dig through other databases, but it will take time and I might not find anything."

"Alright," Leeta got up from the desk. "I'm going to look for the commander. I think he was heading to the prison section recently… Hallie!"

The messenger emerged from the back, where according to her duty schedule, she was currently updating the inventory of cleaning supplies and organizing them, which she detested.

"Do I have somewhere to fly to?" she asked hopefully.

"Not right now. Where's the captain?"

Hallie grimaced pitifully.

"Too bad. Captain? He was in the prison section, now he's with that arrested big shot."

"I'm going there, in case anyone asks. Kendra, prepare the arrest warrant for Thorvald and let Hallie go with it to the judge immediately. As soon as she returns, take two or three officers with you and bring the guy to the station."

Hawaiian woman jumped up joyfully and clapped her hands. At least for a moment, she wouldn't have to return to boring inventory work.

When Leeta entered the commander's office through the ajar door, Symeona Lange was already gone, and the captain was typing something on his computer. He looked up at her.

"Something important?"

"Very. We've identified the guy with the implants and, unfortunately, the bomb trigger. It's Sven Thorvald, an engineer employed at Selenoport and also the owner of an electronic scrap yard."

"Great. Arrest him."

"I've already ordered it."

"Excellent. Do you have some time for your commander now?"

"I'm at work, after all." Lieutenant Ankes smiled involuntarily.

"I'll take that as a 'yes.'" Wilder closed the computer and stood up from behind the desk. "Let's go then. I plan to visit Baby."

"They might not let us in," Leeta warned him for good measure.

"That's why I'm taking you and Monty with me. I need a witness, like for the interrogation. Let Idalgo bring the vehicle out and be ready in five minutes."

She nodded briefly, military-style. Once, she would have wondered what Clint was planning to do; now, however, knowing how the new superior operated, she had a good idea of what to expect.

When they arrived, after pressing the doorbell, an armed staff member in a light blue internal security uniform emerged, carrying a stun gun.

"Is someone injured?" he asked. "Is there some illness?"

"Visiting," Wilder replied briefly and added, "My subordinate is lying here."

"There are no visits. Official directive from management." The guard turned away demonstratively, trying to close the door of the guard booth behind him. Before he knew it, he was pushed against the wall. He cried out in pain and surprise as the officer twisted his arm. Paul Idalgo watched this scene from the parked vehicle in front with an expression of astonishment on his good-natured, round face and silently rejoiced that he did not have to take part in it.

"Let us in, buddy, or it won't be the director going to jail but you for resisting."

"That's an abuse…" the guard groaned, but the captain cut him off sharply.

"No, that's exercising public police authority, which is routinely disregarded here. Or rather, it was. I'm not as nice as my predecessors, and I will enforce the rules without looking at the dissatisfaction of the big shots. Is that clear, buddy?"

"Sure. Please let me go, it hurts."

"It should hurt. Maybe it'll teach you something." Wilder released his grip and stepped back. However, he had to react again in a moment, as he narrowly avoided a zap from a stun gun. The hospital security staff was either very stupid or very confident in who stood behind him. Moments later, he found himself on the ground, hands tied behind his back, with the barrel of a gun pressed against his neck.

"You are under arrest for assaulting a police officer. You have the right to remain silent, but it won't help you. And you are lucky to be alive, you idiot." The captain dragged the dazed man to the guard station and used a second pair of handcuffs, taken from Leeta, to chain him to a chair. "We'll come back for you later, and don't count on your superiors, because they won't get you out of this. Monty, keep an eye on him. Idalgo!" he called out, glancing out onto the street. "Keep your eyes on the entrance and don't let anyone in right now! Lieutenant, the door."

His companion obediently pressed the appropriate button on the console, and the inner door opened silently.

"Is this how you handle everything?" she asked as they were already in the hallway.

"Just what needs to be done," he cut her off. "Salon manners are good for a diplomatic gathering. In our line of work, they are completely unnecessary. You need to understand that."

"Scott managed without them."

"And how did that end? Alright, where is the room?"

Leeta looked around.

"Let's ask the nurse."

Just then, a woman in a white coat and a cap hiding her hair appeared in the hallway. Upon seeing the uninvited guests, she stopped and frowned.

"Who let you in here?" she asked.

"We let ourselves in," Wilder answered her, showing his badge. "Please don't bother calling security, because someone might get hurt, and you will be arrested. Is that clear?"

The woman took a step back.

"Clear," she muttered. "Of course."

It was clear she didn't know how to behave in this situation.

"Where is the injured police officer, Salome Delaforette?" the captain asked, not giving her time for idle thoughts.

"Second floor, recovery ward, room number ten."

"Please lead us there."

"But I…"

"Are you opposing the uniformed services?"

"But the director…"

"Do you prefer to have trouble with the director or with the law?"

Defeated, the nurse obediently led the intruders where they wanted to go and disappeared as soon as they entered the isolation room.

Salome, pale and emaciated, was lying on the bed, looking at a flat press machine connected to the network panel with little interest. Such devices had long since replaced print magazines, which had been so popular before the Ecological Catastrophe. Upon seeing her visitors, the girl's eyes filled with tears.

"Tomcat… You actually came!"

"I couldn't not come, sweetie."

She hugged him around the neck as he leaned down to kiss her cheek.

"I'll keep watch." Leeta volunteered and discreetly stepped out, closing the door behind her.

She didn't want to interrupt them, more for Salome's sake than for Clint's. At the same time, she preferred to keep an eye on the hallway. The nurse's behavior raised concerns that further problems might arise. Perhaps they could have been avoided if Jeanne McCave had been on duty that day, but unfortunately, it was her day off.

She didn't have to wait long. Just a few minutes later, a tall, graying man in a suit and an attractive, dark-skinned woman in an expensive outfit appeared in the hallway. They both walked briskly towards the door of the room and only stopped when Leeta blocked their path.

"Please step aside." The man growled.

"Not a chance, director." She replied calmly.

"Counselor," the woman corrected her sharply. "This is the hospital's lawyer. I am the director, and I ask you to leave, or I will call security."

"I wouldn't advise that. I really wouldn't advise that." The police officer straightened up and crossed her arms over her chest, looking the director straight in the eyes.

"Are you threatening me?"

"I'm just warning you, dear madam…"

"Doctor. Doctor Edna Harris." The director interrupted her coldly.

"Fine. It doesn't matter to me. And I am Juliette Ankes, lieutenant." Leeta indicated the badge pinned to her belt. "Please do not interfere. Commander of the lunnar's police visits her injured subordinate, and no one has anything to say about it."

"There are internal regulations in this facility…!" the lawyer raised his voice, but his speech was interrupted by Captain Wilder himself, who opened the door to the room and stepped out.

"Is there a problem here?" he asked, raising an eyebrow.

For the umpteenth time, Leeta noticed that his height and athletic build made a significant impression on those he spoke to, especially when they felt that they were not quite right.

"You are abusing your power." Dr. Harris spoke up after a moment, her voice much less confident. "And you are violating hospital regulations."

"Really? That's very interesting." The Captain assessed her with his gaze. "Because it seems like you are the one abusing your authority. Visits to hospital patients can only be cancelled in situations of higher sanitary threats. Do you see any such threat? Because I don't."

"I have the right…"

"I don't care. Patients are not prisoners, and you are not the head warden here, just a management specialist. Starting tomorrow, you will restore regular visiting hours under standard conditions, or we will have a disagreement. And believe me, it's not me who will lose out. Lieutenant, let's go." He started towards the staircase, but after two steps turned back. "Oh, and unfortunately you will have to find a replacement for that idiot in the guardhouse. He won't be back to work for at least half a year."

XV
LEETA
Personal Diary

"You know you've just made a few more enemies?" I asked Wilder as we were heading back to the station. He shrugged.

"It's my job. A cop is not supposed to be universally loved, they are supposed to be effective. Doctors have broad powers, that's true, but even they are not allowed to break the civil liberties guaranteed by the Constitution. Obedience to the authorities must be enforced unconditionally, but only within the law. And that was not in accordance with the law. Shut up!" he shouted back to the swearing detainee. "Or I'll have you gagged, and that's all you'll get from it. Getting back to the matter at hand, I don't know why people agree to this here, but it's probably the result of anxiety psychosis. People are afraid because it's a closed space, there's nowhere to escape. They think that the more regulations, orders, and bans there are, the safer they will be. And people like that Harris take advantage of it to feel important. They like to feel power over others."

"You might be right," I conceded reluctantly. "I won't argue. But I think you're exaggerating."

"You'll see that not even a little. I understand, you don't want to admit it, but we are now in a small war, and excessive politeness doesn't fit into wars. As I said before, what people are allowed under the Constitution, no one can take away from them. But rights also come with responsibilities. Loosening the reins on the residents of Lunnar in terms of respect for the uniformed authorities has resulted in this situation. I don't want to upset you, but now I have to clean up after both Cavanaugh and you, and that's why I can't afford to be polite."

I struggled to swallow my resentment. This guy was largely right, even if he didn't have to rub it in.

"I didn't ask to lead. I was appointed." I snapped, perhaps sharper than I intended.

"I know. You did what you could, and if the situation were different, it would have been enough. Don't take it personally. You're really good at what you do, I can't measure up to your intelligence, but we need a strong hand here, not diplomacy. At least not right now."

"I'm not angry." I softened my voice; besides, he was right. "I just don't believe in the rule of terror."

"You'll be surprised, but neither do I. However, you must understand that if the law stops working, then that will be terror because criminals and people for whom civil rights do not exist, only their ambitions matter, will start to rule society."

"I don't want to sound smart, boss, but that makes sense." Idalgo chimed in from the driver's seat.

"I'm not saying it doesn't," I waved my hand. "Okay, let's change the subject.

Actually, there was no longer any reason to change the subject because we had just arrived at the station building.

"Monty, take that jerk to the lockup and hand him over to the duty officer," Wilder ordered as he exited the hovercar. "Charges: attack on the uniformed officer using a dangerous tool, resisting arrest. Call Slavik, let them handle it legally."

"Yes, sir." Monty replied succinctly, pulling the fiercely resisting guard from the vehicle and dragging him towards the prison section. I watched them go. I still didn't understand why this young man was behaving so absurdly. What was he hoping for?

"It's good that you're here!" Kendra called out as soon as we stepped inside. "Look who we have here."

She pointed to two men standing next to her desk, both wearing mining overalls. I looked at them, not comprehending anything. They looked completely ordinary. Both were already over thirty, wore the Helios mine logo, and would not stand out in a crowd.

"Just wait until they tell you why they came."

I stepped closer.

"I'm listening, gentlemen."

They exchanged glances, and one of them turned to me.

"We came here to confess and voluntarily submit to punishment," said one of them finally.

"We're the ones who beat up those cops who came to our district in plain clothes," added the other. "We knew who they were because we were told."

"Who told you?" I asked sharply. "And why did you beat them up? Detective Maru, please start writing an official report."

"I've already started."

"Good, then speak." I demanded. "What is your story?"

One of the men cleared his throat.

"Let me start. Vito Melloni, shot firer. So, there was a plan..."

"We were told there was a plan," the second interrupted him, stressing the word "told." "I'm Jeremy Olsen, supervisor, miss."

"... to suspend certain points of the labor code on the Moon," continued Melloni. "The statutory number of hours, the right to strike, notice periods. And many minor matters. In short, they were tightening the screws on us. We started to organize, formed a secret trade union, and... well..."

"We met and discussed current issues," Olsen took over. "I hadn't seen it before, but after the recent events, I noticed that Polly Greenberg, who was initially just one of our more militant speakers at rallies, began to slowly emerge as the most important person in the union."

"Polly Greenberg?" I repeated.

"Yes. She's a millwright at Juvenille..." he saw my expression and added an explanation: "I mean, she's responsible for the compressor of one of the mines of that company. She became the chairperson at the end of last year. She always had the freshest information, obtained documents, we didn't ask how. When things started to heat up for real, she went into hiding and since then communicates with the union through her deputy, Tanita Ahn, a 'flekarka' at the same mine as she is."

"What is a 'flekarka'?" I asked with a sigh. Every profession has its internal dialect and that sometimes causes serious problems. Juvenille... oh right. That name again.

"It's somewhat like a tallyman. A 'flekarka' calculates the spoil, and Ahn is doing just that. And it was she who pointed out the undercover agents to us."

"They weren't undercover agents; they just went to have a drink in civilian clothes with a mate."

"Now I know, miss..."

"Lieutenant."

"Of course. Ahn told us they came to spy and that all the cops are at the service of those fat pigs from the corporation. We were supposed to give them a proper beating. I mean, to give them a thrashing, so they wouldn't stick their noses in here anymore."

"And you let yourselves be provoked like that? Grown men? Shame." I was not so much outraged as disgusted by such foolishness.

Olsen hung his head.

"Yes, we all messed up," he admitted. "We really thought we had to defend ourselves. That they wanted to make slaves out of us, and who could we count on here? Who would help us if the military and police serve those up top?"

"But they don't serve!" I exclaimed. "You were manipulated like children!"

"Now we know, miss.... lieutenant!"

"When your captain laid it out for us, we sobered up a bit," Melloni interjected. "At first, we didn't believe it, but we started digging into it, and after discussing it, we came to realize that we had been played."

"*Please don't use such words, because I don't understand them. What does it mean?*" I asked.

"*It means we were taken for fools. We delegated a couple of people to the presidency of the Lunnar Company and they were shown all the documents there.*"

"*Where is Polly Greenberg now?*"

"*I have no idea. She disappeared like a stone in water. Her friend did too. I wondered.*"

"*Does any of you know where Ogden Fierce might be hiding?*" I asked another question.

Both vehemently denied.

"*Please think carefully. This man nearly killed my colleague with the tip of a drill,*" I pressed. "*Anyone who helps him or hides him will be charged as an accomplice.*"

"*When we really know nothing about him,*" Olsen assured me warmly. "*When we found out that he tried to kill that policewoman, our jaws dropped. Seriously, they did. It was like someone hit us on the head. We knew him a bit because his shifts at the Hokkaido Pride mine coincided with ours. You know how it is, a shift is two weeks, because I don't think you can imagine daily commutes from Lunnar to the Mare Imbrium area and back...*"

"*I am aware of your work rhythm, please get to the point.*"

"*... So, people, who regularly meet during relaxation time, get to know each other and even make friends, which is how we knew Ogden. We knew he was a hothead, but we would never have thought he could pull such a stunt. No, we don't know where he is hiding. We would be the first to tell you about it.*"

"None of us would voluntarily stick our heads in a noose," Melloni added. *"It's enough that we made fools of ourselves. That's shame enough."*

I nodded. I had no intention of boosting his self-esteem right now because I fully agreed with that self-criticism. I felt sorry for those workers, simple and uneducated people, but what they did could not go unpunished. On the other hand, voluntarily reporting to the police, admitting guilt, and sincere remorse worked in their favor.

"Finish taking their statements," I addressed Maru. "Let them read the protocol and sign it. Then give it to Slavik, let him prepare a legal opinion. Later the captain will decide whether they should wait for the trial in custody or if they can be released on their own recognizance."

Theoretically, I could make such a decision myself, but I preferred not to. Clint Wilder might be right - I lack a sense of timing. Besides, I had things to do.

***

Driving from the hospital to the station, Leeta was convinced that Sven Thorvald had already been arrested and was waiting for her in one of the cells in the detention center. She knew she would have to interrogate him, and she was a bit troubled by it. She liked the eccentric engineer and owed him a lot, but she could not let personal sympathies or a debt of gratitude guide her now. One way or another, Sven was involved in the death of Annabelle Banks, and he could certainly be accused of desecrating a corpse and participating in an act of terrorism. She felt very, very uncomfortable about it, but she could not pass that duty onto someone else. That would be inappropriate.

Meanwhile, having gone to the prison section, she did not find the engineer there. The guard on duty in the detention office informed her that he had not been entered into the detention log, so she returned to the main room, where her colleague was just finishing preparing the protocol.

"Kendra, what about arresting Thorvald?" she called out.

Maru looked up from the form she was filling out.

"I passed that to Kuncz because those two showed up," she replied. "He probably hasn't returned yet."

"He hasn't left yet," Feri Kuncz said, popping his head out from behind the door separating the main room from the economic department. "Hallie was supposed to bring the papers from the judge, but she's still not here, and without a warrant, I can't do anything anyway. That's the foundation."

"Probably Judge Holstein held her up," Kendra added. "Sometimes he needs a few hours to make a decision, plus he likes to chat with Hallie. The old man has his quirks, and she entertains him."

"Yeah…" Leeta sighed. "Listen, I have to take a nap. At least for half an hour, but I have to because I can barely keep my eyes open. Again, I couldn't sleep for almost the entire night." Maru pointed her stylus at the door on the right.

"Use the backup duty room. I'll let you know if something serious happens, but if not, Feri and I should be able to manage without you."

Lieutenant Ankes locked herself in the duty room, and Monty stood in front of her door with his hands clasped behind his back. In situations like this, he instinctively assumed the role of protector and guardian of his lady's peace, which sometimes posed certain problems, as he recognized no authority other than Leeta herself. In this situation, it was clear from the start that he would not allow her to be disturbed unless someone used the "safety password." Only two people at the command knew it: Doctor McCave and Kendra Maru. Both were aware that such a password could only be used in a situation of higher necessity and they must not reveal to others that they had the capability to prompt the android to act according to their will.

Captain Wilder, upon learning that his deputy was asleep on duty, was a bit surprised, but when Kendra explained to him that it was better not to interfere, he only commanded that she come to his office immediately upon waking. And so, it happened.

"Sorry, boss," she justified herself. "I've been suffering from persistent insomnia at night lately and I end up dozing off during the day, and it just caught up with me right now."

"As long as this doesn't happen in the middle of an operation," the captain replied diplomatically. He got up from behind his desk and reached for his jacket. "Now that you're rested, we're going to see the governor. Idalgo is already waiting for us. I need to talk to him. You probably want to as well."

"Wanting is maybe too strong a word," Leeta muttered, following her superior. He turned to look at her.

"You don't like him?"

"It's not that. I'm afraid of him. You'll understand why when you talk to him. He's a dangerous guy, devilishly smart, cold, and ruthless. He can be noble, but it's always calculated."

He stopped.

"You know him well." He stated rather than asked.

"Well enough. If it weren't for him, I wouldn't be here. On the other hand, I wouldn't be among the living either."

Wilder looked at her, intrigued. She waved her hand.

"I'll tell you when I have a free moment. For now, let's focus on what we need to do here and now, because things have really gotten out of hand. Is Monty coming with us?"

Wilder glanced at the usually silent android. He wouldn't admit it for all the treasure in the world, but he still felt a bit uneasy in his presence. Although he owed his life to him, and without a doubt it was Monty's quick reaction that saved Salome after Ogden Fierce's attack, he still couldn't bring himself to trust the "artificial cop." That's what Sergeant Greyfox jokingly called the android, of course, as Monty didn't have the status of an officer. However, he understood that Leeta didn't like parting with him, and he respected that.

"Sure, why not?"

They stepped out onto the driveway, where Paul Idalgo was already waiting for them in the company hovercraft. The captain pointed to the seat next to the driver for the android, and he settled into the back seat beside his deputy.

"We'll be able to talk freely." He said as he closed the transparent, soundproof partition that divided the hovercraft into two cabins – the control and passenger sides.

"Do you want Paul to not hear something? He's loyal and honest, a good cop."

"I'm not questioning that. Why isn't he on patrol duty, though? He's a big guy." The captain looked questioningly at Leeta.

"Too soft for that," she explained. "Our patrol officers have to be tough and uncompromising, or they can get hurt, and at best make fools of themselves. He's not suited for that. He should stay on Earth, but oh well."

"Is he here of his own free will?"

"Yes. Just like Hallie or Kendra. For some, the very word 'Moon' holds something magical."

"Well, I'll be." Wilder shook his head in involuntary admiration. "Alright, never mind that. Tell me something: as I understand it, you'd rather not see the governor at all. Yet you want to talk to him about something. What?"

Leeta clearly became flustered and did not answer right away.

"If this isn't something personal, I would like to know. The police is not a place for internal secrets."

"I know," she replied. "It's just that it's very complicated. On one hand, it relates to the investigation, but on the other hand, it doesn't. This involves an extremely delicate matter.

He looked at her attentively.

"Regardless, tell me what it's about. We need to trust each other since we're running this damn facility together."

"It's not a matter of trust. Besides, I'll tell you, and you'll understand, but I need to clarify something first," the girl decided. "Do you remember how the doctor said he couldn't identify the egg donor for the Medfarm experiments, or rather egg donors, since there had to be more?"

"Yes."

"Legally, it's a complicated issue. I asked Slavik. The law on in vitro fertilization states that the egg donor can contest the surrogate in every case, and also, if adoption is involved, a specific pair of adoptive parents. The sperm donor can do the same. The only limitation of this law may be when either of them loses part of their civil rights during the procedure. For this reason, creating embryos for strictly utilitarian purposes, so that the child produces specific proteins on its own, carries additional risks. Not only can the medical ethics committee unleash hell, but the cell donors could also initiate a civil case. But what if they don't know anything?"

Wilder was becoming increasingly intrigued.

"Is it possible not to know you're a reproductive cell donor?"

"In the case of a father, yes. Samples can be obtained, for example, from used condoms, and our deceased lady with two surnames definitely had the opportunity. However, an egg is a more delicate matter. Hormone therapy is usually necessary before extraction to ensure the material is healthier and stronger. Kelley explained that to me. And the procedure must take place in a specialist clinic."

"And so?" The captain urged Leeta.

"Kell couldn't identify the donor. Only DNA data from people in the government are confidential, but that can be circumvented. Sue Herefort knows how to do it. However, there is always a person whose data is erased from the virtual."

"Who, exactly?" This was incomprehensible to the law-abiding policeman. DNA registration was so common that it seemed like a waste of time to question it.

"Number One."

The captain did not expect that. His eyes widened. He felt as if he either misheard or his deputy was joking with him.

"What are you talking about?" he sputtered after a moment. His handsome, chiseled face paled as he realized that Leeta was not joking at all.

"This is a story you don't know," she sighed. "And I know not only the identity of the current Number One, but also a certain secret that does not belong to me, and I cannot disclose. I can reveal that unscrupulous people used someone who certainly wouldn't take them to court because they have too much to lose and desperately want to regain something."

Wilder pondered what he had heard for several minutes. He was sharp enough to piece together the scant information into a coherent whole that almost frightened him.

"Does the governor have something to do with this?" he finally asked cautiously.

"Probably. In any case, he could explain a lot. He was a member of the government team."

"And… why Kovacs? Why take such a risk, using someone from outside, when anyone from Medfarm could have been the donor?"

Leeta looked him straight in the eyes.

"Because Victor Kovacs is damn similar to… a certain man from years ago," she replied. "He immediately seemed familiar to me, even though I saw him for the first time in my life. It had to be him."

"But he didn't know anything?" Clint checked.

"No, I don't think so. Almost certainly not. He wouldn't get involved in such a story. And if he had known from the beginning, Annabelle wouldn't have been needed as an intermediary. Maybe later. She could have blackmailed him just like she did her murderer. Although the doctor claims she didn't write the letters, that's no proof. She could have hired some scripter, how is it called among fraudsters."

"And what do you think, could she also be behind the explosions underground?"

"Who knows. She worked at 'The Ambassador', had contact with the mechanics servicing the delivery vans, and God knows with whom else." Leeta looked out the hovercraft window. "We'll be there soon. I have a feeling that once we get to Yalande von Stolp, we'll find all the answers, but we won't do it without the governor."

"Probably not," Wilder agreed with her. "The judge did not sign the subpoena for her at the official hearing, supposedly due to a lack of sufficient evidence. However, that does not mean we cannot make the effort to visit her apartment. We'll have a chat with this lady on her turf, and then we'll see."

"Just no stunts like last time!" Leeta was alarmed. "She is very influential, and we currently have no evidence against her."

He smiled indulgently.

"Calm down, my dear. I won't even touch her without a judge's order. I know very well when to do what, and besides, I've never hit a woman. We'll just have a conversation with her. For now."

She looked at him but said nothing more. She only thought that the conversation between her new superior and Citizen Hakata, now Karl Stanton, could be very interesting. Both had strong personalities and equally despised dissent. Clint Wilder, additionally, could not stand people in positions of power, big entrepreneurs, and generally all the wealthy who looked down on those they considered inferior. Their clash could indeed be interesting, but Leeta wasn't sure she wanted to witness it.

The police hovercraft stopped in front of a residence surrounded by a high wall. Two armed guards came out to greet the guests, but upon seeing Wilder's badge, they saluted and, without asking what it was about, opened the gate.

"They are ordered to admit the police chief at any time of day or night," explained a cheerful Leeta, seeing the captain's surprise, who was expecting resistance, as in the hospital or Selenoport. "Karl Stanton has his flaws, but he understands the rule of law exactly as it was established by the relevant law. He won't deviate an inch."

"But as I know life, he probably knows how to manipulate what's allowed well."

"You can be sure of that. Paul," she turned to Idalgo, "you stay here and keep an eye on everything. It got a bit unsafe lately, and I don't want to risk another bomb in a police vehicle."

"Sure, chief."

Wilder darkened at the mention of the bomb.

"This corporal from Colonel Sirtis either really knows nothing, or he has been compromised," he said as they walked to the residence building. "Someone bribed him, but the transaction supposedly took place at night, and he didn't see any facial features. Kuncz and Dakota didn't learn much from him."

"He's a pawn. Greedy and therefore useful. He's still alive because he can't harm his employers; otherwise, he would probably have been taken out."

"What's going on here..." the captain muttered bitterly to himself. For some time, he had the impression that he had been sent not to a post in an industrial city, but to an asylum for dangerous lunatics. Or that he had traveled back in time at least a century. The people living in Lunnar acted so illogically and unpredictably that one could truly come to such a conclusion.

After pressing the doorbell, the doors of the residence were opened for them by a young girl with platinum blonde hair styled in an elaborate do and a beauty apparently too perfect to be a work of nature. An oval face with regular features, beautifully shaped lips, and elongated eyes gleaming a bright green seemed as calm as a lake on a windless day. The fitted outfit she wore highlighted her perfect shape like a second skin and probably cost a fortune. A necklace of peacock pearls surrounded her slender neck, and her delicate ears were adorned with earrings made of the same stones. The stunning beauty extended her narrow hand with long fingers in a gesture of 'you shall not pass" carefully manicured nails.

"The governor is currently sleeping. You can't enter." She spoke with a voice melodic as the singing of birds.

Table of Contents

"But we must," replied the captain, who was not impressed by her beauty. "Please step aside."

– That's impossible. – The girl did not move.

– That's an officer's order, miss… What is your name?

"Allienor. You are not allowed."

Clint glanced at Leeta and gestured with his head. As he mentioned earlier, he did not use violence against women unless he was forced to during police action. Even then, he felt terrible about it. He always preferred that one of the female officers take his place in such situations.

Leeta took two steps forward and tried to push the girl aside, but she didn't budge.

"Get away from here." She said as if she had not heard the words directed at her.

"Please do not obstruct and let us through." Lieutenant Ankes commanded her, impatient and surprised by this sudden resistance. She tried again to push the girl away, this time more assertively, but unexpectedly received a slap to the chest so hard that she flew against the wall. Monty caught her at the last moment, saving her from crashing into the wall, and then leaped into action himself. Grabbing the aggressive beauty by the arms, he suddenly froze. For a moment, both stood still, then Monty stiffly turned his head and looked at the captain.

"She's just like me. We are the same." he said, awkwardly formulating sentences, as always when faced with a situation he had not been prepared for.

"Oh my, it's an android!" exclaimed Leeta in astonishment, discreetly rubbing her arms. The fingers of her artificial friend were tough enough to leave bruises.

Wilder raised his eyebrows.

"Seriously? I thought yours was some kind of anomaly."

"I thought so too. Monty, somehow negotiate with her. We really need to get in and talk to Governor Stanton."

Monty looked at his female counterpart.

"The governor allowed the police commander to come in at any time of day or night." He reminded her firmly.

"The governor is sleeping." Allienor was not about to yield. "He didn't allow himself to be woken up. He clearly said" 'Don't wake me until I've had enough sleep.'" she finished, changing her voice to a male one.

Wilder shrugged.

"When did he supposedly say that?" he asked with exasperation. "I've had enough of one stiff; now I'm going to deal with two." he concluded in thought.

The android turned her glassy emerald eyes toward him.

"Forty-five hours ago." She answered as if it were about forty-five minutes.

"What? Something must have happened!" shouted the captain. "People don't sleep that long!"

"Don't they?" she asked in a tone so innocent that Wilder's hands dropped.

"Do you even know how much sleep a person needs?"

Allienor blinked for a moment with her long lashes before answering.

"I don't have such data."

Leeta shook her head.

"She's very young," she said. "I mean recently constructed. Otherwise, I would know about her. They gather knowledge just like children do, well, maybe faster than they do, but in a similar system. Let's leave that for now. Allie, darling... understand that something may have happened to your guardian. I don't know, stroke, hemorrhage, heart attack. You probably don't know these words, so take note that they are very dangerous failures of the human body and that they usually happen suddenly, without warning."

The android freed her hands from Monty's grip and took a step back. She looked down the corridor.

"The bedroom is that way," she said, pointing in the direction. "If it's as you say... we need to go in there."

"It is as they say," Monty assured her. "I know. I understand the workings of humans; I was taught that."

Allienor suddenly turned and dashed down the corridor. They hurried after her and caught up as she struggled with the locked door from the inside. Unable to open it, she struck the outer coding panel with her fist, triggering an alarm that rang throughout the residence. "Pretty soon we'll have the guards on our backs," Leeta mumbled.

The door gave way and they all tumbled into the bedroom.

It was empty. The rumpled sheets indicated that someone had slept there, but a neatly folded suit hung on the back of a chair, and shoes were set nearby the bed. Bloodstains were visible on the sheet, the duvet, and the rug in front of the bed. The open window left no doubt as to the course of events.

"He escaped?" Leeta looked around, trying to spot any trace of the governor.

"In pajamas and slippers? And why? And where did that blood come from? Good grief, two days... The trail has gone cold." Wilder scratched his neck thoughtfully. "Karl Stanton has been kidnapped, possibly killed," he told the security team that had just arrived. "Turn off the alarm and secure the entire area. From now on, no one is to enter or leave without my knowledge."

"But… this is the governor's residence…" mumbled one of the guards, clearly shaken by the news.

"From now on it's a crime scene," the captain cut in. "Exercising my authority, I am declaring a state of emergency throughout the city. Along with all its consequences."